"

When I put this book *(The City on the Sea)* down it had become
an old friend.
Pat, Mt. Philo

My children and I loved *Becoming Truitt Skye: Book One* as it had
such wonderful elements of creativity, imagination, humor, and
thinking beyond current limits! I enjoyed finding a book that we
could read together and enjoy! Cannot wait to read Book Two
together!
Maria Weesner and kids, age 11 and 9

Truitt Skye is a truly inspirational character who allows you to
see the world in a whole new light. I was captivated by her spirit
in the first book and cannot wait to be enlightened by this book.
Kaylee LeCompte

Truitt Skye is an intense, electrifying literary work that took me
on a journey of deep introspection, challenging my thoughts as I
delved in a world of wonder and intrigue about what is real and
what is imagined.
Jennifer Sharp, author and publisher

Truitt Skye (and Adrea Peters) were masterful in their ability to
weave a bridge between the known and the unknown, to explain
in a way I can understand, what we were, what we are and what
we will become. Tell me MORE Truitt.
J Botelho

Truitt's journey catapults the mind into a realm of endless possibilities. It's nothing short of magical!
Jen Frankenhoff

Magical, like the book's author with her two dogs, Skye and Fig.
Peter Dietrich

"

Truitt is the mirror of life; curiosity, bravery and courage. She represents the love, trust, and possibility we can lose over time and fight to bring back. A true representation of how we are working to raise our 3 teens today.

Jodie Gallant

I am mesmerized by Adrea Peters' writing. She not only captures the essence of a typical Milwaukee winter but makes the reader feel as if you are living in it as you read. We loved reading Truitt as a mother daughter book club!

Becoming Truitt Skye is a marvelous mystery tour of whimsy and wonder. This treasured story takes the reader on a journey of inner expansion and exploration that feels like a quantum leap in consciousness and is wildly entertaining ride the whole way through.

Amber Lilyestrom

A perfect combo of an intro to Quantum Physics, and a living our best lives primer. *Truitt Skye, Book 1: The City on the Sea* is like experiencing The Beatles' 'Here Comes the Sun' in the form of reading a book. Truitt Skye gives us a glimpse, in Truvie's short seventeen years and seventeen days, of lifetimes of curiosity and love, pain and healing, loss, joy and hope. I cannot wait to read *Cave of Souls*, and I agree with Truitt's Dad, as he says about Gram: 'She's earned our listening.'

Holly Hall-Perry

The author, Adrea, knows how to weave a story that is vivid, creative, and brings all the characters to life. A page turner that leaves you craving for the next adventure and now it's here! I cannot wait to read the ongoing journey of Truitt Skye!

Laura Hudman, an avid fan of Truitt

"

It is not only entertaining, but to an open heart, allows the labyrinthian of lessons to filter into the amazing possibilities of 'what if?' one allows oneself to go there. My mind was like a sponge absorbing all the delicious messages as I read through this beautiful story. I laughed a lot and cried too, and nodded as I quietly whispered to my Mother in heaven... "That's what I thought..." Hope is healing. Heartfelt congratulations Adrea L. Peters. What a creative genius you are. Ten stars all the way.

Mickey Martin – Author of The Given Trilogy

While reading *Becoming Truitt Skye, Book 1,* my dreams became more vivid, complex and other-worldly. Truitt is personable, someone you adore immediately. Her exploration of the multi-layers of humanity through quantum physics had my mind expanding as it once did when I was younger. This book is a reminder to allow for the possibilities in life. Let go and trust.

Bella Icenhower

Truitt is absolutely mesmerizing! Adrea found a way to take quantum truths and share them through story in a way that is fun, enchanting, and so beautifully written that no matter who reads it, they will walk away with a deeper understanding of themselves.

Kristen Hubbard, poet

Truitt Skye transcends age, time, and physics. As her name and her story suggest, the sky is not a ceiling, but an aspiration to reach for. Reading this book reminded me that my mind is my box and to work at breaking down the walls and breaking through. I'm excited to see her next adventure.

S. Reed

National Library of Australia Cataloguing-in-Publication data:
The City on the Sea/ Adrea L. Peters
Young Adult Fiction

ISBN: 978-0-6487280-8-5 (sc)
978-0-6487280-2-3 (hc)
978-0-6487280-9-2 (e)

BECOMING
Truitt
Skye

The City on the Sea

1

ADREA L. PETERS

For Nancy

Contents

1
Over the Edge · 1

2
Seventeen Years and Fifteen Days · 4

3
Party Time · 18

4
Seventeen Years and Seventeen Days · 31

5
Grandaddy · 44

6
Flight · 54

7
The City on the Sea · 68

8
Pel Willows · 82

9
Light · 96

10
The Restore · 105

11
Eva Kinde · 117

12
Answers · 131

13
The Glasshouse · 143

14
A Room Above · 156

15
Gaining Momentum · 168

16
Gravity on Water · 176

17
The Physics of the City on the Sea · 191

18
The Wish Listeners · 203

19
The View from Above · 211

20
The Mint Isle · 226

21
Backward · 243

22
Becoming Truitt Skye · 259

23
Fragments · 268

24
There is No End · 277

25
The Glass · 288

26
Breaking Through · 298

27
The Line Between · 307

28
After · 315

29
With Love · 328

Acknowledgements · 340

About the Author · 342

Other Titles by ADREA L. PETERS · 344

1
Over the Edge

Hand quivering, Junius set his pen to paper and let his memory recount the horror just portrayed. The rain skidded in erratic streams down the glass walls enclosing him. A single flame from a candle offered faint dancing light as he etched, "17 years and 17 days," then closed his eyes and saw it all over again.

. . .

Truitt Skye barreled across a narrow, uneven rock wall in the dark of night. The moon illuminated the tips of crashing waves hundreds of feet beneath her. A cool, salty mist rose moistening the surroundings and threatening her footing. She could not fall before she found the silver pool.

"Wait!"

Truitt pressed forward without looking back to the woman chasing her. Eva could not catch her. This was the only way.

"Please Truitt! Don't do this!"

Faster, Truitt demanded. Her toes gripped the wet earth as her calves and quads engaged, giving her plenty of traction to accelerate. The strength of her body fed her momentum.

And then. There it was. The portion of still, shimmering silver sea with no compliance to the crashing waves around it.

This was no innocent stall in the sea. That water carried a descendant to another world. The world of humanity. A world Truitt Skye was responsible for and must protect at all costs. A world she never intended to enter. Her duties resided here in the City on the Sea, a world of souls devoted to humanity.

"STOP TRUITT!"

Truitt fell to her knees. Blood spread into the fibers of her white pants. She looked back. Eva halted. Each begging the other to change her mind.

Truitt stood. Blood trickled down her shins as she raced along the edge.

Eva started to chase her, but—

Truitt bounded off the edge.

"No!" Eva rushed to the side of the cliff just in time to see Truitt Skye disappear into the silver pool where life begins again.

"Oh Truitt," Eva whispered. "What have you done?"

. . .

Junius etched the final moments of Truitt Skye onto his scroll. He could not balance the tiding tears in his eyes. They slid down his cheeks, dropped onto the scroll, staining the parchment with dark, solid marks.

She would return, but she would never be this Truitt Skye again. He could hardly bear knowing the pain she would soon endure. Blurry eyed, he inscribed her last instruction, "Promise me you will help me become Truitt Skye when I return. I won't remember who I am but that cannot stop me. This is the only way to save—"

"Everything," Junius finished, her voice echoing in his mind.

"I'll see you in seventeen years and seventeen days," Truitt had said, then added, "Granddaddy."

Junius set the pen to the table and stared at himself in the glass as the rain streamed down the pane. He saw a man of youth, bald, without wrinkles. "Granddaddy," he said to his reflection. "Quite an honor, my dear. Quite an honor."

2
Seventeen Years and Fifteen Days

Truvie Tucker raised her chin to the October sky. Crimson leaves clinging to maple trees trembled and rustled but did not fall. They held on despite the fragility of their tenuous bond. It was only a matter of time. A raindrop, a breeze and they would let go, drift to the ground and melt in to decay with the others.

The sun lowered behind her, softening the illumination of the gold, crimson and burgundy forest behind the carriage house. On the far edge, near the back fence, sat her father's shed. This shed did not hold a lawnmower and garden supplies, but computers and books and equipment to support her father's physics experiments.

She arched to her tippy toes, trying to get a glimpse of him working, but the shed was dark and still.

A whoosh of leaves sprung to life, startling her.

"Fig!" Truvie pet her beloved black Labrador's head and ears. "You scared me, sweet boy." Fig wriggled and wagged at her knees, always delighted, always ready to love her.

The fallen leaves crackled and crunched as she trekked toward the shed, convinced her father was in there working away. Then again, Truvie would do anything to avoid the main house right now and the fervor of her mother's party preparations.

"Figgy! Come on! Let's find Dad." Fig emerged in full stride passing her then cutting her off to drop his red ball at her toes, forcing her to a stop.

With a playful groan, Truvie bent over and grabbed the ball. Holding it in her palm, she let him know, "One toss. That's it, mister."

He wagged and wriggled backward in eager anticipation. She twisted left and threw it across the yard, exactly in the midline of the wide gap of lawn between her grandmother's carriage house above the garage and the main house where Truvie lived with her parents. A good toss. Maybe forty-five feet with a ten, maybe twelve, foot arch. Fig took off as if his paws had boosters and raced to the ball, leaping up to catch it on a bounce.

She shook her head and said, "Spaz." Then followed the matted path of decaying red and brown leaves to her father.

. . .

Truvie cracked the door to the shed a sliver. She knew better than to knock. He despised interruptions. Her nose, right toes and right eye the only thing inside, she found her father hunched over the keyboard typing at a fast click, periodically looking out to the two 24-inch monitors on either side of the curved 34-inch concave monitor. His eyes never left the screen as he typed. He coded first, then re-read and revised it, then ran it. A perpetual cycle of creation.

Truvie paused. Wondering if it was worth the risk of—

Fig burst through the crack in the door and lunged straight for his chair, spinning her father around to face them.

"Fig!" Truvie hissed.

Fig leaned back on his hind legs and lifted his paws onto her father's thighs and began licking him. Her father gently put his hands to Fig's face and nuzzled in.

"Hello, you two," her father said.

Fig moved his paws up to her father's shoulders, in a full stretch.

"Sorry, Dad," Truvie said. "Fig. Down, baby."

Fig hopped off then sat a couple of inches in front of Truvie's feet. He swoosh-wagged his tail against the wood floor. Eagerly moving his gaze between the red ball resting near her left foot and her eyes.

"Fig," Truvie said. "No, go lay down please."

Fig didn't budge.

"Sit down, honey," he said to her. "I'll show you what

I've been working on."

"I didn't want to interrupt," Truvie said.

"But you didn't want to be in there either, hmm?" He used his thumb to point at the main house.

She smiled. "Not really."

"I don't blame you," her father said.

Fig yelped playfully. Then pawed the red ball.

"In a minute, Fig," Truvie said. She wheeled the desk chair next to her father and took a seat.

He pointed to the screen with his pinky finger. A thin line of permanent grease resided under his nails, which he kept long enough to use as a tool in his work as an electrician. Screwdriver. Knot de-tangler. Wire separator. Plastic wrap taker-offer. Splinter remover.

"This code here is meant to increase the intensity of the images."

"How?" Truvie asked, leaning in to study the lines of code.

"Speed mainly. And I'm expanding the variables. The AI in the code will remember and repeat several more like variables with such frequency that the end-user won't be able to process them. Not at first anyway. Their mind will remember every single one because it wants to. Desire overrides deletion. It will lock in and activate over time. Or that's the intent anyway."

He put his fingers over the top of his head and rubbed the back of his skull.

"Reverse AI?" Truvie asked. "The computer teaching the human."

"There's nothing artificial about human intelligence, and actual artificial intelligence should be bi-directional, despite what most people think," he said.

"And fear," Truvie added.

"This is new code focused on focus, her father said. "For thoughts to convert to energy that can generate matter, a little concentration is required."

"A lot of concentration," Truvie said.

He gave a little laugh. "It provides more focus than any human has ever known."

"Does the repetition help them—us—believe what we imagine for ourselves?" Before letting him answer, Truvie went on. "If you can remove the gap of time caused by an unfocused mind, you can teach anyone to replace possibility with reality?"

He ruffled the hair on the crown of her head. "I love the way your mind works. I get so technical. Yes, that's it exactly, albeit, a little dreamy for me. Here—" he pointed to a few lines of code. "I'm asking particles to connect with particles they're a match to. In my head, I've been calling them soul mate particles for lack of a better term."

"I love it," she said.

"You inspired it," he said, then focused again, "The bond is key. It's everything. The only way that the mind can convert thoughts to usable energy is to connect to energy that is a smidge ahead in time and space. It becomes more and adds to the overall energy of everything. I don't know exactly how I'll be able to achieve it. We're talking about activating millions, if not more, particles and connecting to each and every one of them simultaneously. If I'm honest, I'm a little intimidated.

Gram. Where is she? Find her."

Fig bolted from the shed and ran through the leaves, lifting a flurry of red in his wake.

. . .

It wasn't that Truvie didn't want to go up the steps she stood staring up at with hesitation. She loved her grandmother. That wasn't it. Truvie simply never wanted to leave the shed. The equation meant everything to her. She tried to play it cool and not be a spaz like Fig but that was how she felt. Out of control happiness. When Truvie wasn't supposed to hear, her father bragged that it was all her fault. Four years ago, Truvie had stormed into the shed and announced to her father that she needed a new ball and a new arm, in no particular order.

"What?" her father had said, finally looking up from his computer screen.

"Fig deserves a better thrower," Truvie had said. "I have to be the one to throw the ball for him. It has to be me. I'm his alpha."

Next to her, the broad, whipping tail of her beloved one year old, eighty-five pound black Labrador retriever hit her knees in rhythmic sequence. She reached down and pet the top of his head. "I'm not good enough. But I could be."

Her father looked at her. "That's where the new ball comes in?"

"Needs to be heavier, smaller, hollow and—"

"Pitted," he had cut in. "Like a golf ball."

"I need to take full advantage of turbulence. I need teeny pockets of air to give it hang time. I don't have the strength, but I can master accuracy. The ball has to hold its lift."

"Turbulence," he said

"Turbulence," she repeated.

"You coming up to visit or making an escape?"

Glancing up, Truvie saw her grandmother, Helena, in her red silk housecoat and red sequin slipper boots.

"Both," Truvie said, shaking off the memory.

Fig wedged out from behind her grandmother's legs and wiggle-hustled to Truvie, tail rounding in circles, waist stretching side to side. Fig offered a faint whine of utterly uncontrollable excitement.

"It's been less than ten seconds since I saw you, Fig."

"Love tells no time," her grandmother said.

Oh boy.

Truvie lowered her knees to a stair and nestled her nose into Fig's head and gave him a faint whine of utterly uncontrollable love then raised her gaze to her grandmother, "Ready to partay?"

"Let's go to Paris instead," Helena said. "It's a perfect time for Pair-ee. I had a friend there. She's—she was a dancer long ago. Très elegante." Her grandmother twirled in a wobbly circle. "She kissed me straight on the lips every time we met."

"I'd rather be here," Truvie said, kissing and cooing at Fig. "With you two."

"Come up, dear," her grandmother said. "I have to change."

"Impossible," Truvie said.

"I heard that," her grandmother teased.

. . .

Helena's painting studio took up the half the loft space above the garage they called a carriage house. A broad open rectangle of two thousand square feet. Her grandmother spent all her time here, rarely coming to the main house. Truvie understood why. Sylvie, Truvie's mom, was a force of nature. The spotlight was always on her. She was an actress who got the lead in every show the Community Theater of Milwaukee produced. Truvie was proud of her mom and equally proud she was nothing like her.

Canvases of all shapes and sizes, and all stages of completion, hung on walls, leaned on the walls, and balanced on easels. The long wall along the back was devoted to paintings and photographs of Truvie's grandfather, Junius. Several included Truvie's mother, Sylvie, and a few had the three of them. He was a man of great style, always in a tailored suit and tie with his shoes polished and shiny. Truvie had never met him, but felt she knew him through the vivid memories of her mother and grandmother. He was thirty-seven when he got sick and died a few days later. The cause of his death still unknown, but never dwelled upon.

The dining room table held no placemats, dishes or silverware. Rather it contained, an array of colorful powders in glass mason jars, waiting for their moment to become liquid and be scooped into the bristles of one of the brushes scattered throughout the room.

Truvie reached for a jar with azure blue pre-paint, then a dark turquoise.

"I'm sorry I messed up your work," her grandmother said.

"I don't mind, Gram," Truvie said. "I like arranging them." She moved a royal blue to the top of the table then found a grey-blue and placed it next to a pale pewter blue. She took another turquoise, slightly lighter than the prior, and lined it next to three other shades of turquoise. Her grandmother moved a navy blue and a periwinkle toward Truvie.

"You always start with the blue," her grandmother said. "Darkest to lightest."

"I do the reds last," Truvie said. "Because they're not as easy as the blues."

"You think the reds are harder than the yellows?" her grandmother asked.

"Don't you?" Truvie glanced over at a painting of three young maple trees filled with red leaves in the easel nearest them. There were easily ten shades of red depicting the leaves. Maybe more. A cup of pomegranate-plum paint sat next to the easel on a wooden table dotted with shades of splatter. A paintbrush balanced perfectly across the mouth of the jar.

"Gram!" Truvie said, remembering why she had come to see her grandmother. "Happy birthday!"

Her grandmother didn't say anything at first.

Truvie was afraid to poke the point. She hoped her grandmother would say, "thank you" and they'd be done.

"I suppose I can't say I'll die young anymore," her grandmother said.

Truvie closed her eyes a moment and focused on the listening her grandmother deserved.

"I thought I would, you know?" her grandmother went on. "Die early. So much earlier. Nothing tragic. Just a short life well lived. But dead, nonetheless."

"I'm glad you—" Truvie started.

"Seventy-seven," her grandmother said as she picked up a paintbrush and carefully coated it with paint. A drip lowered to the edge of the bristles and released just as she raised the brush leaving a drop on her grandmother's already paint-spotted house coat. "I thought I might make sixty-seven. Didn't want to," she said she dabbed and stroked the paint into place. "I never wanted to be this old."

She turned to Truvie. "I never wanted to live a day beyond your grandfather's last. Not one minute, actually, and here I've gone and lasted forty more years."

"I'm glad you did," Truvie said, moving away from the table toward the painting.

"I'm not," her grandmother said. "He left me here with a mess. Death isn't about them. It's about us. The suckers left behind. Death's about the living. Nothing to do with the dead."

"I wish you wouldn't talk like this, Gram," Truvie said. "I know I'm supposed to be quiet and listen. But it makes me sad that you're sad. I love you."

Her grandmother smiled. "I love you, too. But if death mattered to the dead, what would be the point?"

"Dad thinks you get a new body and start over immediately," Truvie said. "Mom says you become your favorite flower. I'm not exactly sure what she means though. A seed? Or the actual flower? Bloomed or budding? Or all of it?"

"What do you think?" her grandmother asked.

"About flowers?" Truvie asked. "Not much."

"About dying, dear," her grandmother pressed.

Truvie shrugged. "I don't. I think about living."

Her grandmother paused for a brief inhale. Then said, "Life is a series of deaths. Not just people. Everything dies. I know you don't understand," she said. "I hope you never do. I hope when I go, you're glad. I might even try to piss you off so you applaud when I go. Relieved to be rid of me. At peace, they'll say about me. Rest in Peace. R. I. P. Let's hope that's the truth. Finally get some peace for this old lost and bitter soul."

Tears burned behind Truvie's eyes. She swallowed.

"Mom!" A distant but distinct call sounded. Truvie's mom. Mad. Very mad.

Truvie and her grandmother looked toward the dark window facing the main house.

"This is YOUR PARTY!" her mother shouted. "Truvie! Are you up there?"

"I'm sorry," Helena said to Truvie. "You know how awful I get on my birthday."

"MOM!" Sylvia shrieked.

"Even though it makes me sad," Truvie said. "I like hearing what you have to say."

"You and you alone," her grandmother said with a sweet smile.

"Truvie!" Footsteps stomped onto the staircase outside the door. "MOTHER!"

"She's closing in," her grandmother said.

"We better go," Truvie said.

"This between us," her grandmother whispered. "Okay?"

Truvie pinched the tip of her index finger to the tip of her thumb and drew it from left to right across her lips, vowing silence with an imaginary zipper.

3
Party Time

The party comprised of a room stuffed with people yelling to hear themselves speak, leaning in far too close to their companions in a desperate effort to hear the responding hollering whilst failing to balance a wine glass, a small plate of messy appetizers all blending into one another, napkin and silverware. It would make so much more sense to set up tables and chairs, advice Truvie perpetually offered every time she and her mother set up for a party. Lack of efficiency and efficacy drove Truvie nuts. This was not mingling. It was chaotic fusion.

Fig came in the sliding glass door in step with Truvie, took one look around and bolted through the crowd toward the hallway leading to the staircase where Truvie knew he would race up and onto her bed where he'd curl next to her pillows.

"Smart man," her grandmother said.

"I may—" Truvie felt a squeeze on her upper right arm.

"Don't even think about it," Truvie's mother said in a quiet, but menacing baritone.

"Stop reading my mind," Truvie twisted and said to her mother. "One hour."

"Unless somebody can convince you otherwise. . ." Her mother shot a quick look toward a group of students then raised her arms sending the billowy white sleeves of her tunic puffing out like wings. Focused on the new arrival, she released a giggly-girly, "Jazz-mine Baker! You came!"

Sylvie hopped into the air and scurried off to meet up with one of her actress friends. Jasmine Baker wore a navy silk jumpsuit with a rainbow-striped scarf tied around her neck. Her navy beret sat off to right, covering the top of her ear.

"Why must thespians always wear scarves?" Helena asked but didn't wait for the answer to her obviously editorial sentiment. "They look ridiculous all noosed and neckless."

Truvie glanced around the room, scanning for data about actors wearing scarves and the count was clear proof of her grandmother assertion, eight of eight wore scarves. A small but definitive sample.

"Are you counting scarves?" Helena asked.

"Maybe." Truvie smiled. "You are correct, in case you wondered. They all have on scarves."

"Of course, I'm right!" Her grandmother reached for a glass of champagne from the pale grey granite counter. "Birthday girls are always right. You can count on that."

Truvie frowned, her mind immediately attempting to process the proclamation.

"Just go with it, dear. The proof will come in time," her grandmother said as she stepped into the vortex of partygoers. Truvie silently wished her luck. There was not one slight modicum of chance that Truvie would follow.

The kitchen extended into the living room and both connected to the family room slash television room. When unoccupied or with just the three or four of them, the space was giant, echo-y. The living room lived virtually untouched save for Fig popping up for a nap on the couch. Right now, no space remained empty. Her mother must be so happy. Truvie looked around hunting for her father. Ah, there he was, reading a science journal in the far corner. Hiding in plain sight.

"Bacon, lettuce and tomato hore dee vore?" a familiar voice said. "They've got your name written all over them. I take it you made them?"

Truvie's cheeks burned with excitement. When she turned, she would see her best friend, Eddie. A boy she loved so much when she thought of him inexplicable fluttering butterflies that aren't actual butterflies, but neurons multiplying, erupted. Her chest hurt. It grew penetratingly heavy when she imagined kissing him, which she hoped beyond hope would happen before her eighteenth birthday, only a couple of months away.

She wanted to experience her first kiss from him, and only him, before she was legal. She wanted it before college. She wanted that kiss, and several more after the first. Period.

When she turned to face Eddie, her mouth dried. She licked her lips and shook her head a bit to get out of her dreams. "Bacon is my energy portal," she said. "To infinite happiness."

"Mine too," he said, popping one in his mouth. Eddie had longish blonde hair that fit his surfer-style, which was unique to this Midwestern crew-cut crowd wearing flannel and fleece, cargo pants and tan lace-up work boots. Eddie had on a hoodie with the Burton snowboarding company logo. He had never been snow-boarding, but she knew he'd be a natural.

As he finished chewing, he said, "I see what you mean about the tables. It would help. A lot."

"My mom likes folks to mingle, not sit," Truvie said then took a bite of her slider and to her great horror felt the guts slide out the back and . . . plop. Bacon, mayo, tomato landed on her chest between her breasts.

"Whoops. Guess that's where they got the name 'slider'," Eddie said. "Let me get you—"

Truvie shoved the remainder of the appetizer into her mouth as Eddie reached for the stack of napkins behind him. Her heart ker-thumped with crushing panic. She pulled her turtleneck away from her body to inspect the damage. Her cheeks and neck inflamed with wretched, painful embarrassment for greasy tomato-mayo spray on her boobs.

"He'll never kiss me now," she said in an inaudible,

panicked whine. She fought the urge to rub it, but these types of spills needed to be scooped off and dabbed. No rubbing. Absolutely no rubbing.

Breathe, Tru. Breathe.

Just as Truvie was getting it somewhat together, Candace Little appeared from out of flipping nowhere. Her hair flowed like elegantly illustrated red flames, perfect curvature at the bottom, full and bouncy onto a silky brown blouse that Truvie knew her mother loaned her because she saw them trying on clothes before the party. Candace was in the same theater troop as Truvie's mom.

The whole of Candace stunk of look-at-my-stunningness. Truvie did stare at the actress, all the time. Even though she was a year younger than Truvie, Candace acted much older. She put out an energy that demanded she be reacted to, like all actresses, her grandmother would say. And then add, "It's a disease called insecurity. Don't catch it." Truvie was jealous of Candace's unending confidence. She'd always wished for a friendship, but Candace loathed her. For what, Truvie had yet to decipher, despite her frequent efforts. It seemed to be a game to Candace, which only hurt Truvie more.

It was no secret that Candace would head straight to New York City the day after graduation, if not sooner. Truvie knew that her mother would be devastated by Candace's departure and wanted nothing more than to go with Candace. Not that Truvie wanted her mom to leave, but still, Truvie wished her mom would go and chase her dream while Truvie and her father worked on the Equation for Imagination. Everyone deserved to live the life they imagined for themselves, especially her mom, who wanted to be famous as much as Truvie wanted her first kiss from Eddie.

"You missed your mouth," Candace said, staring at Truvie's chest.

Truvie turned and bolted from the room, Fig style. She rushed to the stairs, eyes squeezed tightly shut, shaking her head. Nearly choking on emerging tears and the dumb BLT slider she'd shoved in her mouth, she paused at the bottom of the stairs to swallow.

"Truvie?"

She turned and saw her dad, holding the closed journal with his index finger marking the page he was on.

"You okay, sweetheart?" he asked. "What happened?"

Gulping, she shouted, "I'm an idiot who loves bacon! That's what happened." And ran up the stairs without looking back.

. . .

Truvie headed straight for her bedroom. Fig raised his head to see who it was, then thumped his tail against the puffy down pillows he was perched against. He rolled to his back and exposed his belly for a scratch. Truvie sat on the bed and honored his wish, then burst into tears, falling on to his chest. He lowered his paw to her back and tolerated her snuggling for a few moments then wriggled free and licked her tears.

Truvie sucked in a few deep breaths to relax. "I should go back down," she said to Fig who licked her chin to nose several times before he paused ever-so-briefly and moved his concentration to her chest and shoved his nose close with a big whiff. He immediately started to—

"No." Truvie stood. Fig hadn't done anything wrong. He smelled bacon, mayo, and tomato. And naturally wanted some. She pulled off her turtleneck and tossed it toward the red wicker hamper in the corner near the open closet door. Her room was tidy but not meticulous. It mostly contained books. A built-in floor-to-ceiling bookshelf covered the wall furthest from the entrance. Few spots remained unoccupied. Thick textbooks and years of yellow National Geographic spines lined the bottom right shelves. Her father's set of Encyclopedia Britannica from when he was twelve, fourteen dictionaries, and more than a hundred physics books were at closest reach. She took notes from the dictionaries and the old encyclopedias then followed up on the Internet to check their accuracy. What was true once in a book was now presented in hundreds of results to a simple Internet query. Truth was hard to find. Or at least ever-evolving.

Above the backboard of her bed was a giant poster of a green crow with the words "Beware of Induction." Just because you haven't seen it, does not mean it does not exist. We cannot induce that all crows are black merely because we have yet to see a green one. It was the premise of quantum mechanics, the study of the smallest particles of the Universe, and to Truvie it meant that often what was true, where we come from and who we are, was not visible. Everything was there. Our eyes simply hadn't evolved enough to see the smallest of the smallest. We didn't yet have the power to see what was behind everything: energy.

Truvie intended to study these smallest bits of energy to show that we were all the same bits of energy. It was our use of our individual energy that mattered. Not some mystery. Energy. Nothing more. Nothing less. Our thoughts were our one—our only—unique trait. Thoughts were energy. Life was our use of them. Harness your thoughts, and the possibilities became instantly limitless.

Truvie sighed and moved to the mirror bolted the inside of her closet door. Her body bulged around the belly and over her bra on the sides. She eyed the little dot of grease on her white tank top. She lowered her chin to look closer, pulling her tank from her neck. She thought about taking it off and putting on her flannel pajamas hanging on a hook a few inches away from her forehead. Beyond her PJs were turtlenecks and flannel button-up shirts, her staples. She wore dark cotton turtlenecks almost daily, except in summer, of course. And skinny jeans. On the floor, two pair of Jack Purcell tennis shoes—one brown and the other dirtied white. She also had snow boots and a pair of flip-flops. And a brand-new pair of purple glitter faux-fur slipper boots her mother bought her last year that she'd never worn. Not once.

The rest of her closet contained costumes. Not hers. They were her mother's. Not from every single show.

These were the fragile ones. The ones that required hanging. Some were in zipped plastic bags. The tougher costumes were neatly packed in boxes in the rafters of the garage. Every couple of years, Sylvie, Truvie and her father maneuvered the boxes down, checked them for moths and mold, then re-folded and gently laid them back into the boxes and placed them in the rafters with tender reverence.

Truvie didn't go for the Marie Antoinette or Catherine of Aragon get-ups. She liked the white dress with the red belt her mother had worn when she played Maria in West Side Story. And all the dresses from Breakfast at Tiffany's. She lightly touched the plastic carrier for one of the silk dresses. They would look incredible on Candace. Without knowing what exactly she was doing, she unzipped the plastic to the long black sleeveless dress and flayed open the bag. She eyed it, calculating the fit on her body. Her mother was five and a half inches taller and many pounds slimmer than Truvie who inherited her father's more solid build in that her torso was wider, like a swimmer. Truvie hated the water, so her build was a waste. She preferred land. She did get her mother's slender legs, but without the height, they were often overshadowed by her bulky top half.

Still.

It might look okay.

And as long as she avoided the BLTs.

"Truvie?" Her mother voice sounded worried. "You okay honey? Your dad said something happened, something about bacon, but he wasn't sure what."

Truvie stayed in the closet when she answered. "I

4
Seventeen Years and Seventeen Days

Truvie glanced around lunchtime in the cafeteria of Lakeland Heights High School. "Wasted ener—" she cut herself off and corrected to, "Potential energy. Lots and lots of potential energy." It was extracurricular club sign-up day. Students fought to sign up at the Talk2Me table and the lacrosse and cross-country ski clubs. No one had paused, noticed, or neared Truvie's Quantum Physics Club table. The lined yellow tablet before her, numbered one to ten on the left side, remained empty, a wasteland.

Eddie walked toward her. He gripped the messenger bag strapped across his chest then ran his fingers through his hair as he smiled at her. He was liked and welcomed by the tribes of Lakeland, but luckily his loyalty to Truvie outweighed the invite to popularity that trailed his every move. Truvie picked up the pencil, readying it for the one signature she'd been promised.

"Eddie!"

Eddie stopped and glanced in the direction of the voice that had called out his name.

"Eddie!" Candace Little skipped to him and grabbed his forearm. "Come sign up! Over here. With me. It'll be fun for you!"

The banner behind Candace possessed an enlarged headshot of her. She hosted Lakeland's Talk2Me, a talk show about their school produced by the school's theater department, a department Truvie's mother started.

Truvie couldn't hear Eddie's response to Candace, but he smiled while she pouted, jutting out her lower lip. He stepped away and she watched him for a second then turned to the next joiner. She flipped her red locks off her shoulder then leaned into a tall boy wearing a Lakeland High sweatshirt Truvie didn't recognize. Their school mascot, a gator, was cartooned with sunglasses and a visor on the boy's torso.

A shadow darkened her gawking.

"Any takers?" Eddie asked.

Truvie shook her head.

"Beyond bummed?" he asked. "Tell the truth."

"Why would I lie? Truth is all that matters. It's why this club should have a waiting list. Physics explains everything." She paused. He smirked. "Oh. You were teasing. Trying to make light of my pain."

"Only because I love you," he said.

A flutter released in Truvie's belly so powerful she felt her cheeks flush. I love you, too. I love you so much.

"Give me that pencil," he said. "I'll sign up ten times under ten different names."

"You'd still only be one person."

Shaking his head at her, Eddie wrote his name on the first line.

The electronic bell chimed three times sending the cafeteria into a flurry of flinging backpacks. Trays clanked onto the conveyer belt, as a loud torrent of chatter crescendoed amidst the billowing student body. Truvie tossed her backpack over her shoulder and grabbed the yellow pad as she let herself be swept into the mix next to Eddie.

As they reached the exit, Eddie turned to her. "Meet out front after school?"

"Three hours and thirty-eight minutes."

"Unless I walk faster," Eddie said.

"You lope. You don't walk," Truvie said.

"What?" he asked with distinct dimples, "And you trek like we're scaling a steep mountain."

"Maybe we are."

He nudged her in the ribs with his elbow. "Oh Tru, always so serious."

"I wish I could prance," she said softly. "Like Fig does when he hears a squirrel but hasn't spotted it yet. It's really beautiful." She curled her fingers toward her wrist, attempting to mimic Fig lifting his front paw and bending it when he was "on point."

"Go for it," he said. "I'll be the squirrel." He surged

forward into the swarm of students then plunged right, ducking between two boys, then jerked left, cutting off a group of girls. Then Eddie froze and attempted to sniff. With a snort, he turned right and raced down the hall.

Truvie turned as Eddie did, but she did not prance. Then, surprising herself, she gave a glance around to make sure no one was looking, then she skipped the few remaining steps that led her to class.

"I saw that!"

She looked down the hall.

Eddie watched from a doorway. "Excellent prancing."

Truvie bowed as the final bell sounded.

Eddie puckered his lips sending her a kiss that burned into her and melted her head to toe. Butterflies took flight in her belly, emptying doubt, and filling her with more anticipation than she could contain.

. . .

"How'd the sign up go?" Truvie's science teacher, P.J. Ramsey, in his staple khaki pants and a pale blue button-up shirt, was her biggest fan.

"Just one," she said, thinking of Eddie and tingling all over.

"One is more than enough," he said. "You know that. One student who cares gets the teacher to show up to teach."

"I could teach this class, Mr. Ramsey," Truvie said.

"Shh." He smiled. "You'll get me fired."

Truvie straightened and put her right hand to her

heart. "I would never tell anyone, Mr. Ramsey. Ever."

"I'm teasing, Truvie," he said. "Always so literal."

"Yes," she said. "Clarity empowers, don't you think?"

"Almost as much as a sense of humor." Mr. Ramsey winked then faced the class.

Truvie took her seat in the front row, closest to the door and several feet away from the rest of the class. Because the content was so far below Truvie's knowledge and cerebral appetite, Mr. Ramsey had long since tossed out the syllabus and created an independent study program for Truvie. A program he didn't understand but had developed with Truvie's father, Ian.

Truvie dug into her bag and pulled out her tablet. A frozen image of Dr. Leonard Susskind, a physics professor from Stanford University, displayed. She positioned her headphones to her ears and pressed play. She leaned in as Dr. Susskind unraveled the complex, but fascinatingly eloquent Second Law of Thermodynamics. A law Truvie simplified by stating that when time moved forward, things got more random, but when things moved backward, things got less random.

The most exciting thing about this law was that the more momentum and velocity applied, the more expansion something, anything, experienced. It made her optimistic to know that things, including people, only grow when they move forward. That law applied to everyday life as easily as it applied to the creation of our Universe. She knew that to get people to understand and worship physics as she did, she had to find ways of making it personal to them. And it was! Physics explained everything. She knew that as she got smarter and better in her knowledge, it would ooze from her and into them. She knew with every fiber of her being that this was true, despite her current lack of tangible proof.

Everything must move forward, or it will cease to exist. Of course, to some, it also meant that eventually mass would grow so hot it would become meaningless and we would all Big Bang begin again, but Truvie preferred to believe that the excess mass would generate a new Universe, maybe even one we could influence.

Tingles spread over her skin. She clapped her hands and rubbed her palms together vigorously. This was it. Physics explained everything. "How can people not care about physics?"

She looked up from her screen, realizing she shouted that a bit too boldly. All eyes concentrated on her.

"Sorry," she said, though she couldn't hear herself over Dr. Susskind. Truvie pulled her turtleneck up over her chin and slid down in her chair. She tried to refocus on the lecture but was desperate for class to end. The other part of the Second Law of Thermodynamics stated that nothing could go from cold to hot spontaneously. Truvie had just proven that. Big Bang time.

· · ·

At exactly three thirty-eight, Eddie loped out the front door of Lakeland Heights High School. Truvie waited at the bottom of the seven steps, a few feet away from him. A north wind gave the air a bite, but autumn held on with deep blue skies and strong sun working to turn the leaves from greens to goldens to reds. He smiled and waved. Truvie gave a slight wave back.

Candace Little exited behind Eddie, flanked by two of her girls. A pang of envy, which Truvie described as a breath-sucking, chest-compressing, eye-squinting misery to herself more than once, centered into her. She wanted to look away but didn't. Instead, surprising herself, she took five steps up, meeting Eddie on the sixth. Candace and her girls arched over the seventh.

"I don't know why you hang out with this mutant, Eddie," Candace said. "She smells like bacon. Eau de porque frite."

Her girls found that ravishingly hysterical.

"I do like bacon," Truvie said. "The way it melts in your mouth. Salty and meaty—the texture is—"

"Do you hear her?" Candace oinked at Truvie. "This is who you want to be with?"

"Leave it alone, Candace," Eddie said.

"We're all mutants, actually," Truvie went on. "Primate mutants. Apes. But we have a thumb. But you knew that, right? Of course. Everybody knows that."

"Are you calling me a monkey?" Candace said.

"Well, technically—" Truvie started.

"Let's go," Eddie could hardly contain his laughter as he took Truvie's upper arm and led her down the stairs and onto the sidewalk, moving at a fast clip. "Mutants, Truvie? You're going to get your ass kicked."

Before Truvie could say anything, a big, goofy black Labrador galloped toward them.

"Figgy!" Truvie ran to him and bent over to receive his kisses.

"Hey Mrs. Tucker," Eddie said.

Sylvia Tucker, with full theatre make-up, including wide crow's feet, glittery-green eyeliner, and über-bouffant pigtails, joined them.

"He jumped out of the window again to get to you, Truvie," her mother said. "Luckily he didn't scratch my ad." Her mother's SUV was wrapped like a Christmas present with a bow on the roof. The signage on the decal read, "Ho Ho Hopeful: A Holiday Revival at the Marcus. Black Friday through New Year's Day." A toothy headshot of her mother smacked across the passenger door, taken by the same photographer that had taken Candace Little's for the Talk2Me banner. Her mother's show started in two weeks but Truvie had been riding around in a Christmas present since early October.

Truvie stood. "He gets excited."

"I saw you chatting with Candace but—" her mother said. "Everything okay?"

"Okay might be a stretch," Eddie said. "But no big deal."

"I have a dress rehearsal." Her mother raised jazz hands to her face. "Obviously. Take Fig okay? Then start dinner when you get home. I put a recipe on the counter. No cereal. If you don't make the dinner, a BLT is fine, but no cereal."

"I heard you the first time," Truvie said. "You have Fig's ball?"

"It's in the car," her mother said.

"I'll get it." Eddie took off.

"The red one," Truvie called to Eddie.

Without turning back to her, Eddie waved.

"Don't bug, Gram, okay? She's painting. Finally. Big meltdown this morning. She's the worst with birthdays. Seventy-seven is a gift, but not to her. Nooo. She put her foot through a canvas then magically found her muse around noon. Let's let her flow with it."

"She put her foot through the maples?" Worry spread through Truvie. "She's been working on that for weeks."

"Sometimes we destroy what we love." Her mother pulled her red Ho Ho sweatshirt over her waist. The glittery green Ho's were mutely illuminated by the fading sunlight.

Truvie involuntarily shook her head and frowned. "Why would anyone do that?"

Raising her brows, her mother asked, "I'm sorry no one signed up for your club. Candace texted me. She said you could do a science report for the TV station. You know like the weather or something? You're always more accurate than the guy on Channel Four."

"A weather girl?" Truvie asked.

"We could give you a makeover—"

"Got it!" Eddie tossed the red rubber ball from his palm, intending to catch it, but Fig leaped into the air and intercepted it.

"Good boy!" Truvie patted Fig. "You see that?"

"He nearly took my arm off," Eddie said.

Truvie smiled and shook her head. "Never. He's way too good to do that."

Her mother kissed her cheek, which Truvie was sure left a red lip outline. "I'll be home late. Call Dad as soon as you get home. He worries."

Candace and her girls arrived. "Hi Mrs. Tucker! See you at rehearsal! Eddie, will you be there later?"

A rush of cold raced through Truvie's veins. Then she remembered that her mother had recruited Eddie's mom to be in the theater company.

"Not tonight," Eddie said. "Truvie's making me dinner."

Truvie suddenly heated up, blood rushed to her cheeks and forehead. "BLTs," she said with pride. "Come on, Fig."

"She named her dog Pig?" Candace asked in a not-at-all-nice tone.

Truvie's mother laughed. "Fig not Pig. Like a Fig Newton."

"Oh." Candace pressed a smile. "Adorable."

· · ·

Dark clouds moved across the lake toward the cliffside of the park Truvie, Fig, and Eddie entered. As soon as they were ten feet into the maple tree-lined path, Fig bounced and barked, begging, pleading, aching for Truvie to toss that red ball. Truvie shifted her backpack off her shoulders and handed it to Eddie. She cranked her arm back and let the ball fly.

"How far?" Truvie asked.

"Left to third," Eddie said.

"Mid center to third, easy. Likely home plate."

"We'll count next time," Truvie said. "Hundred and fifty feet should take about six seconds to land."

"You can throw far, Truvie, okay?"

"Anyone can. It's physics. Velocity. Turbulence and—"

"Follow through and grip," Eddie interrupted. "Form helps."

"Mass helps more," Truvie said. "A standard tennis ball would never go that far."

Fig arrived back with the ball in his teeth and a wriggling body. "Good boy!" Truvie sang.

Fig dropped the ball at her feet and barked.

Eddie handed Truvie her backpack and grabbed the ball. He situated his messenger bag to his left side and threw the red ball into the sky. A raindrop dropped, hitting him in the eye.

"Should we make a run for it?" Eddie asked.

"Nah," Truvie said. "Fig needs to run or he'll drive me crazy all night. I don't care about the rain, you?"

"I don't mind."

He took Truvie's hand. She yanked it away, not because she didn't want to hold his hand. She did. More than anything.

"Sorry," she said, holding her hand open. "Try again?"

He took hold again. "Is this okay?"

"My heart's racing so fast. It's more than okay. I love it. I mean—yes—it's fine. Great. Great and fine."

"You sure stood up to Candace," he said. "What got into you?"

"Sorry if my palm sweats. I've never held anyone's—you're not anyone. I've never—I'm so nervous. I mean—." She inhaled, held her breath for a moment then exhaled. "I'm happy. I've wanted you to hold my hand for a really long time."

"Me too," he said. "We'll hold on until we can't stand it, okay?" Eddie smiled. "I'm sweating, too."

Truvie gave a little skip to her step. A prance. Then settled into the best walk of her life.

"I wasn't trying to stand up to Candace," Truvie said. "I was . . . I . . ."

"Jealous?" Eddie asked.

The rain picked up, forming impromptu puddles on the path.

"Envious," Truvie said, hopping over a water pool. "I wasn't proud of myself, so I tried to change what I was thinking. Thoughts carry energy that we put out, so I wanted to put out nice energy. And get nice energy back."

"She's not worthy of your nice energy," Eddie said.

Fig rushed up to them, shook the rainwater from his coat, then flicked the ball at Truvie's feet. She looked up to Eddie before she released her hold to his hand. She picked up the red ball and gave it a big toss. Fig raced along the forest path, disappearing to the left.

"Must have bounced off a rock," Truvie said as she picked up her pace. Her heart skipped a beat. She didn't like not having Fig in her sights.

"Fig!"

She took off running. "The ravine is right up here. I don't want him—Fig! Come!"

They rounded the left turn Fig had taken and found him sniffing the ground near a wooden bridge. His tail wagged like a fast metronome. Truvie exhaled. "Thank goodness. Good boy."

She moved to the middle of the bridge. A steep,

narrow crevasse expanded below them. Rain drained past her, pelting the earth. She scoured the sides of the drop searching for Fig's ball.

"There." Truvie pointed to the red rubber ball wedged between a rock and a limb a few feet down the cliff. Fig looked to the exact spot then trotted across the bridge and stood directly above the ball. He locked expectant eyes with Truvie. His tail straight up, rigid.

"No, Fig," Truvie said. "I'll get it. You stay put."

5
Grandaddy

Truvie and Eddie leaned over the bridge and eyed the ball. They looked at each other then up to the rain, which doused their faces. Fig shook head to tail. Then barked.

"Okay, Fig," Truvie said. "Hold on."

"You're not going after it?" Eddie asked.

"It's not that far down. He loves that ball. Had it since he was a puppy."

"He's still a puppy," Eddie said.

"He's almost six. And he needs his ball." Truvie lifted her backpack off her shoulder. "Hold my pack so it doesn't get too—"

"Wet?" Eddie asked, holding the soaking pack. "I think we should leave it and get it tomorrow when it's dry."

Truvie stood next to Fig. "It's only ten feet, less than two of me. Back Fig. Let me through."

Fig took one step back.

Truvie rubbed the top of his head. His body gyrated with wiggles. She kissed his snout. "You wait here. Do NOT follow me. Hear me?"

Fig took several steps back and sat. His tail swooshed against the dampened dirt.

Truvie kneeled to the ground then lowered onto her stomach. "I'm going to be a mess. My dad—"

"Come back up then," Eddie said, shaking his head. "I don't think this is a good idea."

"I'm right at home on the edge of a cliff," she said with a bright smile. "Trust me."

Truvie shifted backward, letting her feet dangle over the edge of the ravine. She groped with her toes for a foothold. Her right big toe hit something solid. She moved her toes to the right. A limb. She pressed into it. Solid. She lowered down with her right foot, putting all her weight into it while her left toes searched the cliff for a second hold. She swung her left toes close to the mountain. Her hands pressed to the cliff, but she had nothing to hold onto. She relied on her balance, and her weight to hug the wall.

Rain pooled against her chest and belly. She shifted back slightly to release the water then glanced down toward the ball. There.

Still out of reach.

"Truvie," Eddie called. "Please come back up."

"I got it," she said. "I got it. Though the rain is creating a complication."

"A complication? Don't. Please, Tru."

Truvie's left toes found a rock. It wasn't quite big enough to serve as a hold, but it gave her some reprieve to her right quadriceps, which had started to quiver. She relaxed and inhaled.

Her left toes slipped off the rock and Truvie slid straight down the face of the cliff. She screamed.

"Truvie!" Eddie ran from the bridge to the edge.

Her right foot found another limb.

She started to swing back away from the cliff.

"Truvie!" Eddie cried.

She grabbed hold of a root jutting from inside the dirt, pulling herself back to the wall and slamming her head into a rock. She yelped then groaned but managed to look up. "I'm okay." Her head burned from the blow. Youch.

Fig jetted toward the edge. Eddie grabbed hold of his collar. "No Fig!"

"Shit Truvie," Eddie said. "Are you all right?"

Truvie looked over her right shoulder, the ball rested a few inches from her. She reached for it. Suddenly her vision blurred. Her head started to spin. Her stomach lurched. She blew out a wave of nausea but couldn't focus.

She closed her eyes.

Her head collapsed back into her shoulders.

"Truvie!" Eddie's call muted and too far away. "Truvie!"

. . .

Truvie suddenly stood next to a bald man wearing a bright blue three-piece suit and navy-blue tie with pale green polka dots. Books and maps surrounded them. A library. A giant, lose-yourself-for-days library. Must be a university.

Waves crashed into jagged glass rocks several storeys below their view out to a raging sea. She saw herself in the glass, soaking wet and shivering. Her lips blue, quivering.

Squinting at his reflection, she knew him. "Grand-daddy?"

"Welcome home, Truitt Skye. We've been expecting you."

***

Truvie stutter-blinked. Rain peppered down onto her aching head, face and the back of her neck. She jerked her head back upright and blinked several times.

"Truvie!" Eddie cried.

Truvie leaned back enough to see Eddie leaning over and waving his arm at her.

"I'm okay." She held her eyes shut tight. Her temples throbbed. She was woozy and weak. "Whew. That hurt."

"Take my hand." Eddie's hand was nowhere near close enough for her to grab.

"Hang on. Let me grab—" She arched her ribs to the right, stretched out her fingers and touched the ball. She reached a teeny bit more and her fingers—

The ball released from its spot. And bounced off the sides of the crevasse until it vanished from sight.

Fig stirred at the cliff's edge. He reached his paws

toward over the side. "Get back!" Eddie shouted. "Now Fig!"

"Back up, buddy," Truvie called. "We'll get it tomorrow."

With a couple deep inhales, Truvie maneuvered up the wall, taking her time to find and secure each hold until she put her hand into Eddie's and he lifted her into his arms.

He pulled away ever-so-slightly and lowered his lips to hers. His lips moist from rain. She tasted dirt and mint gum. Her body warmed face to chest, legs to toes. He kissed her. Eddie Rock kissed Truvie Tucker before her eighteenth birthday. Not once or twice, but quite a few times. Each one softer, longer, deeper.

Fig barked, knocking her out of her dream moment. He shook his coat sending water flying.

"We should get you home," Eddie said. "We're so soaked."

"You can borrow something from my dad," she said. "Thanks for helping me up. And for kissing me. I liked that very much."

"We should do it more often." He put his arm around her shoulders.

"I think so too," she said, leaning her head into his chest.

They crossed the bridge and returned to the path. Fig at Truvie's side.

"You scared the crap out of me," Eddie said. "You're one brave girl, Truvie Tucker."

"You're a really good kisser," she said. "I don't—I never—I don't know if I kissed back right."

He stopped and gave her another kiss. "It was perfect."

Hand-in-hand, they got on the asphalt trail that led away from the forest.

"You scaled a wall for a ball." Eddie shook his head. "In the pouring rain."

"And I failed," Truvie said, watching Fig trot a few feet ahead of them. "I'm sorry, Figgy. I bet it's at the bottom of the ravine. No one will find it before we do. I promise."

They walked in silence as the rain dissipated to a sprinkle. Light drained from the sky as the blaze red sun lowered to the horizon.

. . .

They crossed the parking lot and across a patch of grass then waited at the curb for cars to pass. Fig sat to Truvie's left, looking up, awaiting her okay. Traffic hit puddles of rain, splash, swoosh, splash swoosh. When the road cleared, the trio crossed and headed up the curved driveway to the Tucker house.

The houses across from Lake Park tended to be ornate monstrosities. Truvie's house fit with only two others to form the entire block. This corner lot belonged to her grandparents. Her late grandfather, Junius, bought and rehabilitated it in 1973. Since then, her grandmother and mother re-do a room a year whether it needs it or not, in his memory. He loved bright silks, so each room had a splash of smooth, shiny, bright fabric—throw pillow, wall hanging, bedspread, rug, pretty much anything.

"I have a confession about the ball," Truvie said to Eddie. "And why I went after it. My dad and I made it together. Specific mass and divots for maximum velocity and turbulence. Maximum flight. He'd kill me if I lost it. I'd kill me."

"So that's why you can throw it so far," Eddie said. "Trickery."

"Physics," Truvie said.

. . .

They stepped up the wide stoop steps and Truvie opened the front door. The entrance was an enclosed glass porch with a dog bed, several beach towels, built-in shelves for shoes and boots, hooks for coats and a row of cubbies for hats, scarves, neck warmers, gloves, books, and whatever else happened to land in one, like forgotten coffee mugs with stirring spoons, and stained wine glasses. Fig had to dry in here, which he knew, and hated. He yanked a towel hanging on a hook and held it for Truvie. She rubbed it over Fig as he danced and shimmied through her legs.

"You stay here, Fig." Truvie reached up into a cubby and pulled out a dried strip of chicken breast.

"I'll have my mom stop at the ravine," Eddie said. "We'll take the lake way home."

The muted ring of the phone sounded. Truvie checked her watch. Two minutes after four. She opened the door to the house and raced to the trill.

. . .

She rounded the doorframe into the kitchen and snatched the receiver hanging on the wall. "Hey, Dad."

A wave of nausea rose from her belly button to her throat. Her vision blurred and she thought she might pass out. She blinked rapidly to regain herself. She pierced her lips into a small circle opening and exhaled audibly.

"What happened?" Her father's voice deep, calm.

"Nothing, Dad. The rain. It delayed us. Took forever get across the road and Fig is super wet. He's in the mudroom. Don't worry."

"Your cadence is jagged. What happened?"

"Cadence? I ran to the phone." She took hold of the island counter with her free hand. Her head suddenly heavy, her eyes stung from behind their sockets. "I'm winded, that's all."

"I'll be home in a couple of hours, okay? Check in on Helena."

"Mom said—" Truvie winced as a gripping sensation in her skull tightened. "Not to bother her. She's in the flow."

"What's wrong?" His voice suddenly too loud.

Eddie entered the kitchen. "You okay?"

"Shh," Truvie hissed. "I'm fine. Just cold and wet. Okay if Eddie borrows a pair of your sweats? He's going to help me with dinner."

"Mom told me," her father said. "Sorry about Physics Club, sugar. They don't know what they're missing."

"I kind of liked Mom's idea about doing a science bit

on the school TV show." Truvie rubbed her right temple. Throbbing pain crept from behind her right eye.

"A weather girl?" Eddie and her father said in unison.

"No," Truvie said, bending over to look at her socks. "Well, if I have to, I guess. Anything to be able to talk about science. Maybe I can do some features on sports or something? Physics of baseball."

"I like it," her father said. "See you soon. I've got to finish up the job here. Another hour."

But before Truvie could respond, her legs gave out from under her. The phone dropped to the tile with a crash. Eddie caught her before her head hit the floor.

"Truvie!" Her father's voice cried from the receiver.

Eddie shook Truvie gently. "Truvie. Truvie. Wake up."

"Eddie!" Her father's voice wailed from the phone.

Eddie collected the receiver. "She passed out, Mr. Tucker. When we were in the woods she hit her head on a rock."

"Call 911 and get her grandmother! I'm on my way."

Truvie blinked her eyes open.

"She's awake," Eddie said. "Truvie."

"Put her on," Ian said.

Truvie sat against the island cabinet doors. "I'm fine. I'm okay. Maybe I should eat something."

Eddie stood and started to leave.

"Where are you going?" Truvie asked.

"To get your grandma," Eddie said.

Her father continued in her ear. "Have Helena take you to the Emergency Room. I'll meet you there in ten minutes."

"Dad," Truvie said.

"You know very well what a head injury and loss of consciousness might mean," her father said. "Go. Now. No messing around, Truvie."

6
Flight

The Emergency Department pulsed with patients and their families, nurses, attendants, and doctors. Not to mention machines everywhere—computers and monitors and televisions beeping and humming, leaving absolutely no room for silence.

Her grandmother answered questions being asked by a man with a computer on a cart outside the curtain of Truvie's pseudo-room. Eddie stood next to Truvie's gurney.

"You ever been in a hospital overnight?" Eddie asked.

"Never," Truvie said. "Only thing I've ever had was stitches on my calf."

"When you walked backward through the window

at the Museum of Science and Industry."

Truvie smiled. "You still remember."

"It was memorable."

Truvie offered a slight laugh, not the choking, side-aching kind she'd gleaned many times from this memory of her not paying attention to where she was going because she was awestruck by an exhibit on the future of computing.

Eddie brushed a tear from Truvie's eye.

He didn't look away. Neither did she.

"I'm scared," Truvie said.

"They don't make it easy to not feel scared," he said, looking around the chaos. "Let's think about something else. A nice energy. Packer pre-season game this weekend."

"You going?" Truvie asked.

"My mom—" he started. "You know how she does taxes for a bunch of the players, same as she does for the theater. We always get good seats for both. Want to—"

"Yes," Truvie said. "Packers, I mean. I always get good seats to the theater."

"Just us. Not my mom. She's not invited. And you'll tell me every detail on the physics of football, okay?"

Truvie's eyes burned and blurred. She sucked in her lower lip, forcing a nod. "They really should consider deflating the ball or making the whole ball smaller— not sure—I'd have to test. Less porous, more panels."

The curtain opened. Her grandmother entered with her easy radiance. To Truvie, her grandmother always looked like she'd stepped off a sailboat. Her white-gray hair up and back off her rosy-cheeked face, tanned face. She wore black leggings, period, and a variety of printed tunics. Today's was pale pink. Nothing too tight, but enough to show she was in good shape for her seventy-plus years.

"Now what exactly happened to you, dear? I told the—whoever that person was—that you hit your head. Was that at home? On that damn kitchen island your mother insisted we put in the damn middle of the damn kitchen?" she asked. The ride here had been filled with phone calls from her father to her grandmother and then her grandmother to mother.

"I was scaling down the ravine—"

"In Milwaukee?" her grandmother asked, clearly stressed beyond the point of clear, rational listening.

"In the park, Mrs. Stelae," Eddie said. "By the walking bridge."

"Oh for heck's sake, Truvie. Why in the world were you—" She stopped herself and answered her own question. "Fig."

"His ball went over the edge," Truvie said.

"That special flying physics ball?" her grandmother asked.

Truvie pushed herself up higher on the pillows. "I slid a little when I went to get it."

"From the rain," Eddie added.

"And the pitch." Truvie gestured her hand to a vertical angle. "More than a sixty-degree slope."

"Where did you hit your head?" her grandmother asked.

"Front, off to the right a little."

Her grandmother sat on the side of Truvie's bed and lifted Truvie's bangs. She gently touched the small bump. "Does it hurt?"

"I have a really bad headache," Truvie said. "All over."

"They're sending the CT guy or someone to take you to a CT. Something like that," her grandmother said with a loud sigh. "Your parents will be here any second."

Truvie looked away. She opened her mouth, then closed it, hesitant to sound—

"Spit it out," her grandmother said.

"This may sound crazy but—" Truvie stalled and looked at her feet tucked tight under the sheet and blanket.

"Let's have it," her grandmother said.

"When I—" Truvie said. "I saw a man when I blacked out. I'm pretty sure it was—was Granddaddy bald?"

"Yes," her grandmother said, frowning. "Yes, he was. He lost his hair early. Thirty. Maybe twenty-nine. All his hair—" She snapped her fingers. "Gone in a flash. What'd he say?"

"You don't think it's strange?" Truvie said, looking at Eddie, who shrugged and opened his eyes wide.

"Only if he was silent," her grandmother said. "Junius Stelae was not a quiet man. I'm sure he had something pithy and poetic to say. Even as, no, especially as, an apparition, I'm sure he had plenty to say."

"He called me Truitt Skye. And said, 'we've been expecting you.'"

Her grandmother lifted her chin and bit her lower

lip. After several breaths, she said, "Hmm."

Truvie and Eddie exchanged a glance.

After several nods, her grandmother said, "I miss him." Her voice soft. A tear slid down her cheek to her chin. "So smart. Gracious. He was a kind man. To everyone, not just me."

Helena wiped her tear then focused on Truvie. "I see him too. Usually as I'm dozing off. Similar to when one knocks their head against a rock and drifts from this world for a moment."

"He was in a glasshouse surrounded by books with a view that looked out to a blue sea with crashing waves."

"In one of his fancy suits?"

"Blue. And a tie, navy with green polka dots."

"He had those made in London." Her grandmother glanced off into the distance. "Savile Row."

"We should go for a custard after this is over," Truvie said, trying to lighten the mood.

"We can pick up Fig's ball on the way," Eddie said.

Her grandmother straightened and pushed out a smile. "An excellent plan," she said. "We'll get the ball then head to Kopp's."

She stood and pulled down her tunic as she moved away from Truvie's gurney. "Where the hell is this CT person? You two stay put. I'm on it."

Truvie closed her eyes. Eddie's thumb rubbed the top of hers. She opened her eyes. They said nothing. His look said it all: I love you. She blinked and told him the same with every cell of her being.

Within a few seconds, a young, robust man with dreadlocks and a Rasta pin on his faded violet scrub shirt entered with a wheelchair.

"This is Joseph," her grandmother said. "Luckily for him, he was already on his way."

"Or else," Joseph said with a thick accent, Truvie couldn't place. "Let's go den, sweet girl. Take a big photo of dat beautiful head of yours."

Joseph and Eddie gently guided Truvie as she lowered into the wheelchair.

Eddie took her hand and squeezed. Helena kissed her cheek. "We'll be right here. You're in good hands. I can tell."

· · ·

Joseph wheeled her away and into the main Emergency Room hallway. "Dis won't take long, Miss Tucker," he said.

They passed a row of partially closed curtains. Truvie looked away. She didn't want to peek in on people's privacy.

But Joseph stopped the chair and edged her through one of the curtains.

A young black woman, maybe a few years older than Truvie, sat on the edge of the hospital bed. She perked up at their entrance.

"Uncle Joe!" She coughed and heaved.

Joseph went to her side and rubbed her back. "Easy, girl," he said. "Breathe."

The young woman drew in a deep, wheezy breath as she leaned into him.

He dipped his head toward Truvie. "I wanted you

to meet my new girl, Truvie." He faced Truvie. "Truvie Tucker, dis be my beautiful niece, Serena."

Truvie shimmied to the edge of the seat and used her toes to scoot the wheelchair forward. She extended her hand to Serena's. "Nice to meet you."

Serena, shyly tucked to Joseph, reached her fingers to Truvie. "You too."

Joseph kissed Serena's forehead. "You two a match. I can tell."

He slowly extracted himself from Serena and said, "I be right back. Let me go get dis Truvie a photo of her brain. I tink it's a big one." He laughed and laughed. "Might need two dem photos to get the whole thing. I can feel her doin' lots of tinking."

He kissed Serena's cheek. "You rest. I be back."

Truvie nestled back into the wheelchair seat and waved. "See you, Serena. I hope you feel better soon."

"You too," Serena said.

. . .

When Truvie and Joseph reached the end of the corridor, he punched a button to open a set of double of doors straight ahead of them. Joseph turned her around, feet toward the Emergency Room, and wheeled her backward through the doors.

Eddie and her grandmother stood at the other side of the hallway watching her leave. Each forced a smile. A feathery stirring erupted in Truvie's chest followed too soon by a deadening heaviness. Alone, except for Joseph, Truvie sunk into fear.

"I don't want to die." She whispered it. It was out there. Out there waiting for an answer.

"Death don't mean dead," Joseph said. "Means different."

"My brain is bleeding," Truvie said. "A TBI. Traumatic Brain Injury. I know because I read too much."

Joseph wheeled her into a small room with a large, white CT Scanner.

"I have a large capacity for understanding difficult concepts," Truvie said. "I love to read about complicated things, especially science."

"Nuh-ting complicated 'bout love," Joseph said. "And I would love for you to git up here on dis table for me. Okay?"

"Yes. Okay." Truvie pushed herself out of the wheelchair. "I didn't think I hit my head that hard. It was an accident."

Joseph lowered to Truvie's height and took her hands into his. "We gon do dis. See where we at. Okay?"

Tears fell from Truvie's eyes. She couldn't stop them. They came and came.

Joseph lowered onto his knees. "Der ain't nuh-ting cannot be fixed, my girl. Breathe with me." He took in a long inhale.

Truvie did the same.

"Dat's a good girl."

Truvie sniffled in her snot. Joseph stood and got her a tissue. She wiped her tears and sat on the edge of the machine. Joseph gave her a wad of tissues.

"What you like to read da most?"

Truvie leaned in. "I like stories about love. But I

read them too quickly. Not like science books. Those take time, like days. But my favorite romances I finish in a few hours and I—I start them over again."

"Love. I knew it. You got love written all over you, girl. All over. No stopping it from coming outta you like wildfire."

Truvie lowered her back onto the cold bed of the scanner and closed her eyes as it slowly drew her into the tunnel.

"Lay still now," Joseph said. "And tink of love."

. . .

Joseph wheeled her back through the double doors.

He didn't pause at Serena's spot. He kept going.

Truvie and her father saw each other at the same moment. Ian jogged to her.

"Hey, Dad," she said.

Her father leaned down and hugged her. When he lifted away, he asked, "Can she walk from here?"

"I can walk," Truvie said.

Joseph nodded.

"Bye, Joseph," Truvie said. "Thank you. Tell Serena I say hi."

"Will do," he said then wheeled back toward the double doors.

Her father put his arm around her shoulders. "How'd it go?" Truvie reached up and put her hand on top of his. They took a step then he stopped and pulled her into his torso.

"Everything's going to be okay," he whispered. "I

promise."

She closed her eyes. It wasn't. But she kept that to herself. "I love you, Daddy."

"I love you, too, sugar."

As they approached her curtain, a doctor flung open the curtain and spoke to the nurse at the counter. "Can you give me a hand here? The mother fainted."

"Sylvia?" Truvie's father speed-walked to the doctor. "I'm Ian, Ian Tucker. Sylvia's my wife. Truvie's our daughter."

Truvie joined them. "Hi."

The nurse took a wheelchair into the pseudo-room.

"I'll help you," her father said to the nurse.

"Hi." The doctor extended his hand to Truvie. "I'm Dr. Fenwick."

"A neurosurgeon?" Truvie asked.

"Yes." He moved toward the curtain. "Can we talk for a moment in here?"

Truvie nodded. "My mom faints with stress. You told her?"

Dr. Fenwick stopped.

"About the TBI," Truvie said.

"I told her you needed surgery," Dr. Fenwick said. "Today."

"Is the bleed all over or just on the right?" Truvie asked.

"All over," he said.

"Slow or fast?" Truvie said.

He didn't answer.

"Let me just say—" Her voice caught. She shook her head, but tears welled anyway. "Let me give everyone a hug."

He paused as if he had more to say.

Truvie gave him a faint smile and stepped through the curtain. Her mother had come to and now wept in Ian's arms.

"I have to have surgery," Truvie announced. "They'll put drains into my brain by drilling holes into my skull. It's perfectly safe. They'll do their best, but if they can't get it all, they'll leave the drains in so they can continue to drain. I'll be in an Intensive Care Unit. I'll be out of it. But my brain is bleeding. It has to stop or—"

"The doctor was telling us." Eddie took her hand.

Her mother sobbed uncontrollably. "But she's never sick. Ever—"

Truvie held her attention on Eddie. She put her hand on top of his. "It's not your fault," she said. "I scaled the wall."

Truvie tightened all over realizing that she might never see Fig again. She wiped the tears from her cheeks. "I need to see Fig before I go to surgery."

"Honey," her father said.

Tears blurred Truvie's sight. "I'm not negotiating, Dad."

"I'll go get him." Helena slipped around the curtain.

"I don't think you can have a dog—" her mother said in a tender voice.

"Maybe when you wake up," her father said.

"No!" Truvie voice high, pained. She forced herself to calm down with a deep inhale. "I need to see him before—before I go."

"You're going to be fine," Eddie's mother said. "The

surgeon said he's done this procedure many times."

"Dad," Truvie said. "He's my heart. I have to—"

The curtain opened. A man in pale red scrubs behind a wheelchair entered.

"Truvie Tucker?" the transporter asked.

Truvie took a seat in the chair.

"Wait!" Her mother bent over and hugged her. She kissed Truvie's cheeks, her forehead, and her lips. "We'll wait right here. You are brave and strong. We'll be right here." She kissed her again.

Her father came over and kissed her. "I love you, honey. Be good. See you soon."

"I love you, too," Truvie said.

Her mother leaned in for another squeeze and whispered gently in her ear, "I love you to the moon and back then into the sun where I dance in the fire of your light."

Truvie squeezed her mother's neck. "I love you, Momma."

Eddie's mom hugged and kissed Truvie's forehead. "You're going to be just fine." Her voice cracked but her confidence stood tall.

Eddie.

He awkwardly moved to Truvie. Too many eyes. Too much pressure. Too sad. Too scared. He bent down to hug her while she edged up to kiss him. Her lips, and front teeth, landed on his shoulder, still soggy from the rain. He lowered to his knees. They embraced.

"We are going to that Packers game," he whispered in her ear.

"Definitely," she whispered back then added. "You're

everything to me."

He pulled away from their hold, his cheeks and around his eyes red and blotchy. He kissed her. Soft and tender.

When she opened her eyes, he met her gaze. They didn't need to say it. It was known. I love you.

A hand gripped and released her shoulder. She looked up at her dad.

"We'll all be here," he said. "It's all going to be fine."

She smiled and nodded.

The man in red scrubs wheeled her away from them. She did not—could not—look back. They passed the curtain where Serena had been, but Truvie looked straight ahead. They went through the double doors without him turning her backward as Joseph had done less than an hour ago.

. . .

He wheeled her into the long white corridor. They did not speak. They did not share.

Truvie loosened her grip on the arms of the wheelchair. "Relax," she whispered. Her hunched shoulders lowered. She released her taut thighs and stomach. She rolled her neck side to side.

"Fig!" she shouted. "I forgot to—go back!" She twisted to see the man in red—

He was gone.

Suddenly the floor rumbled and shook.

"What the?"

Truvie shifted to the front of her chair.

To her horror, the linoleum tile flooring lifted and rolled in waves. Her wheelchair ebbed up and down with each ripple.

"Earthquake? In Milwaukee?"

The walls pulsed in and out as if they were readying to burst.

"Hello?" she called. "Helllooo?"

She tried to push herself off the seat, but she could not.

The walls fissured with loud snaps and crackles.

A rush of cold air swept in from behind and beneath her. She looked back.

The double doors had blown off their hinges and flew out toward the Emergency Room.

"Fig!" she shouted.

Her beloved lab raced to her with everything he had.

"Fig! Hurry!"

A wretched rip cried above her as the ceiling exploded. Bits of white plaster toppled onto her.

She searched everywhere for Fig, but he wasn't there. For that she felt a wave of relief as her body lifted, gently at first, then with a thrust, as Truvie Tucker rocketed up, and out, into the night sky.

7
The City on the Sea

Truvie flew across the dark sky, confused but curious, worried but free. The crisp wind should have chilled her to the bone instead it enlivened her. She assimilated the clean, rich energy pulsing through her every cell, her headache gone, her fear vaporized. She expanded her arms out to her sides and let herself soar.

The bright lights of downtown Milwaukee sparkled like diamonds beneath her. The water of Lake Michigan stilled, elegant, beneath the illuminated moon. Her body floated over the lake and into the vastness of night. With each breath, she lifted higher until everything below dulled to black.

She glided along for a short wondering how far she might rise when she tasted sweet, soft morsels of sugar on her tongue. The darkness eased with faint light, revealing a meadow of puffy white clouds. Truvie thought she might find someone sitting on the tip of a cumulous beauty. As if on cue, she approached something—some things—of vibrant green perched on the clouds across a pale blue sky.

"Are those..." She leaned forward and her body replied by zooming nearer instantaneously. "Green crows?"

She hovered close to two crows balanced on fluff. Their bodies a deeper green, like basil. The wings were the color of the pulp of a lime. And their eyes. Their eyes shone chartreuse. The feet and beaks, something in between the dark and the light. Sage.

Suddenly several crows took flight. Blips of green across the white sky. A murder. Crows together were not a flock. They were a murder.

"Murder," she said, letting the word sit there a moment before adding, "Death."

"Not going," she whispered. "Gone."

. . .

The clouds flattened to a blanketed mist of chalk white. Truvie's body began to drop and spin round and round as she plummeted into endless white.

She opened her mouth to cry out. But knew no one would hear her. No one would find her way up here in the clouds. They wouldn't know to look up to find her. She left them all behind in that hospital waiting, expecting, wanting, longing for her to awaken and be better.

Truvie longed for that as well.

"Let this be a dream," she said. "Anesthesia-induced hallucinations. I've read that happens more than people realize."

Subtle, tender caws echoed. Not the ear-piercing, groveling bawls of black crows. This call lilted like an elongated mew, reminding her of the low, playful whimpers that Fig would make when he desperately wanted to come up on the bed but knew he needed to wait for an invitation. Not that anything stopped him from plunging onto the bed about three whimpers in, but that was the song the crows offered. A sweet, gentle request to be invited.

She didn't mind if they came closer. She wanted some company. She felt a little unsettled—in between awake and asleep—not sure what was real and what was fake.

The green crows flapped and glided above her until they methodically lowered nearer and nearer, offering the soft call every few seconds, as they surrounded her.

Birds served as messengers. That was a well-known fact dating back far longer than most could fathom. But messenger for whom? Who wanted to reach her?

The crows edged closer still, inches now from her.

The first beak nipped at the tip of her right shirt cuff. Then took hold. Another crow seized the hem of her left pant leg. She quivered with tickles as one nuzzled into the back of her neck to get hold of the fold in her turtleneck. She couldn't count how many had hold of her, but with the firmness of their support, she swore it was the whole murder.

The instant the last crow solidified its spot they flapped in unison. Faster. And faster still. They jetted through the clouds forging a mist that whipped against Truvie's cheeks and forehead. Her eyes watered. The spray tasted salty as the murder descended from the cumulous heaps to a clear sky. Below, at a great distance, an aqua blue sea emerged. She recognized it instantly as the same vibrant sea she recently saw when she hit her head on the rock in the ravine.

Curious, she dipped forward to see more. The murder responded with a dive bomb toward the water. As they drew closer, Truvie spotted little islands, hundreds of them, across the water. "Someone lives here? Wait—"

The crows halted and hovered.

"Oh," Truvie said. "Sorry. I was confused by the—I don't know. Keep going, please. I guess."

The crows resumed flight. The air turned warm and fresh with a fragrance of the sea and something floral, lavender maybe? Jasmine and rose. It smelled like her mother. Truvie took in the deepest breath she could muster, hoping the scent would penetrate her cells and never, ever, leave her.

She pushed away the thought that she was dead. She simply could not think it.

The crows descended once they neared the outer islands. Some had sandy beaches, while others had boulders for shores. Some looked to be straight from the woods with tall pine trees and log cabins. The one directly below her was all grass around the edges with a sweet grey cottage on a hill in the middle.

Other islands rose high with bridges and walkways to reach the houses. The ones to her left had lagoons inside stone walls with houses on pillars. There was one coming into to view with giant eucalyptuses and treehouses built right into them. She wanted to stop and see who lived there.

"Where are we?" she asked the crows, fully aware of the silliness that entailed.

The green crows arched into a full-on plunge toward the sea, then, at the last moment, swooped to hover mere inches above the water. Their flight rapid, purposed. Mounds of islands appeared and were gone in a blink. They ripped too rapidly for her to decipher anything but a blur of sea and clumps of land.

In a smooth lift, they released Truvie. She flailed immediately in horrid panic and dropped like a rock into the sea. Yet to her utter surprise, she instantly zipped from the water and onto an island with an enormous castle with terraced rose gardens and a fountain with an enormous metal statue of drooping tulips, only a few feet away from where she stood.

Truvie should be dripping wet from her little "dip" but wasn't.

"This has to be a druggy dream. Islands and a castle floating on the sea. A turquoise sea. Obviously, I don't do well on morphine."

Her thoughts drifted back to Joseph the CT technician with a Caribbean accent. She imagined him worried. Sad. In great pain.

Suddenly the metallic tulip statues rose into the air. Their copper stems, silver stamens and golden petals blinding against the sun. Steam lilted from the water of the fountain and soon a steady trickle came from each tulip's center. Truvie stepped into the fog of the fountain. There was no barrier bench encasing it, just a smooth marble base. As she walked to the bouquet, some of the stones beneath her feet illuminated into a bejeweled phrase.

"The City on the Sea," Truvie read. The words made of sapphire and diamonds, rubies and emeralds. Twinkling. Shining. Right into her eyes.

She turned from the fountain to view the castle behind her. For a moment, she wondered if a handsome prince would open the copper doors and whisk her into his arms.

Her mind shifted to an image of Eddie kneeling before a snow-covered gravestone under a dark daylight sky. His black knit hat pulled tight to his bowed head. His shoulders hunched and heaving as tears darkened spots on the grave.

She shook her head to banish the image. As if on command, the green crows gathered her into their talons once again.

. . .

In a quick flight across the sea, Truvie suddenly faced the glasshouse she'd seen when she hit her head.

A figure waited behind the glass.

In a blink, the crows reached the house. Jagged glass rocks jutted up along the island's edge. A glass dock stretched over the rocks for a quarter-mile into the water.

She searched for her grandfather but instead saw books and ladders to shelves high on the walls. Maps, chairs, and long, shiny study tables. He should be here. He was there before when she'd hurt herself. He had to be there. It was how it should be. They were so close, why couldn't she see him?

Extremely close.

"Too close!" she screamed. "We're going to crash into the glass!"

Truvie stared at the gaping mouth and wide eyes of her reflection in complete horror!

"Stop!" she shouted. "Please! We're too close."

This time, the crows shunned her command.

She thought quickly and tried again in her most generous of tones, "Please?"

The crows chucked her forward and vanished.

. . .

A whoosh of warm air passed over her as her body hit the glass. The odor went from pungent seawater to a smoldering campfire.

Truvie opened her right eye.

She and a vast array of glass—from big sheets to little slivers—were suspended mid-air inside the library.

"That was lucky." She arched back, hoping to move from horizontal to vertical, which she did, but her feet still hovered. "Granddaddy? Are you here?"

"I wouldn't do that."

Truvie reached her outstretched toes to the glass

brick floor. "Do what?"

"What you're about—"

Her heels hit the floor and glass shot like bullets in all directions.

Truvie ducked and covered, her forearms tight to her head.

Through the teeniest of squints, she witnessed window-by-window, door-by-door and bookshelf-by-bookshelf explode into devastating wreckage. Torn-up books and broken glass covered shredded leather couches and chairs. All that remained was the trembling glass brick floor and a massive glass fireplace against a distant once-was wall.

She lifted her arms from her head and started to straighten. A biting breeze whipped through the exposed room, freezing her nose and ears until they burned.

"Ahuh, ahuh, ahuh." Loud, rough coughing cracked next to her.

Glass crackled beneath the man's polished brown leather shoes as he drew near to her. He wore the same tight-fitting blue suit. Her grandfather looked stern. Important. And highly irritated.

He surveyed the destruction, gave a wimpy cough, then turned to her and said in a deep, formal, but oddly familiar tone, "I suppose I deserved that."

Her body began to shiver beyond her control. The biting breeze now an icy wind. Her body spasmed and her teeth chattered like over-clicked computer keys.

"Come along, dear. Let's not dawdle." He pointed out to the sea but Truvie was too low to see anything above his knees. "We've got company coming."

Truvie shook her head gingerly.

"Please stand, dear," Junius said. "I think we can agree no more damage can be done here." He pressed his hands forward in a stop gesture. "Not that I'm trying to challenge your abilities. I know how powerful you are."

Truvie slowly rose. "Are you my grandfather? Junius Stelae?"

Smoothing his tie, he said, "I suppose I am. But Truitt, dear, that is not where the story begins." He arched his gaze back to the sea. "We really must be going."

Truvie blinked several times trying to shake the flashes of falling backward playing in her mind.

"Truitt?" her grandfather said.

Woozy, she said, "Truvie. My name is Truvie, not, not Truitt. I don't know why you're calling me—" The deconstructed room started to spin. She stumbled back a few wobbled steps.

"Are you all right, dear?" He looked over his shoulder to the sea. "He's nearly here. We should—I insist we leave. Now."

"Cold," Truvie said, teeth clacking loudly. "I'm so cold." Shudders ran through her veins, desperate to warm her, but the cold ran deep through to the bone.

"I got lost in worry of Pel and forgot," he said.

"Forgot?" She touched her lower lip. Numb, frigid. "Are my lips blue?"

"I forgot to right this room." As he turned back to Truvie, glass lifted in all directions and puzzled itself back whole. The books disappeared for a blink then reappeared in the shelves. Furniture returned itself into several reading nooks and the long table, Truvie figured was for spreading out and studying suddenly had several chairs perfectly placed equally on all sides. Copper embellished ladders lifted from the glass floor and reattached to the tall shelves lining the outer walls. The globes spun and tilted back into place. The maps rolled themselves and plunked back into a copper bin next to the fireplace, which suddenly burst ablaze with a roaring fire. The room restored and warmed in less than three seconds.

He walked to her and extended his hand to hers. Still a bit woozy, she placed her hand to his and leaned into his side. He led her from the window overlooking the sea toward the fire where she wanted to snuggle into a leather chair and read for days.

"We haven't the time, Truitt," he said. "Pel will be here any second."

"Why are you calling me Truitt?" she asked. "You weren't even there when I was born. You'd died—"

She stopped as her mind connected dots. He's dead. That must be mean—she shook her head frantically. "No, no, no, no, no, not true! I'm alive! And in a hospital bed recovering from brain surgery."

"Your name is Truitt Skye," he said. "You are most certainly alive. But . . ." he tilted his bald head to the side. "Different alive."

Tears began to well. Her heart started to pick up its beat and her tummy pitted in panicked dread. "I don't understand what's happening. Where am I? Please. You're scaring me."

"This is your world, my dear girl. Nothing to fear," he said. "Created by you to serve the souls of humanity. A whole world that you do not remember, nor will you understand anytime soon. I'm here at your request to tell you everything. But not now. We need to avoid Pel. At all costs. He can't help himself, so we must flee. Follow me, please. Quickly, quickly."

Truvie's mouth was a desert. Even if she had something to ask, or say, she knew she couldn't make a sound.

"Please." Junius pointed to the sea. "We must—"

Truvie focused on the spot he pointed at and found the teeniest of dots. "You have really good vision."

"We need to move."

"I don't understand, Granddaddy. Is this . . . Heaven? Someplace in between? Parallel universe?"

Junius straightened and narrowed his eyes, looking highly annoyed. "Is that what you learned there? Heaven? Parallel Universes? There aren't multiple versions of you. There's only you. Period. People, humans, make up all sorts of malarkey to justify not living in the here and now when they have those beautiful bodies. Even a broken, diseased, hard-to-move-in body is still a body. A body that can be connected to here, to us, to the soul world where anything, and everything, is possible."

Truvie said nothing. Connected to a soul world where anything and everything is possible? What the?

"Pel is closing in," he said. "See. There. We must go."

Truvie spotted this Pel guy running on top of the sea at the rate of a Nascar. "How's he doing that?"

"We need to get out of here."

Junius walked between two stacks of library books, vanishing instantly. Truvie ran after him "Wait!"

"Hurry, my dear," he said. "Neither of us is ready to deal with Pel."

Truvie jogged to keep pace.

"You were to come to the forest like everyone else, but that near-death job you pulled off in the ravine, guaranteed you'd land here. I tried to tell them—"

. . .

Junius took a sharp left into an encased glass cylinder. They descended an endless spiral staircase. Bright light from above streamed onto the staircase, giving it a light purple hue. Looking over the edge, Truvie lost her footing but caught sight of the sandy bottom. "Does this staircase end under the sea?"

Junius started to jog down the stairs at a fast click. "We knew you would forget everything. But I'd hoped you'd have a better understanding of this world. Most—rather all—souls that arrive here are not like you. They are like me. They arrive, they meet a Partitioner, have a wondrous celebration as they return the lessons they enjoyed in their bodied life, then decide to stay or go."

They rounded corner after corner so quickly, Truvie completely dizzied. "Stay or go? Stay where? Go where?"

"Stay and work here in the world of souls, or meet with an Assembler, like Pel, to put together a new soul, new purpose, new agendas then step into the pool and begin again. New body. New soul. New being."

Truvie shook her head. Her vision blurred. She gripped the handrail that was not there prior to her reaching for it.

"Try not to think," he said. "You're not ready."

Round and round they ran until Junius made an abrupt right turn and exited into a hallway. Truvie scampered to catch him. Pale cerise lights came to life under a glass floor. Glass walls shone with a gentle pink tint.

"Why is my soul not like yours?"

Junius stopped and lowered his head as he turned to face her. "You were never meant to be anywhere but here. You were never expected to have a body. But you—"

"What?" Truvie's question more like a yelp than a word. "But I did! I do! I do have a body!"

Junius shifted his weight to the right. His brow furrowed. He ran his hand over his bare head. "That is all I will say. Please, Truitt, we cannot have a face to face with Pel Willows. For all I know, you'll blast him to bits."

"I would never!" Truvie stepped back a bit.

Junius took off at a fast clip again. "It would be unintentional, of course. Simply your energy, combined with his energy." He jiggled with shivers. "I can't consider it."

"Can't consider what?" Truvie asked. Again.

"Once you're settled, we'll figure out how to deal with Pel, until then, please, Truitt, be quiet. We have the plan you left us with seventeen years and seventeen days ago. Let us work the plan, dear."

Pounding suddenly vibrated the walls and floor. It

was coming from the door at the end of the corridor.

Junius stopped.

"Is it him?" Truvie asked. Her body began to heat rapidly. Her heart pressed against her chest. "I feel— hot. And . . . and angry. Really mad. I don't even know this guy. And I don't get angry—I—"

"Please." Junius extended his hand. She took hold. "This is for your own good." He lifted her into his chest as if she weighed no more than a feather.

A rush of cool, relaxing comfort rippled through her. She placed her head on his shoulder, curled her legs into his mid-section and tucked her hands to his neck. Her eyes grew heavy. She had questions, so many questions, but couldn't care less about asking a one.

He pulled her tight to him, as she nestled in and fell fast asleep.

8
Pel Willows

Truvie opened her eyes the moment Junius released her from his arms. He had placed her on the side bench of a small boat—a skiff like the ones in the waterways of downtown Milwaukee. This particular skiff had polished wood panels and suede red seat cushions.

"It's a short ride," Junius said.

Truvie edged over the railing, searching the glass dock they must have walked down moments before her grandfather put her in the boat.

"Where's Pel?" she asked. "Last I remember there was pounding on the door. Did you drug me? Or is that the drugs from my surgery. . ."

"That was me, Truitt." A young man, only a year or two older than her, with tanned skin and short blonde hair, walked up the dock toward them. "Not Pel."

Truvie blinked, trying to get her bearings. The sun low edging toward sunset gave the sky a lavender muted tint, but she could see a young man in the near distance.

"I would never drug you," Junius said. He started the engine and spun the wheel to the right. "Latham, we need to go."

The blonde took one long step then leaped into the air and was instantly seated next to Truvie.

"That—that was—you were . . . You were at minimum forty feet away. How'd you do that?"

Latham looked to Junius, who steered the skiff out into the sea.

. . .

Latham turned away from her and asked, "How do I talk to her?"

Without looking back, Junius said, "I told you, she'll never remember here. Not in any way. Be informative."

"This is bad," Latham said to himself.

"What is? What's bad?" Truvie asked. She studied him closely. He wasn't tall, but he was fit and dressed in a striped navy suit and cherry red silk bowtie. His feet wore wingtips, like Junius. "Do I know you? Are you related to Junius, and me?"

"Related?" Latham's voice went high. "Truitt. No. No one's related here. We're souls, not humans."

"Junius is my grandfather," Truvie said. "He was married to my grandmother, Helena. He died before—

way before—I was born but my gram talked about him so much I feel like I know him. He was always a part of me."

Latham rubbed his palms together then stood and walked away from her.

Junius turned from the wheel and offered Truvie a slight smile, then focused on Latham, "We have to expect questions. She's Truitt Skye."

"She is certainly not Truitt Skye," Latham said. "Tots is going to—"

"She will be," Junius said. "With our help. And patience."

Waves rose and throttled the sides of the skiff sending warm drops of the sea onto Truvie's face. She thought of this person they thought she was, this Truitt Skye. Truitt Skye.

Truvie was an imposter in a world of warm blue seas, glasshouses, dead grandfathers, and anxious handsome boys that could leap farther than human possibility. She ached for Eddie, for Fig, a walk in the autumn woods, a BLT. What she wouldn't give for a hug and a few minutes with her dad. He could explain what was happening to her. Maybe she was in a coma? Or the neurosurgeon put a drain a little too deep and she was losing her mind via a suction tube. She might be unconscious in a recovery room surrounded by worried family. As much as she hoped that was true—

"I never thought about what happened when we die," Truvie said to stop her racing mind. Nervous chatter, her father called it. "The farthest I planned was college. Lots of college. A Ph.D. in particle physics, maybe another in quantum computing or neurophysics. Maybe, if I qualify, work in large hadron colliders. I just had my first kiss. I never—it never occurred to me that I might not—"

"I know, Truitt." Junius suddenly sat next to her.

Latham drove now. He pretended not to listen, but he kept twisting back at them with a pained look in his eyes.

"Why do you think my name is Truitt?" Truvie asked.

"As I told you before," Junius said. "You are the source of this world. A soul never meant to travel beyond this realm. This is your world, a world to serve humankind. You were called Truitt Skye. It's who you are. More than a name. It's your full being."

"But," Truvie said. "You were Junius Stelae there, on Earth or as a human, whatever. And here you are still called Junius Stelae."

"You know me as that, so—" Junius started.

"We don't call each other by name," Latham said, his lip curled and his head shaking a bit—annoyed completely. "We're energy. Not—"

"That'll do, Latham," Junius said.

"Energy?" Truvie asked, trying to sort out his point.

"I've had quite a few rounds in a body," Junius said. "Many names. I was a woman once. But she is gone is now. All of them are. I arrived as one of them, and the Partitioners took the lessons from my soul and added them to the pool where they mixed with all soul fragments to make us all better, perpetually better. Truitt used to call the pool, the soup." He smiled and gave a little laugh. "A soup of souls. I am Junius to you because that is who you need me to be. Give yourself a moment to adjust. It will all become more clear as you become yourself, Truitt."

Truvie understood what he said even though it was like nothing she could ever have imagined hearing. It felt more true than any fact she'd ever known, and she knew a lot of facts. "And once your soul lessons—fragments—go to the soup, who are you then?"

"Everything," Junius said.

"Then how you would know you would want another body?" Truvie asked, getting confused again.

"Pel," Latham said.

"Pel?" Truvie asked. "He decides when souls get bodies?"

"On the horizon," Latham said, pointing straight ahead of his nose.

"Go through the bottom," Junius said. "He won't know where we are in the Expanding Forest. It'll give us time."

. . .

Without hesitation, Latham rocketed thirty feet into the air and tightened himself with no gaps between his arms, torso, legs, or feet. He pointed his toes and came down with tremendous speed. His feet severed the floor of the skiff and instantly all three went into the sea.

Truvie didn't have time to let out the scream rising from her toes to her—

Latham's body spun in fast, tight circles through the water, creating a vortex that should repel Truvie and Junius, leaving them in the dust and sinking, but instead, united them to his propulsion. Ripping through the current in one long line, the three of them dove deeper into the blue. The temperature shifted from warm to frigid. Goosebumps scattered over her skin. She tasted the sea. She opened her eyes and had impeccable vision. The water did not sting, nor did it fill her lids. What the heck was this place?

. . .

Exposed roots and loose stones shifted beneath them. Must be the shore to one of those islands she flew by. Flew by? She had to be in an anesthesia coma.

Latham slowed. Junius and Truvie's bodies responded in kind. The earth expanded across the breadth of the sea.

"Not the shore," she said in a bubbly flurry of water. "We're under an island."

Latham headed for an opening, no wider than a bucket, and pulled them into a tunnel with no source of light whatsoever. She thought of her mother. Of the time when Truvie had awakened from a bad dream and her mother was there gathering Truvie in her arms. No fussing or tucking, only there to hold Truvie in her arms, to sway, and give her soft kisses on her forehead as tears streamed the sides of Truvie's face.

"Everything's okay," her mother had whispered. "All dreams fade."

. . .

A light extracted them from the tunnel and before she could let go of her memory and without warning, the three stood amongst a group of others. A strong stench of pine came off the cluster of giant sequoias that surrounded them. A ring of stones held smoking, grey coals. One of the women, the most petite, with dark hair to her shoulders, circled then headed to her, arms extended. Truvie tried to take them all in, but she couldn't—

"I don't remember the dream," Truvie said. "I was so scared but—it faded like she said it would. And everything was okay. I cried and cried but why? I was okay. My mom was there, and I was okay. I didn't need to cry."

"Tru?" The teeny young woman—Truvie's age or just past—with open arms started. Junius stepped in front of her and gently lowered her arms.

"Wait Totsinda," Junius said then turned to project to the collective. "I need you all to remember that Truitt is not Truitt yet."

"She feels like Truitt," the young woman Junius called Totsinda said. The same girl who was not touching Truvie, but somehow felt her?

"I agree," a young woman with long, shiny blonde hair said. "She feels the same."

"Stronger," a man in his forties of Native American decent said.

"Pel's close," Junius said. "He'll know we came here because of that. He can feel her because she is her."

"She's not the same," Latham said. "Give it a second. You'll see." He smoothed his tie and put his arm around Totsinda's shoulder.

"What do you mean I feel the same?" Truvie said. "We aren't touching. I'm not touching you."

"And there she is." Latham whistled like a bomb descending, then exploding. "Or isn't."

"Feel," Junius said to Truvie. "Meaning energy, dear."

"I feel better already," Totsinda said then talked so fast Truvie could barely keep up. "I'm glad you're back, Truitt. I missed you even though we don't miss I did. I totally and completely did. Ask the Wish Listeners. I was there nearly every day—sometimes more. I hope you had a good time. Did you have a good time? I tried to imagine what you were like as a human with all those other humans. Could they feel you? Were they scared of your power? Did you like being a girl? You must have been so much smarter and kinder and fuller than anyone else. And beautiful. I bet you sparkled. People must have loved you. And I know you loved them. They were so lucky to have had you in their lives. I bet they didn't know. But they will. That's how life is still. Appreciation after the fact instead of in the fact. That's okay! They learn that eventually. Tell me everything."

Truvie looked to Junius.

"We need to get to the plan, Tots," Latham said.

"He's right," the young woman with the long shiny hair said. "What's first?"

"She'll need to learn everything again, Olivia," Junius said. "Of here, of there, as if she never began. But we haven't the time to let her ask endless questions."

"Good luck," Latham said.

"She's Truitt Skye," Olivia with the shiny hair said.

"That's who she is."

"She always asks," Tots added. "On behalf of them."

"It will be at least doubled now," Latham said.

"I can hear her," Tots said with a bounce and a clap. "Her mind is magic. Chatter chatter chatter! She's home! She's backkkkkkk!"

"Truitt." The Native American man reached for her. "Are you okay?"

Truvie took a step to her right. "No," she said, holding her arms out in front of her to keep them at bay. "I don't know any of you. I don't understand why you're hiding me. If this was a dream, or heavy sedation, I should know you or at least recognize you by a clinical uniform—scrubs—a white coat—something. This could—it could be a bad dream—but somehow, somehow I don't think so—"

"Introductions," Junius cut in with a snap of his fingers. "Quickly. Quickly. Truitt needs information. Tots, let's begin with you."

Tots stared at Truitt.

Latham nudged her with his elbow. "Tots. Speak."

"Okay. Okay. I'm Tots, Totsinda. You call me Tots, usually Tots LaRue. You like the sound of both names together." She pulled at her short, raven hair near her neck. Her porcelain skin, rosy cheeks, purple velvet dress, tights, and black Mary Jane's made her look like she'd popped out of a fairytale.

Truvie extended her hand. "Truvie Tucker."

Tots looked to Junius, who twirled his finger in a gesture for Tots to continue. "More information," Junius said.

"I work with you," Tots said. "In the Cave of Souls. Well, it's a castle but you like to call it a cave. It is a cave. Sometimes. I mean, you like to think of souls as cavernous, never-ending twists and turns, dark and quiet, but still, cozy somehow. Safe and contained."

"I think it's a bit too early—" Junius said

"What's the Cave of Souls?" Truvie asked.

"It's where you fix souls," Tots said. She turned to Latham. "This is hard. She doesn't know anything."

"Fix souls? Why would I do that?" Truvie asked. "Are they broken?

"Very," Tots said.

Truvie's eyes opened wide. Her throat contracted and she coughed.

"It's okay!" Tots sang. "Nothing you or they can't handle. They all want you. They wait until you find them—well—that's where I—we—Latham and I come in. We—we help you organize. Otherwise, all the souls rush you—"

"She's never going to understand that," a man wearing a corduroy jacket over a coffee-stained white button-up shirt said. He looked most normal of the group with his afro-textured hair and horned rimmed glasses.

He extended his hand, "Dr. Walter Blick. I'm a researcher here. A scientist, like you."

He calmed her. She didn't care why. She welcomed it and took his hand. "What's your specialty?"

"I gravitate to the more difficult questions," he said.

Truvie frowned. "What does that mean?"

"The questions from humanity never end," he said.

"Here in the City, we answer every question. However, there is often a long delay before they hear the answer. As you'd expect, they ask again and again and again, never quieting or slowing down long enough to let our answers land, digest and become a part of their experience. It can take days to decades. Sometimes the whole span of a long life. Still, we answer, over and over again. They get what they ask for, or they don't. It's entirely up to them."

Truvie stared at him as if he had fourteen heads. What in the world. . ..

"Soul to soul, Truitt," a boy with creamy brown skin wearing surf shorts and a tank top with the word "Aloha" painted on it said. "Our souls are completely connected to their souls. Continuous energy binds us together."

"I was getting there, Keone," Dr. Blick said. "They have to listen to that little voice in their head. Pang in their heart. Gut feeling. Sixth sense. Intuition. That feeling they get when something is right and good for them and they are certain of it, despite logic."

"My dad calls it resonance," Truvie said. "When you know something is true, proof or not, nothing can shake it from you."

A clap echoed high above the forest. A soldier stepped out from between two redwoods, clapping slowly. "And you said she wouldn't understand."

Tots screamed and hid in Latham's chest.

"Pel." Junius cut him off from the group by stepping to Pel. "We need more time."

Latham, Dr. Blick, Keone, and Olivia quickly lined

on either side of Junius, forming a half-moon to protect Truvie. Tots La Rue took hold of Truvie's hand. Two others, who had yet to speak, thankfully, joined the shield. Truvie couldn't see this Pel character. This soul who created new souls and took them to the soup to begin again.

Truvie shook her head and said, "Let him through. It can't get any weirder."

The group tightened.

"Shh, Truitt," Tots hissed. "You aren't ready."

Truvie withdrew her hand from Tots' grip. She stepped to the shield of soul people and without touching them the two in front of her dissolved to white light. Truvie continued walking, into their light, until she was face-to-face with Pel Willows.

He was tall and thin, but strikingly muscled, particularly his clenched, flexing jawline. His hair brown, cropped. He wore olive fatigues and combat boots.

Pel said nothing. The rest of the group dispersed, and two who had turned to light, Olivia and Latham, returned. Truvie frowned wondering how that worked. She did not trust a thing she saw at the moment, but she didn't want to trouble everyone with another question. Still. All she had to offer were more questions. Everything was off. Everything was wrong. She stood in the woods with strangers who could vaporize to light, burst into the air from sitting, swim like fish—and knew her. But not her, her. Someone named Truitt who repaired something she thought was unbreakable, a soul.

Tears rose in Truvie's eyelids. "I—I don't understand what's happening to me. I want to go home. Please. Can someone help me?"

"Truitt," Pel said, stepping close to her. "I'm not here for you, despite what they said. You can never begin again. You hear me? We need you. It's Eva I want. Where is she?"

"Pel, please," Junius said. "Not yet. She doesn't know—"

"Eva?" Truvie scoured the group. "Which one is she?"

"Eva murdered you," Pel said. "She plans to destroy this world. I'm not going to let that happen. And you wouldn't want me to."

"She wants the worlds to merge the worlds," Tots corrected. "Not end. We're not ending." She turned to Latham who pulled her close to him.

"Merging will end the worlds, will it not?" Pel asked Tots.

"Did you say someone murdered me?" Truvie said. "Who'd want to murder me? Plus, I'm right here. Aren't I?" She let out a giggling sigh and laughed.

But none of them joined in.

"Technically speaking," Tots interjected. "Souls don't get murdered."

Pel moved directly in front of Truvie, who immediately ceased giggling.

"Eva, your hand-picked advisor, pushed you over the edge, high above the Cave of Souls," Pel said with an eerily calm tone. "You fell into the silver pool and began again. She pushed you to rid this world of you. And since that day, she's been missing. I've been hunting her for seventeen years and seventeen days, and now I need you to tell me where she is."

"Obviously," Junius said. "Truitt can do no such thing. She doesn't know where—"

"Or who," Latham added.

"Eva is," Junius finished.

"I can see that," Pel said. "But we all know that won't stop Eva from doing it again."

Truvie's mind whirled. Eva. Caves of Souls. Pools. Edges. Murder. Begin. Again?

"You could help, Pel," Tots LaRue said. "You and Truitt used to—"

"Why would anyone want to kill me, or my soul?" Truvie suddenly felt woozy and sick to her stomach. The trees spun like limbs of a Ferris wheel. Truvie's head dropped back to the top of her shoulders. Her legs gave out. Snow flew in every direction, blanketing the ground in an instant to soften her collapse. White flakes covered the pines, the souls, the sky, everything.

"Fix her." Truvie heard Pel demand.

Someone gathered Truvie into their arms and in a steady, crunching march, carried her across the snow.

9
Light

When Truvie came to, she was resting on her side in the back of the skiff again. Her feet tucked to her bum, knees in her chest. Her head on the lap of the velvet dress worn by Tots LaRue. With all she could muster, she rose to sit. She licked seawater on her lips and wiped the trickle of wet sliding down her cheek. The skiff, driven by Junius, pulled into a swampy, narrow waterway. Woozy still, her head swayed to the left. She could not keep her eyes—

"Lay back down," Junius said.

She lowered back down to the bench, head into the lap of Tots again.

Tots leaned close to Truvie's ear, and with warm breath that smelled of cinnamon, she whispered,

"We're taking you to Amelia. She's a healer."

Truvie felt gentle caresses on the top of her shoulder. "I need to. . . wake up."

The harsh scratching of shrubs and tree limbs against the hull kept Truvie aware. The flutter of wings sounded a moment before a soft waft of air lifted Truvie's hair from her forehead. Gripping talons took hold of her right hand then walked up her arm. Mint and lemon circled her nostrils and a feathered head nestled to her temple. She didn't need to open her eyes to see the green crow perched on her bicep offering her love.

"Is she awake?" Latham asked. His voice close by. He must be on the other side of Tots.

"In and out," Tots said. "What are we going to do?"

"I don't know," Latham said. "This is bad. She's so weak and . . . off."

"How could we ever know this is how it would be?" Tots said. "I still don't believe it. I can't—"

"Junius knew," Latham said.

"How?" Tots asked.

"We're here," Junius said.

The skiff tapped into the dock a few times before it parked.

. . .

The crow lifted its head from Truvie's neck and took flight. She worked her eyelids, begging them to open, but they refused.

The skiff dipped as someone unloaded.

"Why have you brought her here?" A woman's voice. Loud but distinctly smooth and playful. Like Joseph's from the hospital. Caribbean.

A sign.

Of the familiar.

Finally.

"Sit me up," Truvie said. Her temples throbbed. She still could not get her eyes to stay open.

"Shh," Tots hissed.

"We had no choice, Amelia," Junius said. "Or we never would have troubled you."

"We cannot help her," the Caribbean woman called Amelia said. "You know dis."

"Please!" Truvie heard Tots scream.

"Child," the woman said. "Do not—"

"Amelia, please," Tots cut in. "She's in real trouble. It's terrible! We need you. You have to! Please, Amelia! Please!"

Truvie suddenly felt heat surround her. Hot heat, fire hot. She thought for sure she'd pass out in seconds.

"Totsinda, my love." Amelia softly uttered then added, "Her soul is not in trouble."

"It is." Tots sniffled.

"Can't you just touch her quickly?" Latham said. "Get her energy back?"

"Touch her?" Amelia shouted. "She'll blow us to bits."

"She will do no such thing, Amelia," Junius said. "You can handle her. You can feel her limit. I hear you loud and clear. Calculating."

"You are pushing in a place you oughtn't," Amelia said. Truvie imagined Amelia must have stood to face

Junius.

"Indeed," Junius said.

There was a pause. Truvie tried again to open her eyes with great hope she would open them and be home. That was a step in the right direct—

"Put her to the dock. Dare. Over dare."

The intense vibration of heat returned.

"Shouldn't we take her inside?" Latham said.

Truvie's body lifted into the air, but she did not feel one hand on her. She opened her eyes briefly but only saw a sea of white hanging somethings. Curtains? Hospital curtains?

"We're not taking her anywhere near dat building. Did you not hear me? Her energy can ignite us." She snapped her fingers. "Gone."

"But you wouldn't be gone," Latham said. "That doesn't happen here—"

"Shh, Latham," Junius said. "They would. She can send anyone straight to the pool. She has no control of her energy. Or her reactions. Amelia is correct. She is combustible."

"Oh Tru," Tots sighed. "It'll be okay."

Truvie's backside ached against the hard planks of the dock. She moaned and tried to lift herself.

"Latham," Amelia said. "Take off your jacket and shirt."

A rustling sounded next to her. "Hold this," Latham said. Truvie imagined him handing his clothes to Tots La Rue.

"Your hand," Amelia said. "Give it to me."

"But I'm fine," Latham said.

"Your thoughts reflect hers. All of our thoughts do. Dis is her world. Let me show you, and her, what kind of power she is," Amelia said.

Latham turned to Junius.

"Do as she says," Junius said.

Truvie squinted a sliver to see Latham place his hand into a dark-skinned hand with long, thin fingers. This healer was correct. She did wonder what all this talk about her power meant. The last thing Truvie considered herself was powerful. Smart, yes. Powerful, not in a million years.

"When I take hold," Amelia said. "I will become my cells and my energy will flow to your energy, giving your cells more life. It will not hurt. Enjoy it. I'll contain it. Won't spread farther than dat arm, maybe da chest."

"But—" Latham started.

"It's a good way for you all to see what I mean by Truitt girl's power."

Through the slightest blur, Truvie watched Amelia's fingers, hand, then arm dissolve into a golden glowing light. In seconds, the entirety of Amelia became the same radiance. She was now only vibrating light. A white silk dress pooled to the dock. Truvie could watch with ease now as luminesce spread into the tips of Latham's fingers and up through the veins of his forearm, then biceps and shoulder. His arm up to the right side of his neck pulsed with light, but his body remained his body. His every vein and vessel, pure white light.

"Unbelievable," Truvie whispered.

Amelia dropped her hold and returned to her body within the white silken dress. The light rushed toward his heart then left.

"That felt . . ." Latham's voice loud, elated. "Surprising. Good, Really, really-really good. Do it again."

"Shh," Amelia said, lifting her thin index finger to her lips.

The heat intensified around Truvie's shoulders. She lowered her head back down to the rough wood of the dock. Dark-skinned ankles draped with white hems appeared.

"Heal her, all the way," Tots said. "Okay? Not just an arm. It needs to last. She's a mess."

"Truitt will be the one to fill me, Totsinda," Amelia said. "Stand back. And keep your eyes open. It will be bright, but you need to see what you are dealing with."

Amelia held her pinky out. "You see? A pinky of me is all I will risk."

A light touch arrived on the top of Truvie's cheek.

Suddenly, Truvie's eyes burst wide as a blinding beam of light shot from her cheek. Before she could take a breath, the beam expanded and swallowed up every inch of space in its wake. Something big flew backward, but Truvie could not see anything but stream after stream of white light emanating from her entire body.

Truvie got to her feet. She felt the heaviness of the ground but could not find it in the sea of illumination. She extended her arms and circled them in teeny rings sending tiny waves of light beaming across the lagoon.

"You see," Amelia said. "She knows exactly who she is."

"Whoa," Tots LaRue breathed.

"She blew you back ten feet," Latham said. "You hardly touched her." He touched his little finger to Tots' cheek, mimicking Amelia. "Do you feel that?"

"Barely," Tots said.

"Truitt, my girl," Amelia said. "Take a few breaths and eat up the light."

"Do what?" Truvie asked with an arch to her tone.

"Please, dear, inhale," her grandfather said. "You're blinding us."

Truvie sucked in a long breath. And another. On the third, the light subsided. Junius stood next to Amelia. Five other dark-toned women dressed exact to Amelia in long white gowns, clustered near Tots and Latham.

"What was that?" Truvie asked. She could not contain her grin. "I feel—I am so awake. And alive. And hungry. And eager. And—"

"Energized," Junius said.

Amelia laughed. She kissed his cheek, which illumed his skin.

"You are energy, girl," Amelia said. "The energy of all."

"No kidding," Tots said.

"You feel it too?" Amelia said. "The giddy aftershock of a blast of Truitt Skye?"

Tots bobbed her head and shoulders. "I could do anything. Anything at all. Where's Pel now? Let's get him! And Eva! Bring her to me!"

Junius smiled. "Easy. It will fade. Truitt is not Truitt."

"Truitt," Amelia said. "Who am I?"

"Amelia Saint Louise Rose." Truvie could not stop herself from continuing, "You are Haitian. You were a doctor. And you lived to be 104. When you came here, you insisted on staying and I reluctantly agreed. I thought you'd be happier in a new body. Your previous one had caused you such pain for so long. But you assured me you had much to teach me about the power of light. And you were right. You did teach me, but I'm sorry, I don't remember any content. I sense it's there but nothing exact."

Truvie stepped back from the group. "How did I know all that?" Then it hit her. "When you touched me, I knew everything. I—I—I know so much more. Who you were married to—James Winchester Rose? A child that died. A mother and brother that—oh, I'm sorry. I'm so sorry."

Amelia approached Truvie. "It's what you do. You know souls. Better dan anyone ever will."

"How?" Truvie asked.

"You should be going now," Amelia said.

"What now?" Latham said with a happy lilt. "Should we let Truitt touch us all, so she gets her memory back? Will Truitt know everything again?"

"Yes!" Tots said. "Touch me, Tru!"

"No!" Amelia and Junius said together.

"Dis was nothing—" Amelia started.

"Let me," Junius said. "Truitt, what's your name?"

"Truvie Tucker." Truvie cupped her mouth and said under the finger muzzle, "Sorry."

"Is good," Amelia said. "Give yourself time or nottin' will be right. Let yourself become bit by bit by bit."

"But—" Latham and Tots interjected.

"Totsinda," Amelia said. "Take her to Sussy Vox.

Only you. She requires a visit home."

"Sussy?" Latham said. "No way. Truitt doesn't need—that's for souls who can't hack it here."

Amelia walked away from the dock. Her mimics in white gowns followed. A few steps from them, she gathered the skirt of her white dress and turned to Truvie. "I know I ask too much. Remember what you already know: Truitt Skye is the most impatient one of all. But, for now, we must take it as it lay. She warned us dis would not be easy. But worth it, hmm?"

The women continued up the steps like a bouquet of calla lilies.

"We don't have time for this," Latham said to Junius.

"Thank you, Amelia," Junius called.

Amelia stopped at the top of a long staircase. Her voice boomed down to them. "Don't bring her back here. I cannot touch her again."

10
The Restore

Truvie followed Tots La Rue across a whimsical set of stepping stones. Each stone had a painted heart or flower that hovered above the stone, making the image three dimensional, but once Truvie placed her foot on a step, the image merged into it and when she looked back, the stone was painted solid red.

Her heart, her cells, her mind still infused with the healing energy of Amelia Rose. Truvie knew she must be close to waking up from surgery now so she may as well enjoy the rest of the dream. Tots LaRue seemed to love her very much. She wished for such a friend but hadn't met one this good yet. There was Eddie, but she like liked Eddie, more than friends.

"Sussy Vox is super nice," Tots said. "But he'll be a

little surprised you're here, okay?"

"Why?" Truvie asked, hopping over a stone and quickly turning back to see if the heart hovered, but the stone was pure red.

Tots hedged with a gentle groan. "You created The Restore for other souls, not yours."

"What's The Restore?" Truvie hopped quickly from one stone to another, trying to make the pretty painted zinnia stay, but it turned to red. "Darn."

"Sometimes souls have a hard time adjusting to here. Can't find a groove." Tots bobbed her head side to side. "So, you created a place for them to ease in."

"Why don't they take a swim in the pool and forget about it?" Truvie heard her tone. Not friendly and quite smarty.

"Soul work is not a joke, Tru," Tots said. "If you were here, you'd be mad at yourself for saying that. They could do that, begin again, but they want to be here to serve you and other souls. They really do, like me, we want to help you. And they want to be there—until they get to know how here works. Once they understand to power of answering humanity again and again, they never look back again."

"I'm sorry," Truvie said. "It's all a little—I don't understand."

Tots turned and smiled then returned to her stride and kept talking. "The Restore lets a soul go back to their life as a human to find the memories that will help them remember why they stayed in the City on the Sea."

Truvie stopped. "I get to go back to Milwaukee?"

. . .

"Truitt Skye!" The voice of a man sounded up ahead of them. "I never—I don't believe it!"

Truvie looked up and was instantly enveloped by two arms. When he released her, he said, "Truitt Skye at The Restore. I never thought I'd see the day. Lucky me, lucky me. Come in. Come in. I'm so happy to see you!"

Sussy Vox was tall and thin and in a coveralls that a mechanic might be in. He had a full head of black hair and at least a day's worth of dark stubble. His small, round tortoise shell glasses pressed to his green eyes because of the notch on the bridge of his nose. His skin fair and a bit blotchy. He had a necklace with a Celtic cross pendant.

The stone path had led them to the stone cottage behind Sussy. The Restore sat in the middle of a meadow. Wildflowers lined a trail that led to a pond. Truvie arched to her tippy toes. Swans and ducks pedaled near a petite island at the center of the water. On the little isle, a weeping willow tree with a swing.

Sussy opened the door to The Restore, gestured them to join him then disappeared inside.

Tots headed toward the pond.

Watching her, Truvie said, "Where are you going?"

"Only room for one," Tots said.

"It looks big enough for more than one," Truvie said. Tots kept walking.

"I'll just go in then?" Truvie called. "You'll wait here?"

After a few more steps, Tots turned and said, "I'm

never more than a thought away."

A chill dispersed into Truvie's veins. "I don't understand what that means."

"Truitt?" Sussy stood at the entrance again.

Tots climbed onto the swing out on the island. Truvie spied the area for a bridge or log, or rocks, but saw nothing that would get Tots to where she was. It was too far a distance for teeny Tots to jump across the water.

"How—" Truvie started.

"Ready?" Sussy said.

She shook her head. "I'm not sure."

"It doesn't hurt," he said.

Truvie took one more look at the water around Tots trying to calculate the math, then gave up and hauled herself up the three marbled stairs of The Restore.

. . .

Blind darkness overtook her as she went from the outside sunlight to the inside of the cottage. Once things came into focus, however, there was nothing to see. No cozy furniture or roaring fire in the fireplace, as she expected a stone cottage to possess. No fireplace at all. No books. No sink or oven. Only a lone linoleum countertop with Sussy Vox standing behind it. He now wore a silver hat and hot pink striped shirt.

"What the?" she asked. "Mr. Sussy, where did your coveralls go?"

"Vox," Sussy said. "Mr. Vox. And you are Miss Skye. Kind of, but not entirely, am I right? Because Truitt Skye would not see my hat, or shirt, or coveralls."

"Why not?" she said then shook her head. "You know what? Never mind. You're right. I'm not this Truitt Skye person. I'm Truvie. Truvie Tucker. I live on Lake Drive in Milwaukee, Wisconsin. I—I had surgery—I think—"

Sussy stepped out from behind the counter. "Truitt Skye only came here once. Boy do I wish I could recreate that for you. Woooo," he sang. "That was quite a visit. Taught me how to look into a soul, but only the periphery, you know, where memories lie. Memories lie." He laughed at himself. "Memories do lie, don't they? That's exactly what Truitt—what you—said. She taught me to find the imprint made on the soul because you said that was the only thing that mattered, not the truth. The impression held the lesson. The truth was the thread of the soul—of here—and was a constant as any law the Universe had."

"I don't have any idea what you're saying," Truvie said. "Maybe we should find Tots?"

Sussy's voice quieted as he said, "I died so long ago, I don't bother going back to my memories. But when I was first here, when you explained to me how important I was to the care of souls, I went back to my memories to master what I do now. When I saw the lessons I had in humanity, it made perfect sense that I am here for you now."

"Huh?" Truvie frowned and felt a headache building at the bridge of her nose.

Sussy Vox went on, "I was a museum curator when I lived last. Always in the past searching for meaning. I have a vast, expansive imagination that spans centuries of study of art and culture. I can create just about anything you release. I brought memories to life then and I do the same now. Except here, as pure energy ever-eager to serve, my precision is impeccable."

"How?" Truvie was not understanding one ounce of what Sussy Vox was saying. Her eyes and head hurt. She wanted a nap. "How do you do this stuff with memories?"

Sussy smiled as he stepped back to his right. "My energy syncs to yours and we open the door."

. . .

The wall melted away, revealing the street across from Truvie's house in Milwaukee, Wisconsin. The night lights twinkled. The air chilly with a pungent, wet scent. Cars drove by sounding loud and intrusive.

"It's so real," Truvie breathed.

"Go ahead. You do the rest," Sussy said. "The memory you need is there waiting for you to arrive."

Truvie paused a moment. Then realized, this was the way back to her body. Her real body. In her real house. In her real life. No more morphine for me.

Losing all apprehension for the possibility of Fig being there to greet her, Truvie walked forward where the wall had been and without any notice, she stood on the curb across the street from her beautiful home. She jutted out into the street. Screeching brakes skidded to a stop.

A young woman in a minivan quickly and harshly shouted, "Watch it, idiot!"

Truvie gasped as she stepped back to the curb.

"I know which memory this is!" Truvie's smile widened. "I remember that woman yelling at me."

When Sussy didn't answer, she turned back to say it again to him, but behind her was the parking lot that she walked Fig across every day after they'd played fetch. The same lot she and Eddie had walked hand-in-hand across this afternoon.

The engine of the minivan revved, bringing Truvie fully present.

"Sorry!" she called to the driver of the minivan. "I wasn't looking."

"No shit, Sherlock." The woman flipped her the bird and accelerated out of sight, exactly as she had the first time they'd met.

Truvie watched the woman drive away then looked left to right. All clear. She raced across the road and straight into the front door, through the mudroom, and into the entryway.

Fig—a teeny puppy Fig—leapt toward her waist.

"Fig!" She lowered to hug him. She kissed his jowls as she chanted his name, "Figgy Figgy Figgy. Oh, I missed you. You beautiful boy. You were such a cutie patootie baby!"

Fig spun in a circle, then another, and did a little piddle onto the floor. She smiled, "I forgot you used to do that!"

She opened the door behind her and got a wad of paper towels from the mudroom. She tossed them to the wood floor and used the sole of her sneaker to clean up the mess. Using one more towel to collect the soiled others, she dropped them into the rubbish bin and sprinted toward the stairs with Fig at her heels.

"Gram will be coming soon," Truvie said to Fig. "Because that's the memory I'm in." At the top of the staircase, she stopped. "I remember I was upset that's why I wasn't paying attention when I crossed the street but—"

Truvie stopped in her tracks.

Her grandmother stood before her. "What was that?"

Truvie reached out to touch her but couldn't move.

"Truvie?" her grandmother said. "Are you all right?"

"Yeah," Truvie said unconvincingly. "You look good. Your hair. It's not all wild and—"

"Why are you home so early?" her grandmother asked. "And why do you look like you've been crying? You aren't hurt, are you?"

"No," Truvie said. "Nothing like that."

Truvie needed to process for a moment. Something didn't seem right. This wasn't how it had gone. She looked around but knew Sussy was gone. She was on her own here. She closed her eyes to force her memory to come back to her. She would have sworn—

"Gram, can you give me a minute alone then you and Fig come knock on the door?"

"You're acting awfully odd," her grandmother said. "But sure, I'll play along. Come on, Fig. Go outside, go potty?"

Fig raced down the stairs. Helena followed him.

. . .

Truvie opened the door to her bedroom and just as she suspected, there she was, age twelve, crying on the bed.

Truvie started to do the math as to why her grandmother was there—she knew what happened immediately. She hadn't greeted Fig like that—he'd peed immediately.

Suddenly she felt a firm pull at her chest and within an instant, her body lurched toward her younger self and disappeared.

Awake inside herself, she could feel both her younger, heart-broken self and her older curious self, but it was hard to hold onto either. Slowly but jerkily, Truvie morphed from her present self and was twelve again.

A tap on the door sounded. Her grandmother entered without Truvie welcoming her in.

"Truvie?" her grandmother said.

Truvie looked up at her grandmother, tears spilling down her cheeks. She shook her head.

"What happened?" Her grandmother leaned back and called out the door, "Fig! Figgy come here!"

Within seconds, Fig pounced onto the bed and began licking Truvie's tears away.

"You aren't hurt?" Helena asked. "Physically?"

Truvie shook her head. "I left."

"School?" her grandmother asked.

Truvie nodded and sobbed.

"Why?" her grandmother asked.

"I'm dead," Truvie said.

Her grandmother cupped her hand to her heart then pulled Truvie into her for a hug. "Must have been something truly terrible to have you feeling this bad?"

"That's what she said," Truvie said. "Dead to them. Dead."

"Candace Little, I presume?" her grandmother asked. "She's a real pain in the butt, isn't she?"

"I want her to be my friend," Truvie said as Fig curled into her lap. "Why is she so mean to me?"

"Can't control her or how she acts or the choices she makes," her grandmother said.

"But I'm not dead," Truvie said. "I'm right here."

"Ever think dead might be a good thing?"

Truvie leaned back and sniffled. "No."

"Opens up all sorts of possibilities," her grandmother said. "Use your imagination. Without a body, you could be so many places all at once. Paris for dinner with Eddie. Reading a physics book by the Medi-terranean in Tuscany with your dad. Movie premiere in L.A. with Candace. Sushi in Tokyo with me and your mother. Swimming off the coast of Africa with dolphins. Endless. You would be endless. Friends everywhere."

"Gram," Truvie said. "This is serious."

"I know, I know it is," she said. "Life is too short to be terrible to each other. Life is too precious to worry about who likes who. Life is meant for you to live your dreams, not squash them. To be smart. To be well-read. To know that above all else, we are all made of the same bits and parts. Every single one of us is made of the same stardust."

"That's what Dad always says," Truvie said. "Carbon and oxygen came from exploding stars. We are all the same settled dust."

"And do you know where he got that?" her grandmother asked.

Truvie nodded. "Granddaddy Junius."

"The biggest pompous arse genius there ever was," her grandmother said. "Who I love as much today as I did when he walked the Earth twenty-five years ago."

Truvie pet Fig who rolled onto his back and splayed his limbs out to the sides. "Do you miss him?"

"Never." Her grandmother grinned. "Because he's always here. Listening. Talking. Completely surrounding me with his theories and interjections about how to live my life to the fullest. Never wasting time on anyone or anything that doesn't matter to me."

"Where?" Truvie said. "I don't see him."

"Can you see energy?" her grandmother asked.

"No." Truvie sat up straighter. "Can you?"

"No," her grandmother said. "But I feel it. I feel you right now. Not at your best but getting better, stronger, brighter, lighter. Do you feel it?"

Truvie shook her head. "Not really."

"How about Fig?" her grandmother said. "You can feel his energy, right?"

Truvie stroked his belly. "He's happy."

"Practice feeling his happiness," her grandmother said. "You need to get comfortable with feeling the energy of everything and everyone."

"Why?" Truvie said.

"So that you have the upper hand with that little br—with Candace," her grandmother said. "Energy is all there is. It's all you are. It's all Candace is. Or me, or Fig, or granddaddy Junius, who taught me about energy being the only source of power there is. When you remember that, nothing hurts for long."

Her grandmother wrapped her arms around Truvie's torso and pulled her in for a squeeze. "Can you feel all this love? My energy to yours?"

Truvie tightened her hold, careful not to disrupt the snoring Fig in her lap. "In my chest and ribs. My ears. Even in my toes and the top of my head."

11
Eva Kinde

The memory in Truvie's bedroom rapidly let go until she could no longer feel her grandmother's hold or Fig's heavy head in her lap. The wall behind her with a giant poster of a green crow with the words, "Beware of Induction," beneath it merged into the empty counter space of The Restore.

"Welcome back, Miss Skye" Sussy said.

Truvie hugged her chest, and with her voice quiet, asked, "How did you know that was the memory to pick?"

"I don't choose," Sussy said. "You do. Your soul takes you where you need to go."

"I . . ." Truvie sighed. "I never thought much about souls."

Sussy found that particularly funny.

Tots La Rue opened the door. "Everything okay?"

Sussy tried to speak, but instead, barreled over with laughter.

"I said I didn't think too much about souls," Truvie said.

"Oh," Tots said. "I'm sorry. It's—"

"I know," Truvie said. "What you all think I live for."

They walked away from the stone cottage and into the meadow toward a wooded area filled with paper birch trees, their white bark curled and flaked from the trunks as their vibrant waxy green leaves shivered in the breeze.

"Not at the moment," Tots said. "But you will. You're Truitt Skye. You can't help but help."

Truvie didn't respond. She thought for sure she'd be awakened in a hospital bed surrounded by her family and Eddie and his mom. And Fig sleeping next to her.

"He means well," Tots said. "It's just—the soul thing you said. Truitt was—well, she was very devoted to souls. Very, very devoted."

"It's okay," Truvie said. Her chest constricted. She tried to raise her arms to her heart; it burned and ached. But they hung at her sides, too much to lift. "I don't understand what's happening to me."

Tots faced Truvie and took hold of her hands. "Stop fighting. Let go."

"I want to go home," Truvie said, tears budding. "Please."

Tears welled into Tots' eyes. "You're where you belong and want to be." Tots lit up with a smile. Her eye sparkled like sapphires. "I have an idea. It might be a little much for you to take in, but I think it might help—"

Tears falling from her eyes, Truvie moaned. "I don't want to see anymore. I don't want to be here. How can you say I belong when I hate it so much?"

Tots threw her whole body into Truvie and squeezed. "I don't know," Tots whispered.

Hugging Tots, Truvie said, "I miss Eddie. And Fig. My family. If I'm so needed and important here, then why would I have left in the first place?"

Tots gently released Truvie. "To save us," Tots said. "And to save humanity from her."

. . .

A tall birch filled with deep green leaves dropped to the ground with a whoosh and thunk. Tots took a seat on a fallen tree. "Sit, please."

Wiping her tears from her cheeks, Truvie sat on the grass in front of Tots. Little dandelions began to bloom around her fingers and feet.

"I'm going to tell you about what happened, okay?" Tots said. "I'll know when you've had too much."

"How?" Truvie asked.

"Just listen, Truitt. Can you do that?"

Truvie nodded. "If you call me Truvie."

Tots smiled but did not call her Truvie. "More and more," Tots said. "Those in bodies, on Earth, hues, I like to call them, but Truitt hates the term. When we work on souls, we only see their energy, their light, not their skin and bones. And depending on what they need, or want, they reveal an array of colors. Their energy illuminates for us so we know what they are asking for. And we answer. We always answer because we're always there. No separation. They sometimes, oftentimes, think there is. Do you understand?"

"You connect to their soul?" Truvie guessed.

"Yes. We do, especially you, Truitt." Tots grinned, and Truvie would swear she saw green light beaming around her head. "See," Tots said. "Green, right?"

Truvie nodded reluctantly.

"And Eva, you remember Pel mentioning her?" Tots asked.

"The one who supposedly murdered me?" Truvie said. "I remember."

"She is an extraordinary soul worker here, one of your most trusted, and she, well, she's a genius at world creation—"

"World creation?" Truvie cut in.

"Truvie would call it, physics."

"Oh." Truvie perked up. "Yes."

"Here we think of physics as a little more . . . immediate. Like a perpetual science laboratory," Tots said. "Eva was a physicist when she was in a body last. Prominent and—" Tots hesitated for a few seconds, then spoke again. "She wants to give hues that connection, the connection to their soul, all the time, not every now and again like they do now. She wants to eliminate any gap between their souls and their bodies. She demanded you merge the worlds, ours with theirs, so that there would never be separation. They would never feel apart from who they really are, or some would say, who they long to be. Every question answered and every wish fulfilled without delay."

"Is there a separation?" Truvie asked. "I thought it was all within. Isn't it in your heart?" Truvie looked away then said, "Wait. Your mind? Which one is it?"

"It's energy," Tots said. "All of it. Body, soul, heart, organs, mind. Cells, chemical reactions, relationships, love." She snickered at that. "I'm quoting you, Truitt. And you don't know it. This is so wild."

Truvie's mind was going now. "Why would it matter if the worlds merged? People probably would like that."

"How would people grow?" Tots leaned forward, closer to Truvie. "You said, 'none of us grow unless the hues and their soul are out of whack on a regular basis.'"

"I did?" Truvie asked.

"If people didn't disconnect from their soul, how would they grow?" Tots asked.

"How can they disconnect when it's right there with them?" Truvie asked.

"I'm not smart like you, Truitt. I know when I see a soul in trouble, maybe that means disconnected, maybe it's something else. That's your expertise. I find them, you fix them."

Truvie fondled the bright yellow petals of a dandelion with the tip of her finger. "I didn't want the worlds to merge for something to do with growing, but Eva did. Now Eva's missing? And Pel wants her. So that means, I need to find Eva?" She took a breath. "I need to find Eva so I can find out what this all means. This is like a dream." She paused, then added, "I'm not responding well to the anesthesia at all."

Tots stood and reached for Truvie. "Ready?"

Letting Tots pull her to her feet, Truvie said, "To meet someone who tried to kill me because I don't want this world to merge with humanity? You know this is crazy, right?"

"Not to me," Tots said.

Truvie had to admit she was intrigued. Who was this Eva, this genius physicist who had some way of bringing souls to life? She could see herself in a dream like this. It made sense. It was quantum mechanics come to life.

As if reading her mind, Tots said, "Truitt Skye loves digging in and figuring things out. Especially when there's danger lurking. And with Eva, there is always danger. You two pushed each other to the brink. As often as you could."

"She was brave, huh?" Truvie asked. "Truitt."

"You are beyond brave, Truitt Skye," Tots said, tears welling in her lower lids then slipping down her cheeks. "You're the one we all want to be, Truitt. The only one. Ever."

Truvie's brow furrowed. She wiggled her head and reached for her constricting chest. "I find that hard to believe."

"I know you do," Tots said with a little happy hop to her step. "That's what's so exciting to me. Now that I know you as Truvie, I can say with all certainty that you would have loved this. Truitt would devour these moments of confusion and pain. Swallow them whole. She was never confused. Never unsure. I know for a fact she never experienced pain. Makes me think Eva had nothing to do with you beginning again that day. Not one thing. My bet? Curiosity pushed you over the edge, not Eva."

· · ·

The back of Tots' dress lit up with the words, "Curiosity is My Superpower," as she pranced into tall stalks of sunflowers. Truvie followed, watching her feet touch the grass. She curled her toes into her sneakers. The ground hard, with a bit of give, like real soil held the blades in place. She reached for a stalk. The edge rough with little brisk hairs and the weight of the tall flower significant, sturdy. The bright yellow petals soft as silken velvet. Real. The sunflower she held exact to the ones in the garden at Eddie's.

Truvie shuffled to catch up to Tots. "Who plants things here? How are we in a meadow and flower patch?"

"Sussy," Tots said. "Here at least. It's his island. Here what we imagine appears instantly. We think it, it becomes. Just like the Glass Isle and the—

A swarm of green crows swooped down and gathered Truvie and Tots into their talons.

"Cave of Souls," Tots hollered back to Truvie as they soared into the dimming sky, "are yours."

"Mine? How can they possibly be mine?" Truvie asked in a voice too quiet to travel.

· · ·

The sunlight faded beyond the clouds, a descent from orange to pink to purple to a subtle twilight of golden blue. The crows soared toward an island. Against the beginning of night, the silhouette of the isle's peak appeared to be a tower or a lighthouse. Below, lights began to dot the sea. Electricity. Homes. Islands with soil and souls. Could such a place exist? Or was she thinking it into being? In a quantum world, that is how it would be. There would be no end to the possibility.

The gentle call of the green crows started as if they offered answers. She wished they could. But doubted she would understand, even if she could suddenly decipher crow song. Truvie Tucker knew she did not dream this well. Fear rippled through her as goose pimples scattered over her skin. A breeze lifted her and the crows higher into the sky.

"It could be new drugs," she said to the wind. "But I'm starting like this dream."

The crows dove for the island with the tall peak. She could see now that it was a tower. The same tower to the castle she found when the crows brought her here. They swooped around the castle revealing the rocky cliffs on the backside of the island. The sea crashed into boulders that served as beaches to the monolith.

Tots and her crows veered right toward the fjords.

Truvie's crows did not follow.

Hers lowered to a few feet above the sea. Heavy gusts of wind sent sea spray to her face. Crests of waves only inches from them vanished as the crows circled a rimless, glimmering, still silver pool. They did not fly directly over it, but close enough for her to see the place where life began again.

Without warning, the green carriers shot up from the water and ripped directly into the fjords. With a cry, they heaved Truvie onto a precipice and continued their flight into the coming of night.

"Hi."

Truvie turned to Tots' voice, sending a handful of pebbles over the side. The ledge barely held space for one.

"I can't see you," Truvie said.

"In here," Tots said.

"Where's here?" Truvie called before she moved. Suddenly it was too dark to see anything. She could hear the waves crashing far below. She had no desire to misstep. She'd already fallen—

"The Cave of Souls," Tots said.

"I thought it was a castle," Truvie said. "Didn't you see the tower?"

"The other side of the Castle is the Cave," Tots said.

"A façade?" Truvie asked as she spotted a silhouette of a petite girl—Tots—near the mountain. She moved toward what illuminated into an arched opening. Her foot slipped on the moist surface. Tots appeared instantly and grabbed Truvie's forearm, steadying her.

"You and edges." Tots pulled Truvie into to the opening. A steady drip echoed from the chamber. And was that—

"Is that hissing?" Truvie asked.

"You can hear it?" Tots asked.

"Can't you?" Truvie asked.

"No," Tots said, taking them further into the darkness. "But you always told me it was there."

"Don't tell me—"

"Not souls, Truitt," Tots said. "Directions."

"Directions?" Truvie searched the darkness but could only make out rocky bumps and root-like protrusions.

"Just a little wind that funnels through here. From the Crest."

"What's the Crest?" Truvie asked. "Or do I even want to know?"

"Trust that sensation you just had," Tots said.

"Not wanting to know?" Truvie said. "But I kind of do want to know."

"You sensed the information would be hard to hear," Tots said. "That's valuable. Helps you be in tune with your you."

"Oh, okay," Truvie said, unconvinced. "What's The Crest?"

"It's not safe for you to be this close," Tots said. "That's why you paused."

"Close to what?" Truvie scratched her arm where a root tickled her.

"Merging the worlds," Tots said. "Come on. This way."

As the two moved deeper into the cavern, small flames embedded midway up the walls came to life offering a warm, flickering glow. Truvie counted ten steps. On the twelfth, Tots took a tunnel opening right and sat down on the ground.

"What are you doing?" Truvie said. "Why stop—"

"Sit down," Tots said. "Quickly. It'll knock you over."

Truvie looked behind her to see what might be

coming, but nothing—

Tots yanked Truvie to the ground as a heavy wooden door from above dropped open. The long, slender side of a red door swung less than an inch from Truvie's nose before it slammed shut, making Truvie scoot backward toward a cave wall. The moment the door closed, it burst open again, then slammed closed. And as it had before, the moment it connected, it released, sending a mean crash booming all around them.

Covering her ears, Tots screamed, "You have to grab it."

The red door banged toward the cave wall.

"And go in!" Tots cried.

"Grab it?" Truvie shouted. "Are you insane? It'll snap my hand in two."

Wham! The door went again. And again.

"You have to go!" Tots huddled into a tight ball and closed her eyes. "Please!" she cried.

"Why?" Truvie cried.

"You know you want to go in and see," Tots screamed. "I can feel it!"

Truvie cringed as the red door bashed again and when it opened her arm lifted and her fingers grabbed hold. Gripping it, she steeled her body and held the door ajar.

Tots unraveled with a sigh and a smile. "Thank you so magnificently much."

"Why didn't you warn me?" Truvie asked. "You could have explained this door and banging—"

"I didn't know until we got here." Tots tugged at her ear with her thumb and index finger. "You won't believe me when I say that. But I move by feeling and asking. You said you wanted to find Eva. I followed the answer to that question."

The door ripped free from Truvie's grasp, slammed then opened again. Before she could react, her feet lifted out from under her as she was hurled through the door.

And hit on the harsh cement floor with a penetrating reverberation.

Flat on her back, Truvie heard Tots' voice called from down below, "Told you you wanted to go in!"

The red door she'd come through melted into a blinding white cement floor. Truvie rose to her elbows and found an infinite line of blood-colored doors mounted in unblemished white walls. They opened in unison.

"Oh no."

And closed with blasting bangs. Open. Slam. Open. Slam. Open. Slam. Over and over and over again.

Truvie curled into a tight ball, her hands pressed to her ears. The slamming pierced into her core, making her feel sick to her stomach. The constant pounding hurt from the inside out.

"Stop, please!" Truvie called. "I don't understand."

A gentle whimper seeped up from the floor in between slams. With the slightest lift of her forehead, she scanned for the sound.

"Hello?" Truvie tried. "Is there someone in here?"

The banging did not subside, but the whimpering grew louder.

"Who's there?" Truvie asked.

No one answered. It didn't sound like an animal. It sounded like. . . a girl.

Truvie crawled on her hands and knees. The cold, hard cement sent jabbing pain from her knees, up her thighs, and into her hips. Wisps of air rhythmically buoyed her hair from her shoulders before each sharp strike of the doors slamming shut.

Head and heart bursting to the point of breaking, Truvie reached a woman, curled into a fetal ball in the center of the pale corridor floor. Truvie lightly touched the woman's ratty sweater.

"Excuse me?" Truvie whispered.

The woman—not a small woman at all—sprang into Truvie's chest and wrapped her arms tight to Truvie's neck. Rocking off balance, Truvie's back slammed into an expanding door.

"Owwah!" Truvie howled.

Truvie quickly pushed her bum forward, still entangled with this woman, to avoid the impending deadly slam.

"Do you know how to stop the doors?" Truvie asked

The woman rolled her head to the right out of Truvie's hold. Her bloodshot eyes and sweaty forehead filled with strands of wet hair gave the woman a savage look that quickened Truvie's pulse.

Truvie pushed her horror away and wiped the woman's hair from her brow. "Please, I want to help you. But I'm—I'm out of my league here."

The woman locked her eyes to Truvie's. Her irises green with flecks of pale orange around the pupils.

The doors ceased.

"Are you Eva?" Truvie asked.

The woman nodded. She glanced over Truvie's shoulder at the closed red doors. They instantly opened with a whoosh and slammed with an ear-piercing bang.

Truvie put her hand to Eva's cheek and gently guided it toward her. They locked gazes.

"Don't move," Truvie said. "I'm not kidding."

The doors stopped again.

"Tru—" Eva's voice cracked. She coughed for several moments, turning her head away, sending the doors into fits.

Truvie rose from her knees to standing then held out her hands. With all her focus she imagined Eva taking hold.

Eva took hold of Truvie's palms and slowly came to her feet. Her jeans tattered and her feet bare, the woman still stood five or six inches above Truvie. Her long auburn hair a ratted mess.

"I don't know what else to do," Truvie said. "But don't let go whatever you do."

Without a blink, Eva gave the slightest nod.

Truvie steadied her mind and thought of helping this woman.

She turned her gaze away from Eva and toward the nearest red door.

This time the doors did not fly open. The room remained perfectly still.

And Truvie knew exactly what to do. She tightened her grip to Eva's and asked, "Ready?"

12
Answers

Truvie didn't wait to hear Eva's reply. She pulled the haunted woman through the door with all the force she could muster.

They fell forward into emptiness and all went quiet. Down and down they traveled. The second Truvie started to worry, they landed with a thud, bums to a plush, but unforgiving, wood floor. Part in shock, part in awe of her triumphant leap, Truvie giggled. Eva did not. Still, Truvie couldn't help herself. This was getting ridiculous. The dream that never ended in a world of quantum mechanics where there was no sense of boundaries, exactly as Truvie would have imagined a world of quantum-ness. No more this or that. It was this and that, and that, and that. This was a dream come true. In the real world, quantum mechanics was theoretical. Here it was everywhere. In everything.

To ground herself, she studied the room, which was a little more than strange, and not all that grounding.

The carpet had intertwined geometric shapes like a modern-art puzzle. The segments colored in electric tones of army green, magenta, hunting orange, cherry, copper, gold and silver. Truvie sat at the intersection of an electric orange circle and a magenta triangle. Her feet on an army green rhombus that touched a gold hexagon. Hideous was the term her mother would have used. Her father would have loved it and feverishly sketched it into his journal.

"You brought us to Sagacious Hall. Terrific." Eva rolled to her knees and into a miniature chair with a red tulip blossom for a back.

"Where?" Truvie asked.

"Sagacious Hall," Eva said.

"Sagacious means wise," Truvie said.

"You want to define simple words? That's what you want to do?" Eva asked. "I told you this would be a disaster. You ruined everything, Truitt. How could you be so selfish?"

"It's Truvie. Truvie Tucker. I don't know anyone named Truitt."

Eva blinked several times. Her mouth opened, but nothing came out.

Truvie got up and walked to a row of windows that opened with a clasp at the top. She knew this kind of window. She unhooked the latch and pulled the pane forward. As expected, its hinges only allowed the air in through a couple of inches.

"We had chairs like that when I was in kindergarten," Truvie said. "And windows like these in all the schools I went to. I guess they think students might jump."

The distinct scent of mint came in with a gentle breeze. She contorted to catch sight of the starry sky.

"I'm not interested in teaching you," Eva said. "Not in the least."

"Is there a moon in the City on the Sea?" Truvie asked before she could stop herself.

"Two or three," Eva responded. "Depending on the night. And the asking."

"How can that be?" Truvie asked.

"Truitt," Eva said.

Truvie turned her attention from the stars to Eva then returned her gaze to the night. "I know you want answers. I don't have any. I need you for answers and you're a physicist. I'm good at physics. I think like I might be in a dream—I hit my head and then—this—it's lasting a long time. Too long. I want to think I'm still under anesthesia. But—"

"You're dead," Eva said. "That is, if dead were real, but it's not. You think you're the dead person, this Truvie Tucker, but you aren't. You are, and will only ever be, Truitt Skye."

"You were once alive, right? You were Eva? How did you die? Are you dead now too? Were you in the hospital where I was? Is that why you're here now?"

"Stop," Eva said. "There is no live or dead. There is. Only is. No end to living. I am Eva Kinde. And before that, I had a different body, name, life. When we go into the pool, we begin again, and who we were before only comes through in the broadest of ways. Ways that are so general, we call them the greater good, or collective consciousness, or essence. But we are completely new."

"So I'm not dead?" Truvie asked.

"I need you to find the Truitt Skye you," Eva said. "You must become who you are or the trouble that comes will devour us all."

Truvie pulled her hand back from Eva with a not-so-subtle yank. "I know who I am. Call me whatever name you want. Truvie. Truitt. Lily. Jill. I don't care. But I can't be anything but me and I wish everyone would stop asking me to. It's not nice. It hurts my feelings. I came here, dream or not, and everybody needs me to be this Truitt person. That all of life depends on it. This doesn't make sense. I'm seventeen years old. I'm supposed to be going to MIT. I got in. To MIT. Do you understand what that means?"

"I do," Eva said. "I went to MIT, and later taught there. Professor of Theoretical Physics."

"Not recently you didn't," Truvie said. "I've followed all the professors there since I was seven."

"Technology has come a long, long way," Eva said. "I was there in the 1940s, Truitt. A bit before your Truvie time but not your Truitt."

"Are you saying I was here? As Truitt?"

"You've been here since the beginning of every-thing."

Eva stood and paced the opposite side of the room near a chalkboard. "I want to be patient and gracious with you because I know you believe you are still a child. You feel less than extraordinary, and for now, you are, but that is merely by choice. You're fresh and highly curious, but very, very stubborn, I can feel that loud and clear. You say you know who you are? Then where are you? Gone are the insights of Truitt Skye, creator of a world that protects the souls. Gone! By choice! It's—it's infuriating!"

Truvie watched this stranger. Hate—hot, itchy waves of anger—oozed from Eva. If Eva had been Truitt's most trusted, they should be working together. Eva should want to help her. Truvie should want Eva to help her. Instead, Truvie's every muscle tightened. Rage had never pulsed anywhere near Truvie Tucker. Not once. Her parents were not angry people, Eddie was the sweetest thing ever, Fig only wiggled and played and ate and kissed. Helena, sure, she could be prickly, but not one ounce of the white heat of fury Truvie was feeling.

"Go on," Eva said. "Let's have it. Maybe there is a little Truitt Skye in there after all."

"You're lying," Truvie said. "I've never once in my life called someone a liar. And it hurts to say it now. But I have no doubt I'm right. You're saying things to me for your benefit, not mine. You only want something from me. You have no intention of helping me become this Truitt. You're against me. Why? I haven't done anything to you. I just met you."

Eva gripped the edge of her tiny chair as she let out a surging scream. Then stood and tossed the chair across the room. "We were so close! How could you do that to me? How could you jump over the edge and begin again when we were so close?"

Truvie picked up the chair Eva had thrown. "To what?"

"I'm not your damn teacher," Eva said.

"Please," Truvie said.

"Please, what?" Eva stepped closer. "Truitt had a very provocative soul, and since souls don't change, her intensity is intact. Naive, uninformed, innocent. . . all states I deplore and always have. And it is who you are now. By bloody choice! Do you know what that makes you to me? To this world? To humanity?"

Truvie didn't know what Eva wanted her to say.

"Useless!" Eva roared. She kicked a red rubber ball. It bounced off a chalkboard and hit her in the nose. "You did that!"

Truvie laughed. She had imagined the ball whapping Eva but only really quick.

Then it whacked her a second time!

Eva stumbled backward landing hard on her butt.

Truvie cupped her hands to her mouth. "I'm so sorry. I didn't—I didn't mean to—"

Eva hunched forward and took in a long inhale. She spoke to the copper octagon rug piece under her feet. "Pel will find us soon. I know he can feel us. I suppose I should go with him and get it over with."

Truvie lowered onto the rubber ball on the floor opposite Eva. "I'm a quick study. I'm curious. I want to be useful. I want to help."

"You can't," Eva said.

"I love bacon," Truvie said. "Did she? I love particle physics. I know everything there is to know about the

Higgs boson. I'm great at math. I can—"

"We aren't girlfriends, Truitt. That's not how it works here. Not then, not now."

"What harm would it do to tell me what you want?" Truvie asked. "Not teach me, include me. Who knows, maybe everything will come back to me with your help?"

"It won't. You're you, but you're a new you. Exactly what I wanted to avoid. By now you must have heard that you and I were working on a plan to merge the worlds."

Truvie nodded.

"That's what humanity is asking for," Eva said. "Us within them constantly."

"Why?" Truvie's heart started to race. Her palms moistened. And her vision turned razor sharp. Everything in the room was in x-ray focus. She didn't ask why because she didn't want it to go away.

"There's a gap," Eva said. "A delay that hurts them terribly. Souls have far more to give to humans and humans want to be more connected to their souls. Merging the worlds means life could be beautiful. Struggles would evaporate. Conflict would be settled in seconds. Wars. Murder. Violence. Inequity. Hatred." She snapped her fingers. Her skin glowed. Her green eyes bright and sparkling. "All eliminated immediately. Souls would lead. Suffering would be replaced by thriving. Generosity would be an epidemic. Love would dominate."

"Why didn't we do it then?" Truvie asked. "What was the problem?"

"We couldn't find a way to do it slow enough," Eva

said.

"Why does it have to be slow?" Truvie asked. "I'm sorry. I know you don't want to teach me—"

"Think about it," Eva said. "We might destroy Earth. Implode the solar system, forge a black hole."

"Gravity could obliterate us," Truvie said.

"Them," Eva said. "Not us. We're energy. Light. We'd eventually emerge from the darkness."

"Why would you push me over the edge like Pel says you did?" Truvie said. "Especially if I agreed this was what we needed to do for humanity."

"I didn't push you," Eva said. "I let Pel and the others think I pushed you because I didn't want to explain the consequences."

"Consequences?" Truvie's vision blurred. She blinked as Eva spoke, wanting the super-sharp vision to return.

"You not being you means all growth has slowed," Eva said. "More souls are fragmenting. More chaos. More pain."

"Why didn't you merge the worlds without me?" Truvie asked.

Eva laughed, her eyes wide and wild. "Don't you think I would have if I had that power? You as Truvie are agreeing because you like the sound of it. You have no perspective. You can only think of yourself and your friends and family. Like humans do. Truitt Skye thinks broader. This is her world. I serve her. We all do. You're the only one who can do such things."

The floor rumbled and pillowed, exactly as it had in the hospital earlier.

Truvie lost her balance on the rubber ball and fell forward to her hands and knees. As she righted herself, she shook her head.

The walls of the room suddenly collapsed with a thunderous crumble. A grey, musty dust emerged from the ground swallowing them. Truvie coughed and heaved. Caked with remains, Truvie blinked her vision free. The room once bright with color, toys, and games, now in ruins.

"Eva?" Truvie coughed. "Are you okay? Did I do that or did you?"

But Eva did not answer.

As the dust drifted to the ground, she saw Eva running into the woods.

"Where are you going?" Truvie asked in a quiet tone, knowing Eva Kinde was long gone.

. . .

Truvie was alone for the first time since she arrived in this bizarre place they called her world. A place of islands on the bluest sea ever to be. Of souls leading the way. Truvie hadn't a clue what to do. She was certain Pel would arrive. And that Tots was not far behind. Probably that blonde guy, Latham. If she could, Truvie would run, hide, do anything to not hear how important and magnificent Truitt Skye, was.

She walked from the destruction down a hall filled with children's art on the walls. Finger paintings and stick-figure scenes. The same kind of rudimentary art Truvie created years ago.

"If the worlds merge," Truvie started, but violent quaking rattled through her legs. Truvie braced herself to the wall, careful not to grab hold of any art. The vibrating stopped. She regained her balance with a long inhale and proceeded down the hall with an exhale. She wanted out of here. Back to her grandfather, something familiar.

She paused her movement to close her eyes, to focus, to remember how to get out of here. "Please," she whispered.

An image of Sagacious Hall formed in her mind. A long hall of classrooms. It wasn't hard. It was a school. Something she already knew well. And then it came to her. One more door to go, turn left, and the main doors await her.

She walked out the right side of the wooden double doors into the light of three small moons and countless shimmering stars.

"Where's Eva?"

Pel stood, one leg up a step from the other, at the bottom of wide marble steps.

"She considered giving in to you," Truvie said. "I'm sorry if that's what I should have let her do."

"Crazed still?" Pel asked, walking up to meet Truvie halfway.

"She's. . ." Truvie paused then decided on, "Passionate."

"Angry," Pel corrected.

"That, too," Truvie said. "But I think I may have made a little progress."

"You know where she went?" Pel asked.

"I'm hungry," Truvie said.

Pel shook his head.

"What?" Truvie teased.

"You are kind of like you still," Pel said.

"Oh yeah?" Truvie said with a lift to her tone.

"Distracted easily," Pel said. "Not a compliment."

Before Truvie could think of a clever reply, Pel whistled.

A pack of wolves charged from the edge of the forest.

They gathered around Truvie with ferocious love and elation. Howling and yelping, nuzzling their heads to her legs, begging for her attention.

"They'll take you to Junius."

"Aren't you coming?" Truvie asked.

"No," Pel said.

"Is Eva dangerous?" Truvie asked, her head leaning on top of a grey wolf.

"More than you can ever imagine," Pel said. "And with you like this, I can't—I won't—stop until it's done."

"I want to understand," Truvie said.

"That's step one."

Pel marched into the woods leaving Truvie alone with a pack of wolves. Some white, others grey, one charcoal, one black, and two tawny brown. Pel looked back and as she lowered to her knees. She gave him a wave. He sort of smiled, maybe.

A sudden wind released a spur of falling golden leaves. She searched for him in the swirl. Gone.

Truvie's arms lifted from snouts. She eased her back to the ground and was immediately covered in kisses and beasts filling her lap. Each three times the size of Fig, these babies carried serious strength and long limbs, but she could not have loved it more. Their meaty breath and stinky, ripe coats should repel her, but instead, made her feel at home. She dared imagine that if she stood outside this pile looking in, Truvie herself might be a wolf, exactly like them.

13

The Glasshouse

After a long frolic, the wolves lined up in two rows before Truvie and without ropes or ties or a sled, the ground beneath her lifted and cupped her into a small cozy, soft seat. The grass and dirt transformed into a velvet green blanket and folded over her lap and chest. With a unified breath, the wolves strutted for a few steps then swiftly galloped across the lush landscape. To her welcome surprise, her seat did not bounce as they moved. It balanced motionless a foot or two above the earth.

In only a few strides, they jumped off the island, easily clearing Truvie in the rear. With a controlled descent, they gently touched their paws to the starlit sea. They raced across the pristine water casting only minute splashes with each stretch, and again her chair did not move. It never came close to touching the water.

She nestled the velvet to her chin. Wolves racing on the sea. Glasshouses on glass islands. "Don't think about it," she whispered to herself.

The wolves hurled from the water and over the jagged rocks lining the beach. They landed with ease onto the glass walkway. The front entrance to a glass-house wasn't ornate, except for the stained-glass sun above the front door. Vertical wide panes separated with copper framing extended from both sides of the corrugated pale pink glass front door. Above her, too many floors to count.

She gave each wolf a kiss and a pat. "Don't tell any-one, but you're better than the green crows."

The wolves walked as one toward the end of the lawn and settled down beneath a grove of aspens quak-ing with golden leaves.

"Truitt."

Truvie did a double-take of the golden leaves then turned to the welcome voice of her grandfather.

Junius eyed the pack. "I see you met up with Pel again. Come in. I'll make you a BLT."

Truvie skipped up the steps and threw her arms around Junius. The bald man staggered back and took a moment to adjust before he placed his hands on Tru-vie's head and back and received her embrace.

With a slight release, her chin to his belly, Truvie said, "Hi."

She rested her cheek to his sternum and squeezed him again. "I love you," she whispered inaudibly. She closed her eyes then louder said, "I'm scared."

Junius pulled away. "Wonderful! You're arriving, dear. I take it you found Eva?"

"She's a lot," Truvie said.

Junius nodded. "Come inside. I want to hear."

. . .

The kitchen was unexpectedly large with a ten-foot table made from refurbished wide slats of thick barn wood and matching benches on either side. In the corner near a gilded glass door sat an extra-large dark leather chair with a reading light and small bookcase painted red. Across from her were tall windows that appeared to roll up with the use of ropes and a pulley. Beneath the window, glass garden beds with herbs and vegetables were planted in narrow rows, roots pressed to the walls.

The sizzle of fat to the frying pan pleased her as the sweet, salty aroma of smoked bacon hit her. A waft of yeast vented from the brick oven near the leather chair. Homemade bread. How good could this place be?

"When did you get here?" Truvie wondered out loud. "I mean—"

"You're having trouble understanding the order of things," Junius said. He flipped the bacon with the prongs of a fork. He picked up a serrated knife and began slicing the tomato. "I died young, as you know."

"When you were thirty-seven," Truvie said.

"But you think I've been here longer?" he asked. "You're right. We don't count years here. I believe we might now, now that you have had a little time as a human. But soon you will forget, and we'll go on back to the answering for them, not you. Back to what we all do. To what you do."

"Do you miss it?" Truvie ignored his rambling about what happens in the City on the Sea. She had enough of that for now. She needed specifics, not riddles.

"I hate to disappoint you." His back to her as he removed the bacon from the flame. "But no, dear. I never miss it. Would you like to know why?"

"Very much," she said.

"Because I'm there equally."

"You mean when you go to The Restore?" A thought grabbed Truvie. "Wait. Eva did say something about being here and there."

Junius handed her a piece of bacon, which she held but did not eat. He took a nibble of his slice. "I don't go to The Restore anymore. I ought to pop by and see what Sussy Vox finds for me. Maybe a nice lunch I forgot I had long ago with your mother in London. I'm usually too busy cataloging you."

"How? How are you there equally?" Truvie returned the bacon to the plate then picked it up again and took a bite. "Energy? Quantum entanglement would do it, but—but that's theoretical, not practical. And in very, very, very small amounts—like particles, not peoples. An electron here could be connected to an electron thousands of miles away. Could be, but you can't see it. And it doesn't have a whole body still—"

Junius donned mitts and pulled the bread from the brick oven. It steamed with fresh heat. "Quantum entanglement. Yes, that is the science of it, true, albeit archaic and silly. I can be there or anywhere and still be here. Connected completely. Energy has no container, you know this."

"And you're always aware of the connection?" Truvie asked. "Entanglement is a theory. Proven only via computer. But you're not a computer, right? I'm not talking to a hologram, am I?"

Junius found that so funny, he dipped forward and almost dropped the bread to the glass brick floor.

Once he collected himself, he said, "My dear, we are souls. Not holograms. Not theories. Not computers. We are, as humans are, much, much more than the imagination can comprehend. We know it. They want to believe it."

"Physical, actual, real entanglement would be a miracle," Truvie said. "Nobel Prize. Teleportation. Please don't mess with me, Granddaddy"

"I am not physically there, Truitt, dear," he said, slicing the bread with the tomato knife. "Energy is far more powerful than any physicality."

"I disagree," Truvie said. "Respectfully."

Junius grinned. "I'm sure you do."

He opened the refrigerator and collected a mason jar filled with what Truvie suspected was homemade mayonnaise. "Pick some lettuce from the windowsill, will you? I like the butter leaf."

Truvie went to the garden rows and spotted the lettuce behind some Tuscan kale. She plucked a girthy leaf of pale green butter lettuce then found a long slice of Romaine for herself. She rinsed them in a huge glass basin that served as a sink. She opened the third drawer down on her left and pulled out a towel to dry the leaves. She straightened. "I knew where this was." She twirled the towel toward her grandfather.

"Because you put it there," he said. "It's easier if you relax. Let things come naturally. Let's have the sandwiches to go. I have something to show you." He laid out four slices of sunflower and herb bread then slathered them with mayo. Next the lettuces, then thin slices of tomato, which he doused with salt and pepper, and lastly four slices on each of succulent bacon.

"Grab some basil, will you, dear?"

Truvie pinched off two large basil leaves and gave them to him.

Junius pressed the basil to the mayonnaise-splayed bread then topped it to the bacon. He cut them through the center, not on the diagonal, just the way she liked. He stacked half to half and gave it to her. He did the same with his and took a bite.

"Follow me," Junius said as he chewed.

. . .

Junius stopped ahead of her in a corridor passed the spiral staircase they'd traveled down after Truvie blew up the library. She watched him as he chomped on the last bite of his BLT. She still had her second half to finish. The flavors of smoky, chewy, perfectly-singed bacon and bright, juicy tomato, the crunch of crisp lettuce and a hint of mayo and basil on the chewy, rich bread gave Truvie indecent pleasure.

"Best ever," he said.

"Mm-hmm." She nodded as she stopped in front of a vase suspended by long, thin rods, about seventy-five feet high. The narrow vase held six long stem red roses. She arched to her tippy toes and took a whiff.

"Beautiful," she said.

"Come see this," Junius said, pointing to a mirror mounted in the glass wall. "Your best invention yet."

Taking another bite of her BLT, Truvie walked down the corridor to meet her grandfather.

He put his hand out to stop her. "Stay out of the reflection for a moment, please dear."

Truvie popped the last of her sandwich onto her tongue. She rubbed her hands together to whisk away any crumbs then flattened her palms to the front of her jeans leaving smudges of tomato and mayo residue. Fig would be licking her pants and hands, if she were home.

"I miss Fig."

"Fig?" Junius asked.

"My lab. He's almost five."

"He's keeping them busy," Junius said. "No need to worry."

"He's good at that," Truvie said. "And love. He's very good at love."

"It's what animals are designed for," he said. "Lean over a bit so you can see," Junius said. "But remember, keep your reflection from the mirror."

"Got it." Without stretching too far to her right, she saw her grandfather in the mirror.

"Please watch the mirror, Truitt." He extended his

left hand up and around with a wave out to the left. And when he did, his reflection changed dramatically. He became a child, a little boy of four or five wearing red and brown flannel pajamas. While standing right next to her, he remained a fit bald man with a grey-striped suit and a pink tie. A man of thirty-seven. The precision caught her off guard.

"What's going on?" Truvie asked. "How—how can—what is this?"

Without a word, Junius waved his right hand out and around, circling to the right. His reflection turned to that of a teenager in a black suit and chartreuse tie. He extended his right hand up and around once again, and there he was exactly as she had seen in photographs of him and her grandmother on their wedding day, black tuxedo with a pastel plaid bowtie, thin black hair slicked back, wingtips and a white rose boutonniere.

"I was twenty-two," Junius said. "We married six weeks after we met. I would have married her six seconds after I met her if she would've have agreed."

"I've seen a photo of you so many times," Truvie said. "It's on Gram's nightstand."

Adjusting his bowtie in the mirror while his hands remained at his side in the Junius next to her, he said, "You created this mirror to take souls through the main events of their life."

"I created it?" she asked. "Truitt Skye I?"

"You wanted to be able to see their lessons—the events imprinted into their soul to share with the future—that exemplified their unique purpose and experience."

"Why?"

"To serve other souls with specificity."

"What connects the souls here to the souls there? How exactly does that work?"

"In the crudest of terms," he said. "They ask. We answer."

"How? I never heard you answer," Truvie said. "Never once."

He raised his eyebrows—both his reflection and his person—and smiled. "You did, dear. Trust me on this, will you?"

Truvie shrugged. "I don't think I'd understand anyway."

"You, and any human, let us know through your preferences, interests, obsessions, likes, dislikes, what they are thinking about and concerned with," he said. "We take it from there."

"But how do we hear?" Truvie asked, uncertain but hopeful.

"How you feel reflects the connection," he said. "The better someone feels, the closer we become."

"For everyone?" she asked. "On the planet? No. There aren't enough souls—I mean think of all the things people like and don't like. Our brains never shut up. Nor do our emotions."

"It's never too much for us. We aren't concerned with the outcome. To us, everything is good. It's all part of life," he said. "Still, we gravitate to our deepest desires, we can't help but be interested in what interests us."

"Like attracts like," she said. "My dad says that controls everything."

"It's rather comforting, isn't it?" Junius tightened his tie to his neck and stepped away from the mirror. "The way I appear to you now, meaning me as me here, not the child in the pajamas or the groom, is the best reflection of what matters most to me. It was the peak of my time in humanity. Me at my best means I give them the very best I have to offer. You see?"

"What is the best of you, Granddaddy?" she asked.

"That will be a treasure for you to discover," he said. "No need to rush. Can you trust me on that?"

"I trust you," she said.

He stepped to his right, further away from the mirror. "I want you to steady yourself. Your soul and my soul are not the same. You will not see what you saw with mine."

"Because I'm still alive?" Truvie frowned.

"As am I. Your reflection may shock you. It may delight you. I leave that to you. You have nothing to fear. You are in control here."

"If only that were true," she said.

He collected her hand into his and squeezed lightly. "Let your curiosity have its way with you."

She gave him a weak nod and sidestepped into the reflection. For a split second, she saw her Truvie self. Strawberry blonde wavy, slightly messed hair. Freckles. Jeans, turtleneck and cocoa brown Jack Purcell's, but in a blur, Truvie was replaced with a series of reflections: an elderly Chinese woman, a young boy with a blue lizard, a man with a full grey beard and all leathers, an

African boy with a water can. The reflected images did not slow. They gained momentum. She looked down to make sure she was still her, and she was, but when she looked to the mirror, she was an older man petting a cat in his lap, an elephant, a very pregnant woman, a fisherman, a golden retriever, a tall, skinny man in a blue turban and a long white beard, a bride, a horse, a female soldier, a little girl in a white nightie, and on and on, never stopping.

"Who are they?" They all looked so beautiful to Truvie. She considered twisting toward Junius and peppering him with questions but was not about to look away.

Junius gently took hold of her upper arm and guided her his way, free of the revolving reflections. Truvie twisted back but the mirror stilled, empty and grey.

"You're them," he said. "Everyone. Every soul flowing through you."

"Everyone ever?" Truvie said. "Including animals?"

"You are them and they are you," he said.

"But—" Truvie stepped further away from the mirror. "But why? Why aren't you them too?"

"Because this is your world, your soul, your purpose, your life, your endless experience," he said.

"You have a world too then where you're everyone?" Truvie said.

"My world is your world, Truitt," he said.

"Why?" Truvie begged. "Why is it my world?"

"Why would you want it any other way?" Junius asked.

"I have a world!" Truvie said. "With my family and Figgy. And Eddie. I have a future I want to get to."

"My dear," he said. "Trust me. You planned the entire experience as Truvie Tucker. Down to the last second. Your world of there has gone nowhere. You simply aren't letting yourself see it."

"No," she said. "I wouldn't—I would have stayed and lived my life. I would never have—have—have—"

"Truitt, you are living your life," he said. "Exactly as planned."

"Stop!" she screamed. "I don't want to hear anymore!"

She paced the corridor, hands covering her ears. Spots of red doors flashed before her vision. The classroom with Eva. The wolves. Pel. Fury. Fear. The images of people and creatures in the mirror. Everything and everyone unwelcome.

"I want to see my reflection as me," Truvie asked. "And go back to my lessons like you did."

"Why don't I show you to your room instead?" Junius said. "Perhaps you'd like to have a rest?"

"What does this have to do with Eva? And the red doors? What was that?" Truvie asked. "Does she have the same as me? An endless stream of beings? Is the mirror how we merge the worlds? If I break it, will the merge thing happen?"

She raised his fists into the air preparing to crush the mirror to bits.

Junius lowered his gaze and moved away from her, at first backing away then he turned and stalked down the corridor, an echo-y heel thud with each step.

She lowered her arms in defeat. Tempted to look, she touched the edge of the mirror. She wanted to see them all again, all the souls that were somehow her. "You are them and they are you," she repeated then took off at a sprint down the hall.

"Granddaddy!" she called. "Wait! I'm sorry!"

Junius halted.

She collected his hand and squeezed it.

"You have nothing to apologize for," Junius said. "I confused you."

"The mirror has nothing to do with Eva," Truvie said. "I don't know why I said that. I know you are trying to help me understand what's happening to me. But—"

"You want answers," he said. "You're piecing it all together. Yet your thoughts are messy and jumbled."

She threw her arms around him and gave him a hug. This time he did not hesitate or have to adjust, he put his arms to her shoulders and returned the squeeze.

Her cheek to his chest, she said, "I would like to see my bedroom."

"Follow me." He continued in the hallway for several moments, Truvie at his side. Almost to the end, he veered left and started up a multi-story glass brick staircase next to a solid glass wall. No creases for frames, at least none she could find. The entire staircase slowly bloomed with golden pink lighting.

"All the way to the top?" Truvie huffed, hands at her hips. "How far is it?"

"Seven floors to the atrium," he said. "Your place to dream."

14

A Room Above

The staircase extended beyond what she could see. At first, she was out of breath, but now, not in the least. Her side did not ache. Her legs remained fresh and eager to climb. Not one drop of sweat. She glanced over her right shoulder. Dizzied, the hundreds of steps below blurred and twinkled. She should be dripping with sweat and begging for a break. She was not in this good of shape.

"Don't think about it," Junius said. "Watch the sunrise instead."

The sky brightened with a haze of orange and blue, awaiting the arrival of the morning sun across the horizon.

Still looking to the sun, she lifted her foot but when she placed it, it fell too far and landed with a thunk.

They had reached the top, which opened to a museum-sized wide-open, high-ceiling room with a glass-domed roof and windows on the sides the size of cargo holds.

Birdsong filled the room, trickling water came next, then a rushing waterfall that she could not spot. The smell of—

"Jasmine?" Truvie sniffed deeply to take in the sweetness.

"Tuberose," he said. "The jasmine is on the far side of the stream. Could be pikake as well. You know, those dinky little white flowers you love."

She smiled. "No, Granddaddy, I don't know, we don't have tropical flowers in Milwaukee, but will you show me?"

"They're through here." He pointed to an over-growth of ferns and super-sized burgundy calla lilies.

Truvie ducked into the fronds, the air moist and heavy. "It's so alive." She touched the deep green leaf of the impeccable coned lilies.

"You wouldn't have it any other way," he said. "This entire city pulses with life."

"How can that be?" She turned and her cheek brushed a wet leaf. "Aren't souls dead?"

"You tell me," he said. "Is that what you think a soul is? Only alive in a body?"

"We have bodies," she said. "Are we ghosts?"

"The bodies here are a new thing," he said. "Something you added when you built the mirror. Believe me when I say it was the best thing you ever did. You constantly astound me with your genius. Constantly."

Truvie stopped amidst chest-high plant life and faced Junius. "I put the mirror in to show you all who you used to be?"

"You built the mirror for you to see who you are in relation to the rest of us. You knew you would not remember."

"Then why would she jump in the first place?"

"Why would you jump, you mean?" he said.

"Why would I jump?" she corrected.

"I've told you, to stop Eva."

"It was planned? Everyone knew? That's not what Eva said." She stopped herself, suddenly realizing the truth. "Only you and I knew. And you told a few people—souls—that was the plan. Or wait. I told you who to tell once I'd gone. Why? Why not tell everyone? If it was to save the worlds—or whatever—wouldn't it be a good thing for people to know?"

"You see, my dear? The atrium is bringing you back to you. But it wasn't quite that simple." He gestured for her to move forward again. "I know this is not something you understand yet, but it is not for me to explain because it is done. Can't change yesterday. Here is where we are. You, curious in a whole new way. Exactly as you wanted it."

"Pel says I'm weak," Truvie said. "And you're all relying on me."

"That is something Truitt Skye would never believe," he said. "Thus, I am ignoring it completely."

They walked in silence. Though it was not quiet. The songbirds tried to out sing the crows, making them cry louder, but neither muted the steady bubbling burble of the stream.

"Truvie Tucker wouldn't say it either," Truvie said.

"Over the bridge," he said. "See them now?"

The cluster of little white pikake flower plants in lovely planters sat on a glass tile floor. More tropical flowers vined along a backdrop filled with glass birdhouses. In the center of the sanctuary, a copper bird feeder with a dozen stations.

"It was genius of you to warn me," Junius said.

"Warn you?"

"Of your imminent arrival."

"You mean the library?" she asked.

"Not the crash," he said. "Prior to."

"That wasn't much of a warning," she said. "I was only there a second." Smelling the sweetness of the flowers she asked, "What did the warning matter?"

"I put Eva in the room with the red doors."

Truvie stood tall. "That was no room. It was a torture chamber."

. . .

Junius stepped to the wrought iron chair near the stream and sat. He smoothed his pink tie, which suddenly seemed brighter than it had before. "I contained her. She's been doing who knows what since you leapt over that cliff. Not to sound melodramatic but I cannot bear to think what she may be capable of at this point."

Truvie sat down in a chair opposite him.

"When you arrived, standing next to me with the only view that overlooks the City on the Sea. She could

not hide. Her energy was easy to see once she saw you.
I did what I had to."

"They could all see me?" Truvie asked.

"Those who were looking," he said.

"How many was that?" Truvie asked.

"You want to know how many souls are here?
Watching you?" Junius asked.

"Not watching me," she said. "How many in general?"

"Why?" he asked. "A moment ago, you were keen
on knowing about Eva and the red doors. I find you
terribly hard to read."

"You told me," Truvie said. "She was waiting. But I
was only there a moment. My guess is she came running straight—round the spiral staircase—but I was
gone, and you subdued her somehow. Hugged her then
gathered her into your arms like you did me?" Truvie
raised her brows. "Transformed her energy somehow.
Little trick Amelia Rose maybe taught you in a few late
nights together."

Junius flushed. "Now you sound exactly like you,
Truitt Skye." He laughed and pulled on his tie. "Something close to that did occur. Yes."

"How many?" Truvie asked.

"The numbers vary," he said.

"But you track them?" she returned.

"In a manner of speaking, yes, but not with bar
codes and computers," he said. "There is a process of
souls in and out. We all have a part in the tracking
depending on what we focus on here."

"Eva, what did she do?" Truvie took a seat at the
edge of the stream.

"She answered requests for pushing humanity forward."

"Pushing humanity forward?" Truvie repeated. "As in?"

"She works with visionaries. Good and bad. We don't differentiate here. They ask. We answer."

A cat, bigger than one of domestication, crept out from overgrown fronds. All white with lavender eyes. It slinked without pause to Truvie and hopped into her upper thighs, purring with delight.

"Meet Sprites," Junius said.

"What is it?" Truvie asked, leaning back with a tinge of trepidation. "I see it's a big cat, but what kind? Looks like a small panther. Is it friendly?"

"Sometimes," Junius said. "You know cats."

"I've only had Fig. He's a black Labrador."

"Sprites," Junius said. "Is a breed you and Saul discovered ions ago from the Egyptians. They didn't make it long with humans."

"Why?"

"Too fierce," he said. "Absolute and utter loyalty to their owner. To the detriment of others, if you get my meaning."

"Is it a sphinx?" Truvie asked, hardly believing the question.

"I've no idea its species, dear," Junius said. "I try to pretend he's not here, but you tend to refer to them as catters."

Sprites stretched his head up and into Truvie's collarbone. He licked her cheek and offered a deep purr.

"Don't worry," Junius said. "You two are good

friends."

Truvie tickled the catter's chin and behind his ears. "Did I name him Sprites?"

"Tots LaRue. I think you call it, Cat, or something original like that."

"I wasn't attached then?" Truvie said.

"You weren't attached to anything," he said. "You prefer movement. Momentum."

"I find that hard to believe," she said.

"It is the nature of your being, my dear. Your pleasure comes from the growth and strength of others. Their success is all that matters to you. You don't see failure, or death, as anything but a great success. You live to help the rest of us believe in our potential."

"What exactly does Eva do for visionaries?"

"Offer a guess," he said. "You're getting better. What are the biggest things the leaders in humanity are concerned with? What keeps them up at night?"

Stroking Sprite's back, she said, "Finding ways to get more."

"More what?" Junius asked. "Get specific. We're specific here."

"Money . . . Technology. Science. Scientific Discovery. Love. Freedom. War. More. Always more."

"Good!" he said. "Driven by?"

"I want to say curiosity, but that's not always true."

"It is true of visionaries. Be specific. Stick to what you know. What do scientists want more of?"

"Science. Umm. Big discoveries."

"Like?"

"Unified Theory. Higgs boson. Quantum leaps.

Universe as finite or infinite. Weight of mass, origin of mass, purpose of mass. Then there's curing cancer, diabetes, heart disease. Healing the body in general."

He sat back against the chair. "Precisely."

"Space travel. New forms of fuel. Mapping DNA. Mapping RNA. Particle accelerators. That's what I wanted to do. Work at Fermilab on the most precise microscope ever created. One that could define the smallest of the smallest and determine once and for all what created us all."

"Yes," he said. "I know what you intended."

Truvie squirmed her left leg free. It pulsed with numbness. The deeper sleep Sprite found, the heavier he became. "How can she help those people?"

"Not only Eva," he said. "You, too, dear. You were a team. We all move as one when the asking is strong."

"But how? If I was helping souls?"

"Momentum," he said. "There are people who are acutely aware of their energy, like Truvie's father, Ian. They know they are energy and thus understand how to attract more energy, more answers, more, just plain more. They understand what we do, not specifically, but they are tapped into the wellspring of their imaginations. They know their curiosity is heard because answers seem to appear out of nowhere. Yet, they know, it comes from an eternal knowing, they just don't admit it. A whisper heard in the unknown stays unknown.

"They ask, how does this or that work—it may be something specific like radioactivity or something more subjective like what is love, but we answer, over and over again in an infinite number of ways until they digest and embrace the answer with no further doubt. It becomes them. The answer merges into their being and then, naturally, they share what they know, what they are. They can't help but teach what they know because they have become it. And equally, they can't stop from—"

"Asking more," Truvie said. "I get it. I was there."

"I know you do," Junius said. "We heard you loud and clear, Truvie, my dear."

"Wait," Truvie said, sitting up and knocking Sprites off her lap. "I was one of the visionaries? Me? Truvie Tucker? And you knew it was me? Eva knew?"

Junius shook his head slowly. "I never told a soul. As for Eva, and the rest of the souls here, it was merely an exchange of energy. They never knew Truitt Skye was the one doing the asking."

"But you knew," she said. "You knew it was me?"

Junius rose to his wingtips and smoothed his tie. "A tale for another day. Let me show you where you dream. Sprites, will you please lead the way? I'm quite certain that's where you came from, you lazy bugger."

The white catter stretched his front paws out and lifted his rear. He yawned and meandered into the thick green foliage.

A chill scattered through Truvie. "But—I have more questions."

"Enough," her grandfather said. "For now."

He followed Sprites path, and so did she.

The passage through the ferns took them to an opening into giant palms. She reached out to the trunk. The rough, harsh bark of the palm surprised her. She'd never touched a palm, not as Truvie Tucker anyway. She lingered behind, not wanting to follow him. She didn't want to dream. For all she knew this was a dream. Or a coma. A shudder ran through her. The eagerness to return home was, for the first time, waning.

"Truitt, do try to keep up, dear," her grandfather said.

She slowed and whispered to herself, "Maybe I'll wake up. Maybe I won't. But if I do, please let me remember here. Please let me know what my soul can do."

"Truitt!"

She jogged to catch them as Junius and Sprites stepped onto a rope and wood-planked bridge that led high into the atrium. A hundred or more feet above them was a small structure made of wood, draped with white curtains, and suspended several feet with thick chains attached to hooks at the bottom edge of the domed roof.

"Is that my house?" she asked.

"More a room," Junius said.

Gripping the rough, earthy-smelling, thick rope railing on either side, Truvie made her way up and up and up to the platform bedroom she supposedly called her own.

"After you," Junius said. Sprites leapt from the entrance to a white bed. White puffy comforter, white fluffy pillows, white throw blanket across the foot of the bed. A white bed skirt of heavy cotton swathed the bamboo floor.

Tented white drapes left an opening in the ceiling

center. Wisps of thin clouds moved quickly across the morning sky giving the sensation that the sky existed on the reel of a movie.

A bookcase to the left of the bed held textbooks, notepads, and dolls. Directly across from the bed, a sizable clear glass screen hung without visible supports. Two suede chairs in a pale grey were arranged to face the screen. Between the seats, a bouquet of pink, red-tipped peonies sat in the center of a small wooden table detailed with carvings of the moon and stars.

Behind Truvie, further left of the bookcase, a small vanity and sink. Where a mirror might be, was a painting of a woman dressed in white pants and billowing white tunic. She balanced, arms outstretched, bare feet, on boulders above a crashing sea's edge. Her long blonde hair lifted by the wind, her chin to the sky. Her eyes open. Her manner, generous, ready, contented.

"Is that Truitt?" asked Truvie.

"You tell me," Junius said. "I've never seen that painting."

"Haven't you been in here?" Truvie asked.

"Never."

"Who comes here then?"

"You and a guest," he said.

"A guest?" Truvie asked. "Who? Who would I have in here?"

"I don't know, my dear." Junius pointed to the clear glass panel. "But I do know what you discover, you place in there."

"What is it?" Truvie said. "A computer monitor?"

"Would you like to find out how it works? How you

work here, Truitt?" he asked. "Are you now curious enough to execute the plan you intended? Because once this momentum starts, it will not end."

Truvie touched the painting with the tips of her fingers. Energy pulsed down the back of her hand, up her arm and into her heart.

"Yes," she whispered. "Very much."

15
Gaining Momentum

Truvie stood in her suspended bedroom. Sprites, curled into a doughnut against the white pillows, purred with a tender snore. Junius had gone a few moments ago, pleased to the point of giddy that she was ready to continue in this world fueled, for now, he had said, by her curiosity.

"I want to get out of this," Truvie spooned Sprite's back. "Can I?"

The big white cat rolled under Truvie's arm and shoulder, exposing his pale pink belly. "Just like Fig," she said as she scratched. Sprites elongated his arms with a yawn, then relaxed, his super-sized paws, floppy and limp.

On her side with Sprites in her chest, she studied

a set of dolls, larger than a Barbie, more like a Plush standing about thirteen or fourteen inches, but not made of fabric or plastic. "Maybe bleached wood?"

They all had the same face and body, similar to her own; blonde wavy hair, blue eyes, pinkened skin, pale freckles across the bridge of each nose and over to the cheeks. "Are they supposed to be me?"

Seven, no, eight dolls in total. One in a lab coat. "Could be." The next in khakis and a blue tee-shirt. A camera around her neck, passport in her hand, hair in a high ponytail. "Tourist." She studied the one above it. "A monk?" The doll had only a brown robe with a rope tied around the waist.

The next doll she liked. "Glamorous," Truvie said. It wore a long, radiant red gown. Hair up in a fancy up-do, make-up, and manicured fingernails. "That can't be me."

She rolled to her other side, closed her eyes, and fell asleep.

Her dreams came with ease. Floating from the white sky, swooping against the sea. Escaping. She spun over and over in sun-drenched air with her arms stretched like wings. She rose, high to the moon, tapping sparkling stars with the tips of her toes. She dipped into a forward flip and dove like a predator into the sea.

Truvie woke with a start. Sprites blinked then returned to slumber. Daylight streamed through the dome above her. Finches zipped across the tops of the trees, their bright yellow feathers like fast-falling leaves.

"Good morning beautiful!" Tots LaRue sat in one of the chairs by the clear screen. She'd twisted it around to face the bed.

"Hi," Truvie said, hoisting herself against the fluffy pillows. "I'm still here."

"I brought you some clothes," Tots said.

"Don't I have some here?" Truvie asked as she searched for a dresser or closet in her room, neither of which was there.

Tots smiled and shook her head.

"Where do I get my clothes? How do I dress?" Truvie asked.

"Hungry? I think Juni is making breakfast."

"Tots?"

Tots hedged by studying the Truvie dolls on the bookshelf. "Cute. Like little yous."

"Tots, where are my clothes?"

"I like the baseball one," She pointed to the doll in a green and gold baseball uniform, hair tucked beneath a hat, glove on her left hand, baseball in her right. Then finally said, without eye contact. "You didn't dress, Truitt."

Truvie eyes grew wide. "I walked around naked?"

Tots giggled. "You didn't wear a body, Truitt. Sorry. Should have been more specific. I forget how un-you you are."

"But that mirror—downstairs—"

"Yes, exactly." Tots stood and started toward the bridge. "Coming?"

Truvie followed. "What do you mean, exactly?"

"You're everyone," Tots said.

"How did you know it was me?"

"Your energy, silly." Tots raced over the bridge. The

rope handrails bounced up and down and side to side. "I love this thing!"

As Tots neared the end, she flew into the air, did a flip and landed on her feet.

"Nice!" Truvie laughed.

"You do it!" Tots called.

"Are you crazy? I'll break something. Ankle. Neck." The memory of her head smacking into that wet rock in the ravine flashed behind her eyes.

"What's wrong?" Tots ran back over the bridge.

"Nothing," she said. "I—I want to take a shower and brush my teeth. Then I'm putting on the clothes you brought, body or not," Truvie said. "Where's my bathroom?"

Tots puckered her lips then pulled them back into a grimace. "Umm." She rubbed her temple with her fingers, each of her fingernails painted a different color. "Don't have one? Just put the clothes on, okay? I'll see you downstairs." Tots took off at a sprint.

"Tots! Wait!" Truvie waited at the top of the bridge, but Tots didn't come back.

· · ·

A folded white tee-shirt, a pair of skinny jeans, ankle socks, and a new pair of pale red slip on sneakers sat on the suede chair. Truvie went to the sink first. "Note, have Junius explain where people go to the bathroom. Very scary to think we don't. But," she said to herself. "If I don't wear a body, what would it matter if I pee and—?"

Her palms moved to her cheeks, her fingers covering her eyes. "I'm done now. I get it. Appreciate what you have. Align with your soul. Trust in the impossible. I want to go home now. Please."

But she went nowhere.

After a frustrated sigh, she reached for the faucet. "Please work," she said as she turned the dial. Water flowed from the faucet. "Thank you." She pooled water in cupped hands and splashed her face and hairline. She turned her head and took a drink. She stared at the woman on the rocks for several seconds before returning to her new outfit.

She held up the tee which had the word, "Recycled" in rose gold lettering across the chest. Tossing her turtleneck to the floor, she lowered the new t-shirt over her head.

"I always take a shower," she said to the sleeping Sprites. "If there isn't one, and I'm this powerful soul, I will be making a bathroom first thing. Just so you know." The panther cat remained completely still. "Fig always barked after I said, 'just so you know.' Woof. Woof. I'll settle for a yawn or stretch."

Nothing.

Truvie swapped jeans, hiked up her socks and slid into and tied her new sneaks.

"Fine," Truvie said, standing.

Sprites stretched up to all fours, turned around, and plunked down into the pillows with a groan, fast sleep again.

Truvie kissed the top of his head. "Good enough. Sleep well, Sprites."

. . .

Before Truvie entered the kitchen, she smelled pancakes and heard upbeat music. Soul music. Eddie loved Marvin Gaye, Stevie Wonder, Nina Simone. It was all he listened to, so she did, too. The singer on now was someone she didn't know. But liked. Violins and a deep drum beat. The singer, a woman with a rich soprano spoke-sang-said the lyrics.

Truvie tapped her grandfather, who gently swayed with the tune.

When he saw her, the music stopped.

"Where'd the music go?" Truvie asked. "I liked it. I don't mind."

"What music?" he asked.

"Tots?" Truvie tried.

Tots shook her head. "Nope. What'd you hear? Share."

Truvie jiggered her head. "Nothing. My mistake. Why don't we have a bathroom, Granddaddy? Very unsanitary."

"We do." Junius flipped a pancake sprinkled with blueberries. "Wait." He lowered his gaze to Tots. "Not funny, Miss LaRue."

"I couldn't resist." Tots raised a finger. "Do you know how many times Truitt Skye played jokes on me?" She chuckled. "She deserves it. Know it all to not at all. Mine to exploit. Happily. Can we have hash browns too? And that chicken sausage you make?"

Truvie opened her mouth then closed it with a sly smile to Tots. "You were teasing? Where is it?"

"Trust now, Truitt," Tots said.

"Trust you? You're going to need to show me. I want proof. And I have to pee now that I've talked about it so much."

"Down the hall," Junius said. "Hurry though. You can take this food with you. Chicken sausage in the oven. Grab and go. Truitt needs to see Keone and Leilani first, then Blick, then Miss Frank."

"You didn't waste any time filling my schedule," Truvie said.

"Momentum, dear," he said. "Crucial at this juncture. You cannot hope to take on Eva until you have the momentum with you. Understand?"

"I want to," Truvie said.

"Wanting is all it takes," he said. "You'll take her to each, Totsinda?"

"Pleasure." Tots stood and took a cinnamon roll from the plate on the table. "Not Miss Frank, but I'll do it for Tru."

Junius gathered a pancake and some sausages from the oven. "Let's let this Truitt make her own impressions."

"Think she and Miss Frank will get along now?" Tots said, taking the food from Junius.

"Getting along is overrated." Junius gave Truvie a steamy cinnamon roll on a wooden plate then added a chunk of butter to the top. "Have a good day, dear."

"Give it to me, Juni." Tots took Truvie's roll. "This way, your highness."

. . .

They headed toward the mirror, but a few feet before it, Tots took a left. The glass arched door waited at the end of the hall. "See it?" Tots said. "I'll be at the mirror. Love that thing."

Tots skipped away, cinnamon bun in each uplifted palm, skirt swaying with her step. "Stop staring and go pee. Or whatever you need to do." Tots peeked over her shoulder and winked.

A grey beret emerged on top of Tots' head, perfectly suited to the petite spitfire.

"Thanks," Truvie said. Then to herself, "For being normal."

"Pleasure," Tots called.

With no door handle, Truvie opted to gently push the door forward, but it didn't budge.

"Slide to the left," Tots sang.

Truvie eased into the glass brick bathroom. To her immediate right a glass bowl sink with a glass faucet, and vases filled with fragrant purple lavender. But again, no mirror above the sink, like in her suspended bedroom. Low lights in a shade close to cantaloupe, illuminated a sunken shower basin. Above it, suspended by glass piping, an oversized square glass head with several spigot holes for water to flow, or douse, in this case. Tucked into the left corner, a glass bathtub and a narrow shelf with pale pink roses in individual vase slots spaced every six or so inches. She quickly counted them. "Sixty roses."

She took a few more strides deeper in and found, at last, a toilet. A normal "porcelain, not glass," toilet. "Thank you."

16
Gravity on Water

Truvie met Tots at the mirror to finish breakfast. She didn't venture a glance at her reflection. It made her dizzy. Tots stared at her reflection and laughed. "I was such a cute baby!" Truvie had a smidge of a look-see. Tots was three years-old in a cute sailor suit saluting the air and eating a cherry popsicle.

"Extremely cute," Truvie said.

Tots stepped away from the mirror and faced Truvie. "I knew I looked best in bright red even then," Tots said as her lips turned cherry red.

With a quick trip down the spiral staircase, they left the glasshouse. The bright sun and clear blue skies gave her pause. The autumn chill of Milwaukee, that crisp threat of the long winter to come, seemed to be fading.

The City on the Sea

She wanted to reach for it but had nothing to grab hold of. Her confidence that she would soon emerge from this—this dream or anesthesia or whatever—dwindled with each passing moment.

"Let it go," Tots said. "Meet my baby, The Whooper."

Tots' straddled a double-wide obviously jet-ski named, "The Whooper." Something Truvie would have been happy not to experience. It wasn't that Truvie was a stranger to watercraft. After all, she grew up on the shores of Lake Michigan, but right now—

"Can't these people come here?"

"No," Tots said. "Hop on or I'll pull you down."

Truvie backed away. "You're half my size."

"And mighty," Tots said.

"I don't—" Into the air Truvie went and with a gentle release, her legs fell to either side of the jet ski and her hands clasped around Tots' waist.

"You're sure I like you?" Truvie asked. "We're friends?"

"Best of," Tots said and with a rev of the engine, they took off across the sea.

Truvie closed her eyes and rested her cheek on Tots' shoulder. The warmth of the sun hitting her face filled her with a lovely sense of calm. Lightened by the silence, she let herself love Totsinda LaRue. When she was with Junius and Tots she forgot the sensation that she should be somewhere else. It wasn't that she wanted to be here—she didn't. With them, she forgot she was here. That felt nice.

. . .

"We're here," Tots said as she pulled into a rock cluster on the edge of a non-island. The "dock" looked like a pile of rocks dumped into the ocean. A few feet behind it, she spotted a narrow rock rim. This was no island. Maybe the remains?

"Where are we?" Truvie asked.

"Hey Truitt."

An athletic young guy with creamy brown skin stood on the rocky rim. Truvie recognized him from the forest but had no clue what his name was or why she was here. Her mouth hung open, hands cupped to her eyes to shade the sun, "Hi," was all she could manage.

"Keone," Tots said. "She's all yours."

He spoke to Tots LaRue. "We could really mess with her. She deserves it—"

"Trust me," Truvie cut in. "Tots is taking full advantage of my obliviousness."

"Let's go then?" he said. "Lay-o's up ahead."

"Lay-o?"

"Leilani. She was in the woods," Keone said. "You staying or going, Tots? I don't imagine you want any part of this—"

"Why wouldn't she stay?" Truvie's head ached a bit suddenly. "Is it dangerous?"

"Extremely," Keone said then turned to Tots. "She is out of it, isn't she?"

Still holding onto the handlebars, Tots twisted to the back to face Truvie. "Scoot or I'll boot you out. You know I can."

Truvie pressed herself to stand, making the jet-ski

wobble enough—

Splash! Truvie dropped to the sea.

Tots and Keone enjoyed a great laugh.

Leilani rushed from behind Keone. "Help her!" But Tots and Keone couldn't contain themselves.

Truvie turned her back to them. Her chest ached. She wasn't angry. She thought it was funny too, but no laughter arrived. The water warm, and light. She sidestroked to the rock pile and lifted herself from the sea. "I got it. I'm fine."

Leilani hopped down to Truvie. "Shake a little," she said. "To dry."

Truvie paused to ponder that one. "Shake? Like a dog?"

"You know," Leilani said, beginning to gyrate her shoulders. "Shimmy. Head to toe."

Truvie held her hands up in surrender. "I'll stay wet. I think I've entertained everyone enough for now."

Leilani, dressed in a white tennis dress and white sneakers, moved her right shoulder forward, then her left. "It's not a trick. You'll dry in a snap."

Tots and Keone gathered themselves. "She's for real," Keone said.

"Keone and I are souls for physical bodies. Agility, Strength. Stamina. Finesse," Leilani said. "I know you're confused. Working with us will help."

"Trust, Truitt," Tots said. "You can trust us."

"Athletes tend to get our focus," Keone said. "But we're not picky. We serve movement and the desire for it to be better. Optimize the energy so it works for a body, not against it."

"Using the body for more than walking or running or wheeling in a mechanized device," Leilani said. "Really using it to its full kinetic potential, however stressed, limited, or free the body may be."

"Yet another Truitt Skye experiment," Tots said.

Truvie shimmied her shoulders and her waist. Her torso dried instantaneously. She jiggled her head. Dry. She shook her left leg and foot. Same. Bone dry. Then jangled the right lower half. Arms and hands. Suddenly dry. As if she'd never fallen in.

"You're in good hands," Tots said. "I'll be back."

"Thank you," she said to Tots. "I don't mind the teasing. Makes me feel . . ." She shrugged, almost too embarrassed but, "It makes me think you like me. Like me enough to tease me. Keep doing it. Please."

Truvie's eyes burned with tears but she blinked them away.

Tots popped off the jet-ski and was hugging Truvie in less than a blink. "I love everything about you, Truitt Skye."

Keone pulled the glued Tots from Truvie. "Okay, Tots. She gets it. See you later."

"Tots specializes in feelings, if you couldn't guess," Leilani said. "Reads feelings with tremendous accuracy, makes her seem clairvoyant, but she's acutely attuned. So much so, that Tots tends to respond accordingly, and immediately, to whatever you're feeling strikes her. She moves too quick to stop sometimes."

Truvie nodded then gave her new-slash-old friend another squeeze. "That's a nice thing. Scary, but good."

Tots squeezed Truvie again then pounced back onto

the jet ski and drove away.

Truvie turned to Leilani. "When I was feeling isolated—"

"Lonely," Keone corrected. "You were lonely."

"She teased me to make me feel welcome?" Truvie said.

"Must be a way that you felt you fit in when you were human? People, or someone special, liked you and wanted you around because they laughed with you? Maybe even at you but out of love, not malice?" Leilani carefully suggested.

"Eddie," Truvie said. "He liked to tease me."

Keone patted her back and grinned. "If we have to tease you to make you feel at home, we're happy to suffer through it."

"You, Truitt you," Leilani said. "Were, well, let's say, abundant in your teasing."

Truvie leaned away, eyes wide, head shaking side to side. "Gosh, I never tease anyone."

Leilani and Keone exchanged broad grins.

"I don't believe you." Keone laughed. "A serious, stoic Truitt Skye?" He shook his head and laughed again. "Oh, I can't wait to see this."

"Come on up," Leilani said. "We'll show you how to use your body."

Truvie climbed over the rock pile and onto a very narrow rim. "I thought this was wider."

"You don't need rocks to stand on the water," Keone said. "It's all in your energy. And concentration. Or lack thereof."

Truvie wobbled. "I don't want to be shimmying myself dry all day."

A wave of wind whooshed against Truvie's face as the gentle cry of the green crows sounded. One by one, a green crow soared out of the horizon.

"Go away!" Keone shouted and waved them off.

"Truitt," Leilani said. "You don't need them."

"I didn't call them. They came on their own."

"You did," Leilani said.

"Your fear did," Keone said.

The crows landed on the rocks circling a turquoise pool of rolling sea.

"Send them away," Leilani said.

"How?" Truvie said.

"Ask," Leilani said.

"Tell," Keone added. "Tell them to go away."

"Shift your thoughts," Leilani said.

"Use words," Keone said. "Until you get the feel for it."

Truvie lowered to the nearest green crow. Several nearby hopped Truvie's way. Her fingers caressed the top of the crow's head then slowly cupped the back of its wings. "I'm good. I'll call you if I need you." She closed her eyes. Go. But not too far.

One by one, starting from the one she touched, they took flight.

When Truvie stood, Leilani and Keone's feet were on top of the water.

"How—how are you doing that?" Truvie asked. "Don't tell me it's all in the soul. I can't—it's not tangible, or meaningful to me. I can't believe it. Be specific. Not thoughts or feelings. Exactly how are you two standing on the sea? Are there rocks under there I can't see?"

Truvie gingerly shifted to get a look underneath the slight waves.

"This island," Leilani started.

"Blue Isle," Keone said.

"Blue Isle," Leilani said. "Shows the possibility of water. One of your experiments," she looked to Keone, "I guess you would say."

"Your body, any body," Keone said. "Can adjust to anything. Agility relies on the mind knowing that. Owning it."

"Seawater has many purposes—" Leilani started.

"Weather patterns, cooling, support of sea life, boundaries, the formation of land," Truvie said. Her mind and heart racing. She couldn't seem to slow herself down. Breathe. She inhaled but kept going, "Transport, food, medicinal purposes, birth, a variety of sports—"

"Now you're Truitt talking." Keone bolted across the pool, over the rocks and way out into the sea.

"Is he wearing something special on his feet?" Truvie squirmed to get a view of Leilani's sneakers. Each floated on and slightly beneath the surface but didn't look special. "Where'd he go?"

"He expects us to follow," Leilani said. "Go on. Take a step."

Truvie tapped her toe to the water.

And fell directly through into the chilly blue.

Truvie flapped her arms and gasped for air. "Cold! Cold!"

The crows took her by the hair and tee-shirt, lifting

her to the rim of rocks. Truvie wriggled and shook until her dryness returned.

"Again," Leilani said.

Truvie thanked the crows with a nod as she pulled her tee-shirt over her waist.

"This time," Leilani said, "Imagine your body as light, able to rest on the water without sinking. Imagine adjusting gravity to the top of you, instead of the bottom."

"Imagine gravity is no longer law? You do mean the constant, unchanging gravity that keeps feet on the ground?"

"Gravity is different, planet to planet, world to world, depending on what is expected of it," Leilani said. "Pretend you have full use of gravitons and they can hold you upright when organized accordingly, with the expectation that they can."

Truvie let that sink in. Expected of it. Not bad. Gravity on Earth expected to go to the core of the planet. "Space," she said, mostly to herself. "Expect to float away."

"It is not gravity you will change," Leilani said.

Keone raced up to and catapulted over the rocks, landing without any splash and floating next to Leilani. "It's you."

Truvie was suddenly hit with, "Are you two related?"

"Brother," Leilani said.

"Sister," Keone said.

"Did you die young?" Truvie asked. "I'm sorry, that was rude."

"No, it wasn't," Keone said. "Ask anything you want.

Souls don't get offended."

"No," Leilani said. "We died old. We're from the island of Hawai'i. The Big Island."

"Kona side," Keone said.

"We were always part of the sea," Leilani said.

"The Blue Isle of water's possibility," Truvie said. "I worked with you to do this? To manipulate the water?"

The siblings exchanged a glance. "That's one way of putting it," Leilani said.

"Try," Keone said.

Truvie stared at the gentle, but moving, pool. "Gravity, gravitons, totally impossible anywhere but here in the top of my head, enough to keep from floating away but not enough to send me to the bottom of the sea."

Truvie checked Leilani and Keone's feet once again. They looked like they belonged standing on water. Like wading at the edge of a beach. "I expect to stand like them," she said.

"Expect to run," Keone said.

"One step—" Leilani started.

Truvie stepped from the rim and on to the water. She did not fall. She stood. Then hopped with a clap. "I'm doing it."

And under she went again.

This time though, she took a moment to gather her thought—expectations—then shot straight up from the pool and onto the ledge, dry by the time her feet hit the rock. Without pause, she stepped onto the water again. Then another step and another. Gravity up. Expectations high. Gravitons lifting me, one reaction at a time.

"Create momentum," Leilani said.

Keone clapped. "There she is. Let's roll." He took off running. Leilani joined him, passing him within moments. Truvie, never one to sprint, suddenly felt like the only thing she ever wanted to do, ever again, was run as fast and as far as she could across the sea.

And so she did.

The water had give. She dipped and was lifted, into a firm jelly and out with springs. Exhilarated, she searched ahead to see where they were leading her. An island to her left a quarter-mile ahead must be the destination. Before she could guess again, she ran right next to it. Unlike the others she'd seen so far, this island had a nice, white sand beach. She imagined her mother sunning herself and reading fashion magazines. Her father would be in cargo shorts and a Brewers baseball cap next to her reading a thick physics textbook. They'd both randomly share discoveries with Truvie as they read. Yet this beach was empty.

"Truitt?" Keone unexpectedly stood next to her. "We don't have time for sunning."

Truvie looked down at her feet. "I didn't realize I'd stopped. Sorry."

"Lay-o is probably already there." He lowered his left shoulder, ready to race, but Truvie took hold of his arm, halting him in place.

"Where are we going?"

"The edge," he said and took off running.

Truvie followed, gaining on him easily until she passed him. A low island to the right, no, three islands, small, connected by little bridges arched over the water, came into view. She could make out what looked to be a restaurant with tables and chairs set up to overlook the sea. There were several structures, little cottages, spread across the three isles.

Keone caught up and grabbed her left hand. "Isles of Necessity," he said. "Shopping, eating, you know? Stuff you need. Come on. You're too easily distracted. Very you. But we don't have time right now. Let's move."

. . .

He pulled her forward, faster, faster. Her feet like motors across the blue. Islands blurred on either side. She wanted to know what and who lived on each one, but Keone was not letting go. Truvie pushed herself to keep up with him.

Without warning, Keone halted and pointed up a mountain.

Leilani sat on a cliff, legs hanging over, fifty feet high. She waved, then stood and scaled up the face of the cliff like a professional free climber. Above her, a couple hundred feet waited Keone.

"How did you do that?" Truvie shouted then dropped directly into the sea.

Sinking into the water, she thought of Lay-o climbing and Keone already there, he must have jumped from the sea to the top of the cliff. A mere one hundred and fifty feet or more to something he called, "the edge."

"They're giving me a choice." Her voice garbled in the water and bubbles from her mouth blinded her. "Sink, climb, or jump." She took a moment to envision what she wanted to do then rocketed straight up alongside the rock face and onto the ledge next to Keone.

. . .

"Yes!" Truvie shouted. "I did it!"

Leilani's hand groped the earth near Truvie left foot. Without thinking, or doubting, Truvie pulled Lay-o next to her.

"Well done," Leilani said. "Fast learner. Proof you are, without a doubt, the one and only, Truitt Skye."

From the top, the silver pool shimmered below. "The silver pool," Truvie said. "I saw it with the crows."

"It's why we're here," Keone said. "See it? See the shiny pool?"

"I just said I did," Truvie said.

"Stay out of it," Keone yelled. His voice echoed. "It, it, it," diminished slowly.

"This is where you fell," Leilani said. "Or were pushed by Eva."

"Or jumped to mess with us," Keone said. Leilani shot him the evil eye. "Don't tell me you didn't hear Tots mention it."

"Junius said that you requested we bring you here when you returned," Leilani said. "To show you the ways to avoid the pool."

"Before you mean?" Truvie asked. "When I was Truitt?"

Leilani nodded.

"Remember," Keone said. "You are much stronger than Eva. I don't want to hear you—"

"Keone," Leilani cut in.

"No more beginnings for me," Truvie said. "Got it."

"Wasn't supposed to be a first," Keone said. "Now things are really—"

"Let's stick to the task," Leilani said. "Without scaring her."

"I'm not scared," Truvie said. "I'm sorry I upset everyone. I know I don't know you or remember this place, and I don't think I belong here, I am sorry to have upset everyone. I don't like upsetting people."

Keone clenched his jaw. "Just when I think you might be Truitt, so agile and quick-witted, you do all mushy and—"

"About the pool," Leilani said.

"I was there," Truvie said. "With the green crows. They swooped so closely, I thought they might drop me in."

"The pull," Leilani said.

"Resist it," Keone said. "Don't let the crows fly there."

"Do you feel it?" Truvie asked. "I didn't but I can understand—I think—"

"Most of us, except Pel, avoid it," Leilani said. "It makes me want to dive in even this far away from it. I will be so happy and alive and refreshed—here is great, but a body! A body! To test all that I know now! It makes me want to—"

Keone touched his sister's hand.

"Sorry," Leilani said. "Yes, the pull is strong."

"Not for you?" Truvie asked Keone.

"Oh no," Keone said, eyeing the silver from the corner of his eye. "All I want to do is dive into it. I know how good my life would be in a body now." He tapped his temple. "I would gladly suffer and fail a thousand times to experience life with what I know now."

"Are you saying you remember?" Truvie asked. "You'd remember working here on behalf of souls?"

Both shook their heads. "We'd rely on evolution. Every essence of every soul goes into a soul when they begin again. Everything here is possible there when humans let it become. Things only get better. Bodies are far better now than when we lived."

Beneath her skin, Truvie felt the prickling, jerking pull, her every cell wanting to go. To begin all over again better and stronger, more connected to the whole. She dipped forward—

Keone bear-hugged her from the back and lifted her away from the edge, facing the inner part of the island. "Easy, there."

"Come on. We don't need to fuel this momentum any longer." Leilani walked toward a grassy path a few feet inland. "Let's get you to Dr. Blick."

Keone set Truvie down. "Wasn't I supposed to meet Tots back at the Blue Isle?" Truvie asked.

Keone patted Truvie on the shoulder. "You're thought is way ahead of you."

With that, Truvie spun until she vaporized.

17
The Physics of the City on the Sea

With a breath, Truvie stood alone at the entrance to Dr. Blick's, which mimicked a plantation house. The wide, wrap-around porch adorned with rocking chairs and a couple of sofa swings held age and an intense "come on over and sit with me" appeal. Each plank of the steps bowed to the point of breaking as she climbed them. Her dad would have reinforced each one from below with two by fours.

The front door was held open with an antique basin filled with dusty books and magazines. She knocked on the screen door and called, "Dr. Blick? You here? It's me, Truvie—I mean, Truitt. No, Truvie. No—Truitt. Forget it. Hello? Anyone home?"

Bounding down the sweeping, broad staircase, pushing his horn-rimmed glasses back up to the bridge of his nose, was Dr. Blick. Leather-patched elbows on his olive corduroy jacket and wrinkled slacks, he came right to her, hands extended. "Come in, come in."

He looked around the worn-out hallways and asked, "Recognize anything?"

"Looks like the set of Gone with the Wind which we had to watch for American Lit last year," she said. "Plus, my mom played Scarlett too many times to count. Took her weeks to drop that annoying accent." She stopped and cupped her hand over her mouth. "I'm sorry. I hope I didn't offend you. I just—I feel kind of comfortable with you."

Dr. Blick grinned to his eyes. She could tell he was pleased. A softness in his everything. "I'm from Pawley's Island, South Carolina. My people were slaves there for many generations. Can't quite shake the accent myself. But it's not too awful, is it?"

"I like it, Dr. Blick. Yours suits you. My mom was. . . acting."

He gestured for her to come up the stairs. "All right then, Miss Skye. I'll keep it."

Midway up the stairs, a stern, male voice said, "Excuse me."

Dr. Blick and Truitt rotated back to the tour in unison.

Pel stood at the door. "May I have a word?"

Truvie unexpectedly blocked Dr. Blick from Pel's view and held her arms out in protection.

"Truitt," Pel said. "I meant you, not him."

Dr. Blick stepped down a few stairs. "Give us a chance," he said. "She just got here."

"A word." Pel was not going to leave.

Truvie walked down the steps. Craning her neck to the six-foot, muscled soldier in front of her, she said, "I haven't seen her. I swear."

"She hasn't been following you?" Pel asked as if he knew something more.

"Has she?" Truvie asked, mind racing through where she'd been. "I—I don't know. I don't think so. I've been—learning I guess."

"We're proud of you," Dr. Blick said.

Truvie went on, "With Keone . . . and Leilani. About my body—and the pool—"

"I know who they are and what they were doing."

"Oh," Truvie sighed. "Right. Of course."

"Eva was at your heels," Pel said. "When Keone was at the top and Lay-o was scaling the cliff, she was about to snag you, but you went under before she could."

"That was clever," Dr. Blick said. "Well done."

"I fell in," Truvie said to Dr. Blick. "I don't understand. Why? Why is she following me? To push me in the pool? But she said—she said I jumped so . . ."

"Stop talking," Pel said. "When are you seeing Miss Frank?"

Truvie stretched her lips side-to-side. "I think I see her after Dr. Blick."

"I'll see to it," Dr. Blick said. "She's a quick study. We won't be long."

Turning her attention away from Dr. Blick and

back to Pel, Truvie asked, "What's so special about Miss Frank?"

Pel was gone.

Truvie faced Dr. Blick.

"Pel is . . ." Dr. Blick started. "Incredibly focused."

"That's one way to put it," Truvie said with a faint laugh.

"Ready for a little physics?" Dr. Blick said.

"If this is going to be about physics, I may never leave."

"Pel will toss me over the edge if I don't get you to Miss Frank," Dr. Blick said.

. . .

"It must be hard," Truvie said, following Dr. Blick up the stairs.

"What?" Dr. Blick topped the stairs and moved straight down a copper-walled tunnel.

"For you all not to know whether Eva pushed me or if I jumped," Truvie said. "It's hard not to know what happened."

"It's impossible to believe that Eva would push you." He ran his fingers through his messy, thick hair. "Almost as hard to believe that Truitt Skye wouldn't want a round in a body in order to learn how to better serve humanity."

"Would it be like Truitt to not be clear about her intentions with her people?" Truvie asked.

"We're not people. We're souls. We don't clear things with each other," he said. "They ask, we answer.

We serve. That is all."

"But?" Truvie smiled.

Dr. Blick returned the grin. "But it would be like her to want to experience for herself what humanity wonders about their connection to here."

"And?" Truvie smiled broader.

Dr. Blick gave a little laugh. "And then concoct an extraordinary experiment that gave her time with them as one of them." He paused, then added, "If that's what it was. I wouldn't know. None of my business."

"I'm not sure that's true," Truvie said.

"Probably best for you to draw your own conclusions, Truitt," he said.

She knocked on the wall which released a lingering ping. "Copper, right? Not trying to contain a meltdown, are you?"

"It's meant to contain high heat, yes," he said.

"Dad and I went to CERN—you know the large hadron collider in Geneva—the Higgs boson—when I was 14," she said. "To run the particle accelerator, they line everything with copper. It melted once—that we know of. That's what slowed them down. Got people thinking they might generate a black hole right there in Switzerland."

"Would have swallowed all of us," Dr. Blick said. "I was here when you told them to try copper."

Truvie stopped. "Told them? Told who?"

"All of them," Dr. Blick said. "Whoever would listen."

"Are you saying you had something to do with the discovery of the Higgs boson? Of making the collider functional? No. No way. Wow. That is so cool."

"Not me." He pressed his fingers to his chest then extended them to her. "You, Truitt."

"That can't be," Truvie said. "It was only a couple of years ago."

"Peter Higgs' vision for CERN was far before the actual CERN," Dr. Blick said. "You, the Truitt you, were with every contributor every step of the way. I don't think you've ever been so excited. Maybe Einstein got you a little more fiery. And you did love John Maxwell. Oh, how you adored that man."

"John Maxwell?? Truvie squealed. "The Scottish philosopher and scientist? Electromagnetism? Most underrated genius of all time? He got it. He really really really really got it. I knew him? Truitt and he—they worked together? How? How could that be? I don't understand."

"I'm going too fast." Dr. Blick opened a door on the left. "Let's slow down. I don't want to overwhelm you. Amelia would kill me. Not to mention Pel. I hate to think. . . in here, please."

. . .

The room Dr. Blick entered had ten walls with a framed picture window in each one. She counted them the second she walked in the room. Almost too quickly. Her mind moved fast here with Dr. Blick. A long table and chairs made of smooth ruby with short backs stretched in the center of the room. Must be room for twenty—no, thirty-three attendees. There was that fast count again.

"You understand what we do here?" Dr. Blick asked.

"Here? In this room?" she asked. "No."

"Here in the City on the Sea," he said as he walked toward some picture windows opposite them. "I'm not great at you like this. I see what Latham was saying. Don't get me wrong. I don't mind. It's thrilling!" He ran his fingers through his hair again. "How I can say with one hundred percent confidence that you were instrumental in all the discoveries I mentioned, and many more?"

"I have no idea how you can say that with a modicum of confidence," she said. "Because it can't possibly be true."

"You created this world to serve humans. When people ask," Dr. Blick said. "We answer. Period. We care for them no matter what. We answer until they know the answer. We never waver."

"How? They can't hear us. Can they?" Truvie felt her pulse rise. "Where are we anyway? Where is the City on the Sea? If we're not on Earth, how far away are we? I mean, are we invisible? It's—it's crazy."

Dr. Blick pulled out a chair at the obnoxiously giant marble table. "Please."

She stepped away from the chair.

"You're upset," he said. "Because you believe me, not because you don't."

After a few breaths, Truvie took a seat, sinking in and getting a whiff of rose-scented fabric.

Dr. Blick clasped his fingers together and rested his wrists to the table. "I lived in New Jersey. I was a science teacher at Stuyvesant. It's in New York City. My roots were in the south until I fell in love and replanted them in the north with the woman I love more now than I ever could have then. I didn't know love like the love I know here."

Truvie listened intently. She couldn't explain it, but she could feel, head to toe, that he was about to understand everything a whole lot more.

"The City on the Sea is a crest, as far as I can tell. Truitt explained it as an infinite wave cutting through the Universe, always available, always here, since the beginning of everything. I've come to think of the City as a wave woven in between the layer of time and space. I don't think it's a separate wave. We seem, in my observations, to be a peak of a wave closest to humanity, yet, we move faster. By my guess, we're closer to the sun. Truitt would say, had I ever dared tell her these things, I was clinging to my limitations. She would say we are souls who are everywhere, not planets or waves, possessing no matter whatsoever. But I struggle with that."

Truvie smiled. "I can understand why. If we're everywhere, where are we? We can't be everywhere and here."

They laughed.

"It hurts to think about," Truvie said.

"I've tried mapping us, but we shift too much to be sure I'm on track. We morph to their asking. If more ask from India, we shift in a wave-like manner to India to answer. Traveling to the strongest asking without stopping our answers flowing everywhere. As I hope you can imagine?"

Truvie sat up, elbows to the shining marble table-top. "How? That's the thing. How can we answer all the questions? Minds don't stop."

Dr. Blick leaned toward her. "There are many myths in humanity, you know this?"

"Myths explain things. Stories we tell," Truvie said. "Which are usually false."

"Misinterpretations, yes," he said. "One myth, a widely-held one, is that they are downloaded from above, from Heaven or angels, the great unknown. Suddenly, they have been given a brilliant idea, or heal from an incurable disease, or are called to write a book, or have a sudden profound understanding of something hardly anyone else understands. You've heard of this happening?"

Truvie nodded. "Of course."

"Do you believe it?"

Truvie shrugged. "I think sometimes we do suddenly have ideas and deeper understandings that we can't explain. Physics came too easy for me not to have—"

"Absolutely," he interjected. "But they do not flow from above, they come from below. From the bottom, through the feet, from the earth, from the center, the core. When this happens, everything that you were and thus, are, and everything that you have asked for is waiting, eager to find a home within you. You let it rise within you."

"Are you saying that souls from here put answers in the earth like seeds?"

The picture windows shuttered and snapped. A gusting wind threw caps to the waves on the sea. Dense, grey clouds huddled a few miles offshore.

"Did you get sad there? Enough to need a good cleansing cry?" Dr. Blick said. "I haven't felt sad in so long. It's become a mystery. I don't think I miss it, but with the storm—" He stopped himself for a moment then went on, "Truitt, my friend, we never get storms—not until today. Forgive me for asking about your sadness. It—it triggered something in me. It's not my business how you—"

"Will it make me seem pathetic to say I feel sad every day?" Truvie asked. "Including now."

Rumbling thunder startled them and they both fell over backward in their chairs. They laughed until lightning cracked, temporarily illuminating everything with streaks of violent electricity.

"Did you see that?" Truvie cried.

"Wait until the lightning hits the snow," he said.

"You think it's going to snow?"

He shrugged. "Do you? That's all that matters, you know?"

"No, I don't know," Truvie said, standing.

"You will," he said as he lifted their chairs and righted them to view the storm.

The lightning struck the water again and again, as if it wanted to ignite something. Each snap, searching for the right spot. The snow replaced the rain, illuminated still with cracks of bright flashes of lightning strikes.

"To answer your question," Dr. Blick said. "The answers are sort of seeds. Seeds that were always there. Souls nourish the finding. Everything humanity needs exists in their cells, always there, always on offer. We add energy, our souls to their soul, like the lightning to the snow. We shoot bolts of energy in the form of knowing. They ask and ask and ask. We offer, offer, offer. Each time embedding more potential within them. When they're ready, they let the answer in. Most rarely hear us, but we never stop offering. Ever. Truitt says— you say, 'absolutely anything is possible with energy, and a little concentration.'"

"The answer to any question?"

"Any," he said. "From the ones they already know like one plus one to the seemingly unanswerable—"

"Like proving the existence of the Higgs boson," she said. "Or life after death?"

Dr. Blick smirked. "Life and death, we always answer the same way. There is no such thing as a thing called death. There's only beginning again and again. With every new start, we all become more than we were before. A constant revolution of evolution."

Truvie didn't have a response to that. It made her quite itchy and uncomfortable to know how forcefully that answer resonated.

Dr. Blick got up from his chair. "Would you like to see how we catalog the asking?"

The snow blanketed the entire view. The lightning quieted, storm clouds subsided. Only piling white flakes remained.

She nodded, a lump in her throat. Here was getting clearer, which meant—

"Follow me," he said.

As they exited, Truvie unexpectedly asked, "Why is this room so large?"

"This is a place where we figure things out together," he said.

"Who?"

"You, me, Eva, Junius, Tots, Latham, Olivia, Miss Frank, Pel, Stanton. Many more you've yet to meet."

"Team of thirty-three?"

"Used to be," he said.

"You think it will be again?"

"I don't know, Truitt," he said. "You tell me."

18
The Wish Listeners

Following Dr. Blick down the hallway of copper Truvie, of course, had no answer to give. Would she be there, answering questions like the rest of the City?

"I highly doubt it," Truvie said. "I have nothing to offer humanity. I'm only seventeen and I—I wasn't—I didn't—I only had one friend. And Fig. I studied a lot. But it's not like I was famous, or anyone knew that I was good at physics. People didn't care."

"Oh, Truitt. Please don't say that." He shook his head. "You have everything to offer them, especially now, because you were so loved. It's extraordinary to consider you now. You may not know it, but I trust you will and when it hits, oh Truitt. Nothing will ever be the same again."

He gestured her down the corridor, opposite the front entrance. "This way."

"Thank you," she said, slowing down. "Thank you for being kind to me."

. . .

He gave her a minuscule nod and led the way down the copper tunnel. The floor made no sound with their steps. Then suddenly, it did. She had to wonder if it was her attention to it that gave it sound. That wasn't a new way of thinking. If no one heard the tree fall in the forest, the tree never fell. Quantum mechanics one oh one, thanks to Schrödinger.

"Can I ask you something?" she said.

"Anything," he said.

"Do you have a bathroom?" she asked.

He paused, head jerking back into his neck. "Pardon?"

"A toilet. Do you have one here?"

He searched the tunnel. "Here? In the tunnel?"

"Never mind," she said. "You go ahead. I'm following."

"Do you need a toilet?" he asked. His pace picked up significantly as he searched ahead.

"No," she said. "Just wondering if you had one. In case, you know, someone needed one. You said there used to be regular meetings of thirty-three people—soul. . . people."

"Of course we do," he said. "It's just that—well, I thought we'd go to the—if you need a restroom—"

"It's all right. Promise. I can use the one at the glasshouse," she said.

They both knew there was no bathroom here. Though she figured she could create one in a few focused thoughts. How, she had no idea, yet knew it was perfectly true.

They moved through the copper tunnel for several more strides until it ended at a small wooden door.

Dr. Blick placed his hand on the knob.

"Don't we need coats?" Truvie asked. "I only have a tee-shirt on. It was snowing—"

"Trust me?" he asked.

She nodded. "It's not a bathroom you conjured in the last few seconds, is it?"

He laughed. "That would've been good. I'm not that clever."

"I think you're more clever than you're admitting," she said.

"Only because of you."

. . .

He opened the door and they stepped outside into warm sunshine. No sea to be found. No snow. No dark, ominous thunder clouds.

"This way," Dr. Blick disappeared into a swarm of tall silky stalks of billowing yellow grass.

Truvie found his path of matted debris and jogged to catch up with him. The blades brushed her arms as she passed. Above her, through their feathery blooms, a pale blue sky with streaks of white whispering clouds.

"Only a few steps more," Dr. Blick called back. The grasses leaned and swayed with a gentle breeze sending out soft whistles.

She eased a handful of pale grass to the right in order to pass and nearly collided with the awaiting Dr. Blick.

"Sorry," she said, stammering back.

They'd reached a vast green meadow of clover and moss. A clear trail cut straight through the center toward an endlessly stretching grove of aspen.

"It's there." He started down the trail.

A freshness, like early morning in the first days of spring after a long winter, filled her—not only the smell of moist dirt and emerging green, or the little budding crocuses lining the path, or the slight chill to the air. It was the energy, the sense of the field that filled her toe to head.

"Stay back." Dr. Blick extended his arms to halt her. She hadn't even realized they'd reached another end and stood before the tallest aspen trees she'd ever seen, not that she'd seen an aspen grove in person. Still, these were—

A high-pitched growl-slash-roar shattered the moment.

Startled until she noted it was the sound of a catter, like Sprites. A variety of them stalked the grounds before the grove.

A black one, the vocal one, reared onto its hind legs and swatted at them with a hiss.

"What the—" Truvie started but Dr. Blick shushed her and took her arm.

"Take a couple steps back," he said. "Slowly."

Truvie and Blick moved as one, back, back, back. The catter lowered to the ground and crouched back into the rhythmic line of stalking large cats before the trees.

"You met Sprites?" Dr. Blick asked.

"Those are bigger than Sprites," Truvie said.

"I try not to get close enough to measure," Dr. Blick said.

"Why are they here?"

"To protect the Wish Listeners. See, here." He pointed to a large piece of round glass tilted slightly up into the trees. "Take a look. They're not hard to spot."

Truvie moved to the glass, which up close was the size of a school bus steering wheel and magnified.

"Pull it to your face," Dr. Blick said. "It moves. It's not attached."

"How is it floating mid-air like that?" Truvie asked.

"It doesn't weigh enough to do anything else," he said. "Take hold, you'll see."

"Then it should float away, like a balloon," Truvie said.

"Should it?" he said. "What if energy didn't work that way?"

"What if it worked the way I need it to?" she said. "Is that what you mean?"

"What if?" He raised his brows in a teasing way.

Truvie's heart stirred. She liked the way he egged her on without pushing. "Energy, and a little concentration. Isn't that what you said?"

"Try it," he said.

When she grabbed hold, it was light, not like a giant magnified piece of glass should be, but once she had a grip on it, heavied in her hands.

He cupped his hands to a floating magnifying glass and pulled it close. Looking through it into the grove of trees, he whispered, "See them busily collecting wishes?"

Truvie lowered her gaze through the glass. At first, she didn't see anything but the blur of tree limbs, but as she started to pull away, a little something zoomed passed her nose. And another. Two more.

She jerked back and searched the aspens for anything flying—bees, beetles, gnats—but saw nothing except trees. She put the glass to her face. A kaleidoscope of color appeared. Moving color. Busy flying color. Purple and pink and red and orange and gold and green somethings dashed about too fast for her to see what they were. Whatever they were, they were smaller than flies, no, smaller than gnats, teenier than flakes of melting snow but equally transparent save for the color each one held.

"What are they?" she asked.

"Wish Listeners," he said. "Look! Did you see that? A wish fulfilled! When one spontaneously rockets up, it means a decision that serves the person was made. Back there—another!"

"What?" she asked. "Where? They're so many! How many are there?"

"I couldn't begin to guess," he said. "Every wish is captured, no matter how many times it's asked."

"Asked?" She pulled away to look at Dr. Blick. "I

thought they were wishes?"

"I wish I could lose weight. I want to lose weight. Please let me lose weight. I feel so fat. Can I lose weight? When will I lose weight? I wish I were different. Why can't I be different? All those are a wish to be more of who the person truly is: healthy, content, and free. But the Wish Listeners gather each one just the same. One person might say that same thing a million times a day."

"Maybe more," she said. "But why capture them?"

"Momentum. Desire is everything," he said. "Momentum brings it to life. We can only serve them when we listen to what they wish for. More adds to more. If they can see proof that what they wish for, they get, the possibilities are endless. They begin to believe in the power of their soul, the power they have within."

"I agree," she said. "Your logic is sound."

He beamed with a toothy smile and flushed cheeks. "Thank you."

She scanned right to left, so many puffs of life zipping about. "Wow," she said, lifting her head to see deeper into the grove. "How far back do the Listeners go?"

"I suspect it never ends," he said. "No one gets past the catters, so we'll never know."

Millions of teeny puffs of something zoomed into blurs. Up and down and side to side. In white and blue, purple and red, gold, violet, magenta, and green.

"Do the colors mean anything?" she asked.

"The color corresponds to the nature of the question," Dr. Blick said. "Miss Frank will explain. She's a bit possessive about her expertise."

Truvie let go of her magnifying glass, noting he was the second soul to not want to deal with Miss Frank, but staying focused on the Wish Listeners. "If these things hear the wishes, do they grant them too? Are they answering the questions?"

"They listen then transmit out to the rest of the soul world," he said. "The interested souls answer. It sounds complicated but it all transpires in less than a second. Would you like to see?"

"How can I see something that happens so quickly?" Truvie asked. "Can you slow it down?"

"You are one brilliant being," he said. "Correct. I can't show you exactly that. But as you have seen here how they are heard, nothing specific, so too can I show you how they are answered, or better put, where they are answered, not specific, but you'll get a sense. Will that serve?"

"Are there Wish Listeners on Earth?" she asked.

"They're everywhere," he said. "Minute molecules bounding and collecting through all that is. Made of energy, just like us. And them."

"Show me more, Dr. Blick," she said. "Please."

19

The View from Above

Dr. Blick and Truitt returned to the door and re-entered the copper corridor. Truvie lowered her hand to her side, imagining hundreds of Wish Listeners swirling through her fingers.

"Who keeps track of all the questions?" Truvie asked.

"We don't track," he said, a few steps ahead of her. "We answer."

"But how do you prioritize?" Truvie asked, still raising and lowering her arm in hopes of feeling the little ones on her skin.

"We don't," he said. "Everything is constantly in motion. Constantly growing. No need to track. We don't compare in order to measure. That would be counter-productive. It would slow the momentum, not add to it."

"How do you know how often your answers are right or wrong?" Truvie asked.

"You won't like the answer," he said.

"There's no wrong answer to their questions. You just answer, they decide the right or the wrong," Truvie said, slightly disappointed, slightly intrigued.

"You catch on too quickly not to be Truitt Skye."

"I think it's you," Truvie said. "I feel more me with you than anyone else."

. . .

Dr. Blick made a left turn and in a few steps opened a door. The two of them stepped across shiny mosaic tiles onto a terrace high above the sea. A white adobe wall served as a railing. It looked like a photograph from a Greek island villa.

"Junius tracks," Truvie said. "He told me he did."

"Evolution is a tracking system," Dr. Blick said. "Is it not?"

"Are you avoiding my question?" Truvie asked.

After a moment or two he said, "Eva."

"What about her?" Truvie asked.

"When you left," he said. "Junius tracked one question—how I don't know, but I know he did because you told him to."

"What?" she asked. "What question did he track?"

"The wish from humanity to be more aligned with their soul," Dr. Blick answered.

"He thought she might be merging souls?" Truvie asked.

"I can't say," Dr. Blick said. "Not my business."

"Maybe she's right," Truvie said. "Why have a delay in the connection to the answers? Why not let people have access to their soul?"

Without a pause, Dr. Blick said, "We're not the ones creating the separation."

"You think if we merged, the separation would form anyway? It's a human tendency?" Truvie asked.

"We don't know what would happen." Dr. Blick started down the steps.

"But in theory?" Truvie leaned her rear on the edge of the adobe wall. The strong sun beating down on her shoulders and head.

"We don't theorize when it comes to humanity," he said. "Ever."

Truvie reached out to him. "I'm sorry. I didn't mean anything. I—I'm asking to understand."

He tried to smile as he crossed his arms over his chest, holding them tight to his torso. "I'm letting you know that we don't guess. Eva's out of line to suggest something so drastic."

"Why is she? If no one else here wants that."

Dr. Blick sat down on the wall next to her. "We answer. We never determine. They ask more than they listen, wouldn't you agree?"

She nodded. "Of course. It's impossible not to. It's how the mind works."

"Anything is possible," he said. "With focus."

Truvie nodded thinking of her father's Equation for

Imagination.

"As you deduced a moment ago," Dr. Blick said. "It's the human 'way' to feel apart from who they are, what they want and desire, trapped in a sense of being incapable. They have habits of being less rather than habits of being more."

Truvie shifted to face him, straddling the wall. "Wait. Are you saying humanity isn't evolving as fast as it could?"

"It's not mutating. Too much symmetry, not enough diversity," he said. "Difference and diversity are being destroyed. Would you not agree?"

Truvie lost her breath, her heartbeat. She went cold, frigid. She closed her eyes to ground herself.

"Truitt?" He touched her arm.

"I—I wasn't expecting that—it's true. More true than I realized until this moment."

Dr. Blick stood. "It's my fault. You're not ready. I apologize."

Truvie wiped tears that had spontaneously arrived from her eyes. "No, it's good. It's okay. I wanted to—I wanted to know the answer."

"You ask too many questions that intrigue me! Stop it at once," he teased.

She sniffed and managed, "Sorry."

"I have a task to fulfill, here, Truitt," he said. You're going to get me in deep trouble with Junius."

"Can't have that," she said, still fighting tears from flowing.

He handed her a pale pink handkerchief and said," Watch this." He lifted his arm out to the sea and bent his four fingers toward his palm in a 'come here' gesture.

With alarming speed, an island—a whole and complete island—rushed into view.

"Whoa!" She gave a little giggle. "Zippy."

"All the islands are eager to meet you," he said.

"An island wants me to meet me?" Truvie said. "Come on, Dr. Blick."

"The islands are gathered souls," he said. "They want to show you what they do."

A barren island of rolling sand hills lifted from the sea. Chunks of beachy debris dropped like boulders, hitting the water with impressive splashes.

"The souls here on Sandon Isle respond to wishes regarding survival," Dr. Blick said. "Basics like food, shelter, safety."

"Like starving people?" Truvie searched to find a soul but saw only streams of sand falling into the sea.

"Everyone is starving for something," he said. "Even those who are fed, starve."

"Homeless people?" Truvie rubbed her throat, suddenly feeling thirsty and sad.

"Your perceptions are limiting your understanding, Truitt," he said. "The requests, wishes, and questions regarding shelter may be as simple as fixing a window or hoisting a sail. They may be for a bed to sleep in instead of the street, or a soldier needing to avoid an ambush. They may be someone longing for a loving companion. We don't judge. We answer."

"What do they say when they answer?"

The island moved closer to the white adobe terrace.

The humming of voices—hundreds and hundreds of voices grew louder and louder. Some spoke in whispers while others yelled, but most sounded normal and clear.

"What are they saying?" Truvie asked.

The island tilted and twisted so that a corner presented more forward than the rest.

Truvie heard a child's voice say, "Two more blocks. Two more blocks."

Truvie shook her head, not understanding.

The same voice suddenly hollered in a high pitch, "He's right there! Look! Look! The man on your right."

Truvie looked to Dr. Blick. But he studied the barren island.

A woman's voice whispered, "Open the newspaper. There's a sale on beds. Keep turning. Next page. Next page. Yes! There! Well done! Rip it out. Come on. Ripppppp. Good! Yes!"

"If we were able to connect that answer with the Wish Listener who heard the request," Dr. Blick said.

"We would see it shoot straight into the air," Truvie cut in. "A wish fulfilled."

"It's only the beginning," he said. "The souls here never leave. The wisher will be encouraged to go to the store, find the right one, purchase it, get it home and put it together, and so on. All wishes fulfilled along the way. Very precise. Very specific."

"There are souls and Wish Listeners with them every step of the way?"

He nodded. "Every single moment of everything. Never apart. Never separate."

"What if they only need a nudge to the sale?" Truvie asked.

"Where's the fun in that?" He winked. "We want to see that bed in place, join them in their dreams. That bed could spark transformation. We're interested in everything. Nudge upon nudge upon nudge. Never-ending nudging."

"Wow," she breathed.

Sandon Isle whipped back and zipped across the sea.

A new island, this one lush and green with several lakes spun in circles from her right then stopped front and center.

"Energy," he said. "And a little concentration. You're focused and the energy responds."

"No kidding," she said.

"The island before us, Acuity, is an island for adventure, for taking risks, and experiencing the thrills of life."

The island did a fast spin to the left, then one to the right.

"Can we hear?"

But instead of voices, this island upon closer inspection, pulsed.

Truvie turned to Dr. Blick. "What's happening?"

"These souls answer from within."

"Within bodies?" she asked.

He nodded. "They encourage the right responses within the body. Foot to the brake or accelerator for a driver. Quick turn to catch a pass. Spine in line for a cyclist. Lightning-quick balance for a tightrope walker.

Silence at just the right moment for a person about to be attacked. Keen vision for a hunter. And on and on. You get the idea."

"That is—" Truvie wanted nothing more than to dive into the vibration. She leaned—

Dr. Blick thrust his arm against her chest. "Ut ut. Stay put, please."

Acuity backed away and spun out of sight.

The next island arrived before Truvie could complain. This one was a perfect square. No beach. No dock. Just a floating square made of wood. On the wood were too many souls to count. All busily creating . . .

"Clothes?" Truvie said.

"The Seaming Isle," he said. "Easy one to guess."

"These are the souls that help make clothes?" she asked.

"They're interested in creativity and the economic knowledge required to sustain it."

"This is where Tots got my outfit," Truvie said.

"Likely," Dr. Blick said. "Shall we move on?"

"How many islands are there?" Truvie asked.

"No idea. More are forming constantly."

"How did you know which ones to create?" she asked.

"Questions," he said. "What else?"

"You must have a way to organize, to figure out the best way to respond? And don't tell me it's all energy. Energy can be wasted. That doesn't seem to occur here. There has to be something more. What aren't you telling me?"

Dr. Blick smiled wide. Then he turned from the wall

and walked away.

Truvie chased after him. "Wait! What did I say?"

He stopped before the door. "Overwhelming you will only slow your progress."

Truvie studied him. He held very few wrinkles on his face. Rosy cheeks and neat with no stubble. His eyes, gentle, soft.

Out of nowhere, she asked, "Did you have children?"

Dr. Blick cocked his head to the side. "What brought that to mind?"

"Your energy," she said, in a teasing tone. "You're protective of me. I'm not complaining—it makes me feel like I'm home—it just—it reminds me... of my dad."

"I have two children. Findlay and Richard."

"Did you live long, Dr. Blick? As a human?"

"I'm still alive," he said with pride. "No body, but more alive than ever."

"You didn't live long," she said. "I can tell."

"I died when I was 42. I had a heart attack on the subway. Too much barbeque. I was taking my children to school. I hate they had to see my pass, but we all signed up for overcoming tragedy before we entered the pool. They're so beautiful now. They have children of their own. Smart. Hungry in all the right ways."

"They listen to the answers?"

"Oh yes," he said. "Because you taught them to."

"Me?" Truvie asked. "Don't you mean you?"

"I'm not the one who mends souls." He collected his breath and said, "The day I met you, Truitt, you sat me down and beamed your light on me. Told me you were so proud of me. I never felt so much love. Extraordinary love. So incredible. To this day—"

Tears fell to his clutched hands. He swallowed and continued, "You ignited your light so bright I thought I might catch fire. You told me how you met my babies. You knew all about them. Every detail of their lives, of their heart's desires, of who they truly are. You knew us all so well. My wife, too. Our forgotten hopes. Our secret dreams. You reminded me of what life was meant to be. Told me nothing was gone. Nothing lost. Showed me how to talk to them all the time. Send them energy in things they love. They will pause, you said. Love grants the grace to pause. It is in the pauses, you said, that the soul comes to life.

My daughter, Findlay, she loved elephants. I lit up every single one on the planet. Stuffed, alive, drawn, painted, on tee-shirts, on signs, new ones, old ones, any elephant I could find. I never stop. She talks to me sometimes. Calls me Dream Daddy. She tells me what's she's up to, and what she's interested in: her children, scrambled eggs, the color pink, a book, a way of thinking, a song, sand in her toes, glass of red wine. I send all my energy to everything she loves, letting her know I hear her. That I am there with her.

All the souls here feel me sending, so they do the same. They can't resist joining me. So bright, so strong, we send her all we've got. When she moves on, changes her interest, I follow accordingly. I'm with her far more now than ever before. Same with my son, and my wife."

Truvie squeezed her eyes shut and wiped her tears. She sniffed and heaved. "I know you do. I know you do that. I know that's what happens here—us to them,

them to us."

She sniffed again and pinched her nose. She took several short, sharp breaths. "I don't know how I know that." Her voice muted from weeping. "But I know it's true." Tears spilled out from her again.

Dr. Blick wrapped her in his arms and swayed. "I told you that you were close to overwhelmed." He gave a small laugh. "I'm sorry, sweetheart. I didn't mean to get you going."

She shook her head and inhaled. "It's okay. I'm glad you told me." She wept until she emptied.

Exhausted, yet calmed, she released from Dr. Blick and looked out to the sea. The water could no longer be seen. Hundreds of islands had rushed in to be with her.

"Ready for a little more?" he asked.

"I promise not to ask too many questions," she said. "Like what all these islands mean."

"You wouldn't be you without endless inquiry," he said, stepping away from the white adobe wall. "Those islands are here to offer you comfort. They are giving you all they've got, whatever you ask for, it is yours."

"What should I ask for?" Truvie asked, hesitating to follow him.

He reached the wood door they'd traveled through to get out here. "I've got something that you'll find far more interesting."

. . .

They walked down a hallway with red cloth walls. After a couple of minutes, he went down a ramp that zigzagged through darkness lit only by tiny recessed lights in the floor. After a few switchbacks, they arrived at what looked to be a laboratory.

Rain pelted the windows. The storm that brewed before they went to see the Wish Listeners had hit mightily. She didn't want to try to understand the variations in the weather. It hurt her head.

The water now black with angry waves crashing into each other chaotically. A whip of lightning cracked the sea close to them. Thunder moaned, spurring the storm on more.

Dr. Blick had gone to the far side of the room where he fiddled with a small electrical box. There were no computers or monitors. No beakers. No microscopes. No notepads. No desks or cubicles. No chemicals. No microscopes. No books. Not one chair to sit in. Still, it had the distinct feel of a laboratory.

"What kind of a lab is this?" she asked.

"Step back a few paces, will you please?" Dr. Blick held a silver remote control.

She did as he requested. He pointed the device to the high center of the room. Pixels emerged. More bits filled in, outlining a three-dimensional image that covered nearly the entire room. Without thinking, she reached up and touched a gathering of light. They diminished. She released her touch and they replenished.

"Sorry," she said. "What is it? A map?"

"Wait, please," he said.

The image continued to create itself.

"It's two maps," she said.

Then it hit her.

"Oh," she breathed. "It's a holographic representation of us, and them."

He nodded. "I created it because I wanted to know how worlds formed. How they connect. Are there only two worlds we serve? Or are there more?"

The pixels completed revealing a rotating replica of planet Earth. "I've never seen an image of Earth like this. The coloring. What does it mean?" She held out her hands. "Don't answer. Miss Frank. I know."

He nodded. "I don't do it justice. For our purposes, color clarifies requests."

"Clarifies?"

"A color corresponds to the asking," he said. "Let her explain it. It's not my area."

Encircling the Earth was an iridescent band that stretched like a silky piece of ultra-wide ribbon. No beginning, and no end. No tie holding it together. The crests on it, subtle ripples, no peaked mountains, no sinking valleys. It had a nice flow, a gentle rhythm.

"How do you use it?" she asked.

"I watch to see how we move," he said. "Big disasters, tsunamis, earthquakes, are the only things that demand a lot of energetic attention. Only time it rises or lowers of significant note."

"We care for the whole planet, then?" she said. "Not just people?"

"What's the difference?" he asked.

She pointed to a miniscule bump in the wave. "These little ripples, what do they mean? Like here, over ... Chicago?"

"Could be an event. Sports. Musical. A convergence

of energy. Could be something tragic, a mass shooting. I never bother to guess. Our energy is the same. They ask. We answer."

"We give with all we have, whatever they ask?" she said. "And hope they listen and follow the guidance we give?"

He smiled and nodded. "They get as many chances as they need. We never stop being there. Even if they shun us and tell us to go away."

"You never go away?" she said. "No matter what?"

"We wait," he said. "Until they ask again."

"How long does that usually take?"

He shrugged. "A second, maybe two."

Truvie watched the silky ribbon representing where she was in a world of souls. She did love the notion that there was a distinct and ever-present connection between humanity and all this love and knowing. What a thing to exist? Someone, some way, she knew it had to be true.

"Tots is outside waiting," he said. "It's time for you to go."

"I'm not going to ask how you know that," she said.

"Energy," he said.

"And a little concentration."

Truvie slid her back down the wall nearest the door. "She can wait a bit. I want to watch the wave. We're kind of like a force field. Is there anything to measure the chemicals here? Are we made of waste from the beginning of the Universe?"

"It's time to go, Truitt." Tots tapped her painted red nails against the wall above Truvie's head. "Miss Frank is not meant to be kept waiting."

Dr. Blick raised his eyebrows. "She's more impatient than Pel."

"Understatement," Tots said. "Let's roll."

Truvie slinked her back and bum up the wall. "Thank you, Dr. Blick. This has been better than I ever could've imagined. Can I come back?"

"It's your world, Truitt Skye," he said. "I'm always here for you."

. . .

Truvie and Tots walked down the steps of Dr. Blick's porch and alongside a long line of palmetto trees. After a few moments, Truvie turned back expecting to see Dr. Blick sitting in one of the rocking chairs, sipping on an iced tea, but he was not there.

"Look again," Tots said.

Truvie paused, hesitant, but looked and there he was. He held his glass up and shouted, "Have fun!"

Tots took Truvie's hand and started to skip. "You ask, we answer. Simple. Perfection. From the beginning of time to the never end."

20
The Mint Isle

Truvie hugged the belly of Tots La Rue as she maneuvered the Whooper across the sea.

"The one thing to remember with Miss Frank is," Tots hollered over the roar of the engine. "No questions. She hates questions."

"But I thought—" Truvie started

"She hears you without you speaking," Tots said. "Like me. But she's—she's different. Just no questions, okay?"

The air started to chill. Tots slowed the jet ski and shouted, "Hang on. It gets a little tricky as we make our way to Miss Frank's."

The blue sky instantly started to cloud over until it became a white wall of mist on all sides. The sea crackled as it froze. Tots revved the engine as she bounced the jet-ski and broke through the ice with ease. Snow plummeted as a whip of wind turned the scene into a frigid blizzard.

. . .

She slowed to a stop in what seemed like the middle of the snow-drenched sea.

"I'm going to drop you here," Tots said.

"Here where? Where's here?" Truvie cried. "I can't see anything but white!"

"The Mint Isle," Tots said.

"You see an island?" Truvie searched in a spin. "I only see a blizzard!"

"Slide off," Tots said. "I promise we're here."

Truvie did so and stepped onto a slick icy shore, losing her balance and immediately landing on her bum. Whap!

"I didn't mean literally slide!" Tots cried out.

She looked over to the sea and found snow pummeling Tots, caking her beret.

Tots turned the Whooper around to face the sea. "Remember! No questions!" Tots called out as she sped through the ice sending giant chunks of ice flying and splashing into the sea.

. . .

Truvie got to her feet and walked toward an empty chair lift waiting at the base of a snow-covered hill. She rubbed her bum as her head filled with questions. "I can't seem to stop myself," Truvie said, presumably not loud enough to—

"Try!" Tots shouted from way too far away for Truvie to hear yet she heard Tots LaRue loud and clear.

Energy. And a little concentration.

Truvie waved her off and tried to get a sense of what this island was about, other than a deep freeze. The sea for a half-mile surrounding the island was composed of thick ice. Truvie felt a chill wriggle up from her heels, up her calves and hamstrings to the back of her neck. Shivering, she cupped her hands and exhaled her breath into them with a loud whoosh.

The chairlift had only one chair. The rest of the chairs must have been removed, or never existed. While snow fell, this exposed chair remained dry as did a sheep shearling seat cover and a white fur blanket draped over the back.

Creepily inviting.

Three green crows descended to a mound of snowy rocks.

"I'm all right," she said to them. "Didn't mean to send out the alarms."

One of the crows lifted his beak and offered a fluttering soft cry. With the rise of its wings, the brilliant pale green birds took flight. Woo-whoosh, woo-whoosh, and they were gone.

"Miss Skye," a woman's deep voice said. "Am I to bow? Get on my hands and knees? Lie supine? Or may we begin?"

Searching the chair, the ground and the hill, Truvie

could not find the owner to the astringent voice.

"Gaze higher, Miss Skye."

It could have been the angle, but to Truvie, this was the tallest woman that ever lived. She had pixie cut grey-white spiked hair and pale skin. Her refined cheekbones, light eyes, fitted grey leather dress, and severely-heeled leather boots, made it clear she was more than in touch with her feminine strength.

"Truitt Skye impressed? By me?" the woman said. "That's certainly an unpleasant first."

"Miss Frank? Is that you?" Truvie's voice unexpectedly girlish.

"Please board the chair," Miss Frank said. "Olivia will meet you at its end." The stilted, steely woman stalked away from the ridge.

Truvie lifted to her toes and edged onto the chair where she found a warm, cozy heated furry seat. The blanket rose to her shoulders as the chair took flight. Big, white flakes that brought Wish Listeners to mind drifted to her open palm. Perfectly formed extra-large snowflakes rested on her skin as if they'd been made to thrill her. She pulled the fur tight to her chin and snuggled into it.

She thought of her mother readying for her big Christmas show. The snowflakes on stage would be fluffier, and faker, but from a distance, they looked plenty real. Her mom would be knee-deep in final rehearsals with Eddie's mom and the rest of the crew, including the snarky, but talented Candace Little and her sidekicks. Truvie and her dad sometimes helped out, pulling curtains or working the light board. She collected tickets once. She liked greeting everyone and fed off the excitement for the show. Her mother dressed her up like a Christmas elf last year in a green dress and red patent leather boots. Truvie had insisted on no fake ears, but in the end, wore them anyway. Her mom had a way of getting the Truvie's shy to shine.

The chairlift arched up and over the hill revealing a wintery landscape. However, where she thought a lovely log cabin would be stood some sort of industrial contraption.

"What is that?"

She leaned forward to try and make it out. The shape was a right triangle. It reminded her of weird homes in New Mexico that her grandmother cut out of Architectural Digest magazine.

"You'd love this one, Gram." She shook her head, not loving, but fearing it.

As the chair neared the monstrous triangle, it sped up. Two steel columns housed the metal landing at the end and standing in the center was a young girl with shiny hair that looked familiar.

The girl crossed her arms over her chest. Minus her straight long blonde hair, she was dressed identically to Miss Frank. Fitted grey dress and strikingly high boots with spiked steel heels.

"I might be in trouble here," Truvie whispered.

Truvie jogged off the lift and stumbled out of control. Just as she was about to face plant, the girl caught Truvie with one hand.

"You're strong," Truvie said. "Thank you."

"Stand up straight, please, Truitt."

Truvie regained her footing and started to speak but the girl beat her to it.

"Please follow me." The girl of steel rotated on her pointed heel and marched across the snow whilst introducing herself. "I'm Olivia. We met in the Expanding Forest."

Truvie jog-walked after her. "The forest! Right. I was a little foggy then, not that I'm crystal clear now. How are you not sinking? Those heels. They should penetrate the surface. This snow is soft. See." Truvie pointed back to her footprints. Olivia had not left a one.

Olivia continued walking. She did not answer. She did not acknowledge.

"My sneakers are sinking. And sliding. Leaving indentions. Hello?"

Olivia said nothing.

Truvie stopped all movement. "Gravity? No." She paused with an injected idea.

Before Truvie took a step, she imagined the bulk of her energy shifted up, as if her chest and shoulders offered her solid ground instead of her feet, like Leilani taught her. She took a step. Then looked back to see. "Yes," she hissed. "Not one mark."

She hurried up to Olivia, glancing back to witness no evidence that she had. "See, I'm learning."

"You're imagining things into existence," Olivia said. "We both know you can't shift your weight up like that, Truitt."

Truvie's jaw had dropped open and was suddenly dry, vacant.

"Imagining thing into existence," Truvie whispered

to herself, searching for more information. "I tricked myself?"

Crunch, crunch, crunch, their feet to the icy fluff. Cold, biting air with cloud-steamed exhales. Truvie hugged her arms to her chest. Olivia moved like a soldier marching in a parade.

"Are you mad at me?" Truvie asked. "Have I done something wrong?"

More silence.

"Thanks for showing me the way," Truvie said. "I'm sorry to be a burden."

Olivia stopped with a low sigh. "You are no burden. I love seeing you, but Truitt, no questions. Don't speak. Listen. Tots was supposed to explain it to you. Miss Frank is not like the rest. You need her more than any other. I can't protect you, or help, or indulge you. If I do, she'll send me away."

Olivia hugged Truvie. When they released, Olivia pulled her dress back into place, steeling herself once again.

"Promise?" Olivia asked.

"No questions," Truvie said. "I'll do my best."

"Do better," Olivia said.

. . .

They reached an elevator embedded into the vertical side of the right triangle-shaped building. The doors opened.

"After you, Truitt," Olivia said.

"You can go first," Truvie said.

Olivia shook her head.

Truvie stepped in. The door's slammed shut and the elevator shot up without warning.

Within a second, the door flew open, crashing with a loud clanking as they hit the shaft.

Miss Frank waited with arms crossed. "Pathetic. Go again."

Truvie drew in a deep breath. "Hi."

The doors slid shut with ease this time and slowly descended. When the elevator hit the ground, the doors opened.

"Tell me you said nothing," Olivia said. "And showed you were open to listening."

"You could have warned me," Truvie said.

The doors crashed closed and bulleted up once again. At the top, when the doors opened, Miss Frank looked grim, and boiling.

"One more try," Truvie said, knowing she was still scared to death and had a bazillion questions starting with all the steel.

The doors slammed shut. The elevator lowered and when the doors opened at the bottom. Truvie grabbed Olivia's wrist and pulled her in.

"Stop elevator!" The elevator obeyed Truvie. "What is this? A test or something? It's not about gravity—what is it about?"

"I told you," Olivia said. "No questions."

"Fine." Truvie paced the small space. "I'll figure it out myself."

"No," Olivia said hopelessly. "You can't. Stay calm. The elevator responds to your emotions and thoughts—"

"Like Tots La Rue?" Truvie guessed.

"Tots, Miss Frank and I have the same interests," Olivia said. "You talk to souls, we read emotions. We help you do what you do."

"Then why can't you and Tots help me?" Truvie said.

Olivia's eyes grew wide. "Shh. Never say that again. Are you insane? No more questions. You promised."

"I can't help it!" Truvie cried.

"Shh. Relax," Olivia said. "Trust me, we all need Miss Frank. She is beyond a great teacher. Okay?"

"Okay," Truvie said, nodding. "I believe you."

Truvie leaned against the elevator wall. The elevator's doors closed without disruption and rose up to the top floor. They opened with ease.

. . .

Miss Frank turned and walked away.

Olivia nudged Truvie forward. They followed Miss Frank in itchy silence. Careful not to glance at one another. Truvie was trying her best not to feel a thing.

However, what she saw next was so disturbing, she had no control over anything for several seconds. The room had steel walls and steel desks and at the desks, children, eight and nine year-olds she'd guess, all dressed exactly as Miss Frank and Olivia. The boys in little tight grey suits and ties, instead of heels and fitted dresses like the girls. She shook her head to see things again, but the image did not change.

"Come in, please, Miss Skye. We are here to serve."

Truvie backed away, "The-the-that's okay. I'll—um—

I'll hook up with Junius. Tots is probably waiting."

"You will do no such thing," Miss Frank said. "We prepared specifically for your return."

Olivia put her hand in the middle of Truvie's shoulder blades.

"Are you trying to help her, Miss Born?" Miss Frank stalked toward them. The click of her heels echoed off the metal walls.

"She's more of a mess than I presumed," Olivia said. "But help her? How could I? One can only help oneself."

"Accurate, still, I agree, she needs help," Miss Frank said as she hovered over Truvie. "Give me your hand, Truitt Skye. We are here to educate you."

"On?" Truvie asked. Her stomach emptied, danged it. No questions!

Miss Frank turned her hand sideways and extended it to Truvie. "Viveca Frank. Etiquette Professional to The City by the Sea."

"Etiquette?" Truvie questioned but recovered quickly, "I mean. Etiquette. How important. I'm ready to hear everything."

Truvie looked to Olivia for approval. Olivia stoically gazed at the front of the room.

Miss Frank clicked back to her large gold desk situated at the front of the classroom. "Everything is a tad broad, and since you know so little, we will fill you in quickly on the most pressing details."

"Great," Truvie said. "Right? That's a good thing? My fillable-ness?"

"No questions!" Miss Frank screamed. "You are

here to listen. This is my final request for you to come to the front of the room. It's rude to make us torque and turn! Do it. Now. Now. Now."

Truvie jogged up to the front of the room, spun on her toes and faced the creepy little fancy children. "Sorry. Ready for duty."

"No," Miss Frank said. "It is we who are here to serve you."

"Serve," Truvie said. "Go ahead."

"Are you being sarcastic?" Miss Frank moved in close to Truvie's left ear. If she didn't know better, she would swear Miss Frank suddenly licked the air under Truvie's nose with a serpent tongue.

Truvie did her stellar best to not run for the elevator. "No. No, ma'am. I apologize. I didn't mean to sound sarcastic. I was merely stating my readiness and availability."

"Apologies? From Truitt Skye?" Miss Frank did not back away. "Are you afraid?"

Truvie nodded. "Terrified."

Miss Frank stepped closer to Truvie. Her throat at Truvie's nose. "Of? Your own world? Your own soul?" She waved her fingers around as she spoke. Her voice raspy, deep. "Your own rules? Your life here? The life you revere? The one you created?"

Truvie wanted to collapse more into herself. "Could you back away a little, Miss Frank? I mean, please back away. I need some air."

"I'm nowhere near you," Miss Frank said, suddenly several feet from Truvie.

Truvie blinked rapidly. "What are you? Your fingers. They look like talons. Are you a lizard? A dragon? A monster?"

Olivia gasped and cupped her hand to her mouth. The minions did the same.

But Miss Frank. Miss Frank burst out laughing. After much guffawing, she huffed out, "This is the best moment I've ever shared with you, Miss Skye. Talons." She laughed more.

The creepy kiddos attempted to laugh. Olivia simply couldn't do it. She kept her hand to her mouth and shook her head back and forth. Eyes wide, but gaze to the ceiling.

Truvie relaxed and sat on a metal desk chair a few feet away. "I guess I'm more fun than I thought."

Miss Frank stopped laughing. "You're too fun. One of the so many problems with you."

Truvie involuntarily said, "Here we go again."

"Excuse me?" Miss Frank asked.

"I feel like—like I've said that to you before."

A child in the second row said, "You say it every time."

Miss Frank crept down the aisle of desks. "Thank you, Mr. Favreau. I'll do the talking until you're called upon."

Mr. Favreau bowed his head. "That was rude. I apologize."

"Simply raise your hand," Miss Frank said.

"You are so . . . so . . . bossy," Truvie said.

"And you are so ill-behaved." Miss Frank rested her hand on one of the desks. "I'm going to do my stellar best to let your behavior slide, as I always do. The lessons you need outweigh your crimes."

"My crimes?"

Miss Frank stalked toward Truvie.

"Poor manners are criminal. If I could only punish you, I would. But light doesn't feel. Only humans do."

"I feel," Truvie said.

"Truvie Tucker feels. Truitt Skye serves. As energy. As light. In accordance with what is asked of her. If not for me, and my ability to teach the sensations and thoughts of humans, you, Truitt Skye, would cease to be. You would blast around and burn out, like an exploding star who knows no home, no life, nothing to shine for."

"We all come from the dust of stars," Truvie said.

"We are not dust!" Miss Frank shouted. "We are all that humans have protecting them. Not police or government or weaponry. The soul is what protects the human being. They think and feel. We deliver all they need. We connect them to the whole of the eternal power within them. If you do not understand the rules necessary to talk with a soul, you will do more harm than good. More harm than you ever could know."

Truvie frowned deeply. "Wait. . . You and I? We work together?"

"When you built this world," Miss Frank said. "I was your first recruit. To help a soul, you must connect to it properly. There are rules you must obey. You cannot barge into their soul and fix it. That is why you failed time and time again in the earlier ions."

"How exactly do I connect with a soul? I don't actually talk to them, do I? Who could do that?"

The child next to Truvie slid down into her seat.

Another slapped his forehead and with a groan, said, "No questions."

Miss Frank snapped at the little girl sinking away then turned to address Truvie.

"It's what you do, Miss Skye. By your choosing, Totsinda La Rue works with you in the Cave of Souls. Latham is there as well, taking notes and keeping you on schedule. You are a team of three, as it is meant to be. However, once you are connected with a soul, you, in essence, disappear. But in order to connect in the first place, you must know the rules."

"I disappear? Where do I go?"

"The Crease." Miss Frank puckered as if metal had caked her tongue. "Your crude name for the thin layer separating the worlds."

"I still don't get what I do."

"Miss Skye," Miss Frank said. "I only know how you must treat a soul, not what you do to repair it."

"But they must be linked," Truvie said.

"That's the first intelligent thing you have said," Miss Frank said. "Possibly ever."

"Thank you?" Truvie stared, completely off balance.

"Students," Miss Frank turned to them. "What is the best clue we have to knowing a soul is in trouble?"

Every hand lifted and held in tight, straight lines.

"Miss Sharp, please inform us," Miss Frank said.

The little girl who had recently attempted to melt under her chair stood and faced Truvie. "Too much of one color."

"When there is an excess of a particular hue of light, or energy, it indicates what, Mr. Vasilly?" Miss

Frank asked.

A little boy diagonal from Truvie, near where Olivia was, stood. "It indicates leakage, Miss Frank and Miss Skye. A place where the human is out of balance. Where they've left their soul behind because the connection was severed."

"Very good," Miss Frank said. "Miss Skye, have you been seeing an excess of red lately?"

Truvie instantly saw the red lights of the glass dock, the slamming red doors with Eva, the red roses in the glass bathroom, red boots in her elf costume, Tots' cherry red fingernails. "Yes." Her voice loud. "So much I—I can't remember it all."

"Mr. Porter," Miss Frank said. "Would you offer us insight on the color in question?"

"Red," the small boy in a suit and steel loafers said. "It is the base of humans. Feet to top of the buttocks. It is where life comes from. It is birth. It is learning to survive among one's kind, their family, most specifically, but also those things of likeness, gender, race, birthplace, things unchangeable."

"Unchangeable?" Truvie cut in. "Sorry. No questions. But I want to get this."

"Go on," Miss Frank said to Mr. Porter.

"Things that humans don't control. Those are decided here, by the soul, before they go."

"With Pel?" Truvie asked.

"With the Assemblers, yes," Miss Frank said.

"Before you're born, you're saying, you—er—I—the soul whatever—decides if they'll be a girl or boy, what skin color they want, where they'll be born?"

All in unison, the children turned their attention to Miss Frank, who said one word, "Obviously."

Truvie stood and walked toward Miss Frank's desk then she moved past it to a small sliver of a window out to the snow and sea.

"The red," Miss Frank said. "Tells us the human is asking at the most basic of levels. They may have experienced separation from parents, a diseased state in the body, tragedy, loss, violence, extreme circumstances regarding home or living conditions. Usually, it leads to isolation from peers, schoolmates, siblings, or friends. Humans need other humans. It is in relationship that we thrive, souls, humans, cells, planets, suns, moons, all the same. We must learn to love and respect each other in order to thrive as we intend."

Miss Frank did not pause for a breath, she went on, totally captivating Truvie.

"In the Cave of Souls, Latham and Tots find the humans with the most profound asking. You then you meet that human's soul and recover the bit they left behind back into the fold. This is why you call it the Crease. Because they're—"

"Stuck," Truvie said. "Part of them can't move forward, no matter how hard they try. They are energy, Waves of energy. Of course I would call it a crease in the fold. Genius."

"You understand?" Olivia said.

"I lived it," Truvie said as she turned her attention to the snow-covered sea.

No one made a peep.

Good. Truvie wasn't sure she could handle anymore

anyway. No doubt Miss Frank was prepared to rattle the children through recitations of orange, yellow, green, blue, indigo, violet and who knows how many more. She hadn't thought about her anesthesia or hospital bed in so long. This wasn't a dream. She shook her head. Then rested it on the cold steel window frame.

"Too much," Truvie breathed. "I'd like to wake up now, please. I want to see Fig."

Truvie concentrated on hearing the beeping monitors tracking her vital signs. She tried to conjure the bustling sounds of the Emergency Room. She ached for the feel of her mother's hand in hers. Her father tucking a loose hair from her forehead behind her ear. She touched her stomach, desperate to have the heaviness of Fig's head nestled in it.

"Tru!" Tots La Rue panted.

Truvie couldn't move. She pressed her forehead into the metal.

"Truitt."

This time the voice was male.

Truvie raised her gaze and faced the room. Latham and Tots stood beside Olivia.

"It's Pel," Latham said. "He's in trouble."

21
Backward

Truvie didn't rush off with Tots and Latham. She looked to Miss Frank.

"You're not ready to help any souls, Miss Skye," Miss Frank said. "They will swallow you whole."

Truvie's mouth fell open. She glanced to Olivia but—

The click, click, click of Miss Frank's metal heels against the metal floor took over whatever words Olivia may have uttered. "However, you have no choice."

Truvie lowered her gaze. "I know."

"It's time you become who you are, Truitt Skye," Miss Frank said. "Only when you go, will you be free."

"Go?" Truvie asked. "Go where?"

Miss Frank tightened her jaws, flexing her chin line. "You must get through Truvie before you can hope to help Pel. It's time for her to go."

"Truitt!" Tots cried. "Please! We wouldn't be here if we didn't need you. And only you. Now!"

"Miss Frank will never think you're ready, Truitt," Latham said. "She never agreed—"

"That's enough, Mr. Bell," Miss Frank interrupted. "Miss Skye, please. Go. I'll see you later to offer you more, if you survive."

"Survive?" Truvie asked.

Tots scurried to Truvie and grabbed her hand. "Truitt! Now! Please!"

Truvie started then stopped. "Miss Frank, do you—"

"I do," Miss Frank said. "I do prefer you survive." She offered a stretched, awkward, squinty smile. "Do try to do so."

Truvie moved toward the elevator then turned back once again as if asked to.

"Don't break the glass." Miss Frank said. "Or you will destroy us all."

"We have to go." Tots clutched Truvie's hand and pulled her forward.

. . .

Latham held the awaiting elevator. They descended in silence. The moment the trio exited, a murder of green crows swarmed in, collected each one, and took flight.

"Good luck!"

Over Truvie's right shoulder stood Olivia and the creepy children waving in unison from behind thick red railings of a snowy balcony.

Flight felt good. Safe. But soon thoughts formed that were particularly upsetting. Survival. Wasn't she dead? And what about this glass? Don't break what glass? In the glasshouse? I already did break the glass, didn't I?

. . .

The crows dropped the trio before more thoughts could form. They landed on their feet near the rose gardens and drooping tulip fountain. The castle façade to the Cave of Souls straight ahead of them. Truvie felt dinky beneath its intimidating, grand copper and wood plank doors. A double-decker tourist bus could fit through them with ease.

"Why the front?" Truvie asked.

"Didn't you hear Miss Frank?" Latham said. "We have to sneak in."

Truvie shook her head. "I don't remember her saying that."

Latham and Tots spoke together, "They'll swallow you whole."

"Your plan is to sneak in through the giant, and I assume, rather loud upon opening, front door?" Truvie asked. "That's your whole plan? The whole thing?"

"No soul expects you to enter the back way," Latham said. "Most important, Eva. Eva won't expect it."

"Eva? She's in there?" Truvie asked. "I thought she ran into the woods."

"She knows the only safe place is here," Tots said.

"Safe? With the banging red doors?" Truvie thought about walking through the maze of roses and smelling each and every one.

"Focus," Tots said.

"Can't you smell them?" Truvie asked.

"Truitt!" Tots yelled. "Please! Pel needs you."

"Junius put Eva in with the doors," Latham said. "It's not standard to the Cave. We would never do that to a soul."

"You know that, Truitt," Tots said. "Please. Trust us."

"I don't know anything!" Truvie gave a nervous laugh as she pressed her sweaty palm to her forehead.

"We three always go in together, Truitt," Latham said. "We'll guide you through this."

"Guide me through what?" Truvie said. She waved her arms at the monstrous castle walls. "I don't even know what I do in there. I can't save Pel or Eva or you or me or anyone or anything. This is ridiculous. Incomprehensible!"

"All the more reason to focus," Tots said.

"This is important," Latham said.

"Try," Tots said. "I can feel you want to try."

"Your sensors must be off, Tots, because the last thing I want to do is try," Truvie said. "I'll be swallowed whole, remember? That sounded pretty definitive to me. And not in my favor. Not to mention this glass I'm not supposed to break."

"You'll have to swallow first," Tots said. "That's all."

"We're going," Latham said. "Either all three, or us two."

The doors creaked and grumbled forward and slowly moved away from each other, creating a dark, dusty opening.

"Did I do that?" Truvie asked.

Tots nodded.

"At least I stirred her up," Latham said.

"I don't think this is such a good idea," Tots said, backing away.

"Wait a minute," Truvie said. "You've been begging me to go into this castle. Telling me I had—had to save Pel—who, by the way, has a been a real pain in the—"

"I'm telling you what I feel," Tots said softly. "It's what I do."

"Tots." Latham circled her and held her by the front of her shoulders. "What changed?"

"She's never opened the doors," Tots said. "Ever."

"You said that's how we were going to get in!" Truvie lifted her arms to the air and flung them down to her sides.

Tots pointed to a smaller door down to the right. "That's the only opening I've ever seen Truitt use. These doors—I thought they were fake."

"What does it matter?" Truvie asked. "They're open. Let's go."

"You're afraid her power is dangerous?" Latham asked.

Tears fell from Tots' eyes.

"You're crying?" Truvie filled with heat. She fingered her palms. Wet with sweat.

Tots heaved. "It's too much."

"But Pel," Latham said.

"It's the pull of the souls making her power surge, not Pel." Tots rocked with her arms cradled to her chest. "Pel knows better."

Truvie's body vibrated from the inside. She flicked out her hands, jittered and bounced on her toes. "Let's go, let's go, let's go."

"Wait!" Latham yelled. "Calm down. Everyone."

"Can't." Truvie took off running, straight for the unknown.

. . .

"Truitt!" Latham chased after her into the castle.

"No!" Tots' voice faint.

Truvie didn't care if she came or stayed. They got her into this. She would not stop until she had Pel and Eva in her grasp, swallowed by souls or not.

Latham caught up to her within seconds. Tots right behind. Truvie slowed to speed walking. The manicured marble walls of the castle entrance now long gone, replaced with the muddy, rocky walls with hair-like roots protruding, and distant drips kerplunking in the dark crevasses.

"I'm enraged," Truvie said, her arms boldly pumping along her sides. "I don't know why I am so amped. I don't think I can stop myself. From anything."

"It isn't you," Tots said.

"It is," Truvie said.

"No," Latham said. "It's the pull of the other souls. We're a little off balance here. You've been gone a while. No one else recovers soul fragments. I have a long, long list for us to get to. They—I didn't expect this—but Miss Frank—the souls—they're calling you to help them."

"Fine!" Truvie picked up her pace. "Let's help them.

Where are they? Let's get this done."

"TRUITT!" A walloping young boy's cry sounded.

All three stopped.

"Pel," Tots said.

Truvie immediately took off at a sprint. The walls blurred into blackness.

"Faster!" she demanded of her legs. They obliged and her velocity tripled. The path turned from flat to a steep slope. Her fast-working legs started to rise, pumping her knees to her forehead. Jumbled and frantic, she began striding like a stilted tricycle until the pitch turned too great for her speed and she toppled over and over like a crushing boulder in a ferocious avalanche.

She popped up from the ground and ricocheted wall to wall.

"STOP!" Truvie shouted at her legs.

Truvie instantly halted, but before she could try to find Tots and Latham, the floor disintegrated into sand and swirled into a dust storm.

Truvie hugged her elbows to her belly and pressed her hands over her eyes and nose. She spat out sand then shut her mouth tight. Grit grains cut her cheeks and tongue. Whirling wind drowned out her moans for Tots and Latham.

"TRUITT!" The boy's horrid cry echoed again.

"Pel," she called through her muffled mouth. "I'm coming!"

The gusting dust did not relent, though she focused with all her might and will, begging it to quit. She leaned her right shoulder forward and blindly fumbled ahead into the sandstorm.

"Tots, what do I do?" Truvie wailed.

No answer arrived. She heard the words of Miss Frank. They'll swallow you whole. But that would not stop her. Fear was no issue here. Truvie Tucker, on her own, was not brave. But in here, with Pel's haunting call, and that pull, wherever it came from, meant Truvie Tucker was unstoppable.

The ground beneath her suddenly gave out, releasing Truvie through the unexpected hole in the sand.

. . .

She landed on her feet in a vast desert. Sand fell like a deluge of rain until there was no more. A heavy fog of dust ballooned from the ground. Hills of sand scattered the grounds. No walls. A pale blue sky above, as if she were outside, and no longer in a cave behind a castle.

"Latham? Tots?" She scanned the emptiness then yelled, "Pel? Pel, are you here?"

"Dig!" Tots cried. "Hurry!"

Tots and Latham dropped to their knees and frantically shoveled away sand.

"Where did you—how could you—where'd you come from?" Truvie twisted her torso, searching, searching. "What is this? Is Pel here? Under the sand?"

"DIG!" Tots screamed but her focus was on the horizon, not on Truvie.

Truvie turned to see what had Tots' attention.

People of all shapes, sizes, ages, races, and cultures raced toward them.

"Are they coming for us?" Truvie could not stop herself from walking toward the oncoming hoard. She wanted to know them. Her arms opened wide, her chest and chin high.

"Truitt! Put your hands in the sand and dig! Now!" Latham's face and shirt caked in white dust.

"Or your pockets," Tots hissed. "Don't you dare touch one of them!"

"They're souls?" Truvie said, stepping further away from Latham and Tots. "For me?"

"TRUITT!" This time Pel's voice sounded muted and far behind her right shoulder.

Truvie faced the call.

"He's here!" Tots banged the side of her fist on glass. "Truitt! Look! It's Pel!"

Truvie ran to the hole Tots had dug, but her focus immediately returned to the oncoming souls.

"Truitt!" Tots cried.

"Look!" Tots and Latham shouted at the same time.

Truvie glanced down and found Pel's face pressed to the glass.

Truvie fell to her knees. The whole of her devoted to Pel.

"Help me!" Pel cried.

Truvie searched the small glass box Pel was in beneath the sand. "Where's Eva? Is she holding you there?"

"Yes!" Pel called, his voice sounding like he was underwater.

"Truitt," Latham said. "We have a problem."

A mass of souls surrounded them.

Pel pounded the glass. "Truitt!"

The souls reached for Truvie, pulling on her hair, shirt, hands, arms, feet, and ankles.

Tots faced the souls, as did Latham, but the souls pushed the two of them out of their way.

Truvie looked to Pel, but he was not there. Instead, Eva stood in his place.

A sharp pain hit Truvie in the knees and rocketed up her thighs, chest, and neck. With all her might she shook off the souls and raised her fists into the air.

"Do it," Eva said. "Come get him."

Truvie took in a deep breath and lifted her arms even higher, she wanted to garner all the force she could before she punched them to the—

"NO!" Tots screeched so loud Truvie's eyes watered.

Truvie stopped, arms and chest still arched and ready.

"Remember what Miss Frank said!" Tots yelled.

Truvie eyed her sweet friend as she lowered her arms and repeated the warning Miss Frank gave her, "Don't break the glass."

"They'll swallow you," Eva said, counter-repeating Miss Frank. Her voice not muted, clear. Crystal. Clear. "Whole."

The souls moved in closer and closer, piling on and tugging every part of Truvie.

"Swallow!" Tots and Latham screamed in unison.

"Swallow!" Truvie cried. "Are you insane?"

"Do it!" Tots cried. "Swallow them!"

"Now!" Latham yelled.

There was no time to figure out what else to do.

With an inhale, Truvie took the souls into her. Man after girl after boy after woman. On and on and on until—

She burst backward like a cannonball on the battlefield. Tots and Latham evaporated from sight as she propelled back. The middle of her spine crashed through a rock wall, making Truvie cough violently. Thousands of souls thrust from her mouth and back into the Cave as Truvie blasted out the back entrance and hurled toward the sea.

. . .

Truvie quickly spun to face the water and instantly saw nothing but shimmering silver.

With a gasp, she pulled her body up before crashing into the silver pool then plunged feet first into the waves, inches from the still silver water.

Down and down, letting the water have her, Truvie let go completely.

Tears fell but the sea gathered them before her cheeks could. She wanted to go home. To be free of this soul world, a world she had never known but was expected to become part of.

Please take me home.

Further beneath, she let herself descend. Intervals of warm and cool touched her skin until she felt nothing. Not the hairs on her head. Not the water. Not sadness. Not fear. Nothing.

. . .

Truvie opened her eyes.

Because suddenly she was no longer sinking to the bottom of the sea.

"Come in," Junius said, holding the glass door open for her. "I heard you had quite a fall."

Truvie was somehow at the front door of the glasshouse. Night had arrived but no stars, or moons tonight. She hadn't the energy to ask how she got here, how she left the sea, or how the sea left her. All she knew was that she hadn't awoken surrounded by doctors and nurses, her family and Eddie, as she'd asked to be, so she simply could not care.

. . .

The only sound in the kitchen came from the gentle crackle of wood succumbing to fire in the exposed brick oven. Junius was not cooking. He waited by the windows, unmoving.

"I'm not going to wake up there, am I?" Truvie asked.

Junius did not hesitate. "No, my dear. You are not."

"Will I ever go back?"

"Not as you long to," he said. "Not as you were."

"Not as Truvie, you mean?" She sat in a garnet red velveteen lounge chair near the fire.

"Not as you were in any way." Junius moved further away from her and the windows. "Only as more."

"I don't want to fight it anymore," she said.

"It will get easier to let go," he said. "Unfortunately, we're in a bit of a crunch."

"Pel?" she asked.

"Eva," he said. "She's using Pel to get to you."

Truvie raised her shoulders. "I don't know him."

Junius gave her a soft smile. "Still, you want to save him from her."

"Yes!" Truvie said, straightening. "Very much."

"It's her," Junius said. "She's the one you most want to help. Don't try to understand. Let yourself do what comes to you."

"How did Pel get trapped beneath that glass?" Truvie asked.

"Eva would have tricked him," Junius said. "Pel's focus is unrelenting. Would have been easy for her."

"Good thing Miss Frank warned me about the glass—unless she's in on it—is she? Miss Frank? Out to get me? I can't tell with her."

Junius stayed silent. He fiddled with his pink tie, checking the seam then nestled it into his belly again.

"Granddaddy?" Truvie pressed.

He looked up at her. "Have you considered the science of here? Really thought it through?"

Truvie gave it a thought then said what came to mind, "You mean the map that Dr. Blick has? That gravity, a constant, is all whacked here, I think, I actually tell. I would like to know the elements that make things up here—hydrogen, obviously. Iron? Not sure. But I'm thinking carbon might not—"

"Not the particulars, dear," he said, leaning his elbow to the rough edge of the table. "The biggerness."

"Biggerness?" she repeated.

"This world is a part of that world, would you agree?" he asked.

"I can't," she said. "I have no proof."

"How do you explain me? Your grandfather here for you. BLT waiting."

She pressed her feet from beneath her bum to the ground. "I don't know how they connect. I mean, Miss Frank said something about a crease. But—" Truvie leaned back into the plush cushion. "Is the Crease the glass?"

Junius jutted his lips forward with a nod. "Indeed, but let's stay where we are."

"Can't you tell me how to penetrate the glass without breaking it so I can get Pel back. And Eva, since you think I want to help her, too."

"That's not the point," he said.

"It's not?"

"The Crease is where the worlds combine, but if you don't respect what it means, of the need for the worlds to stay apart, I'm afraid we'd all be better off if you returned to the pool."

Truvie's hand moved to her heart. She clutched at it. "You want me to leave? Because I don't understand? I thought you were supposed to help—"

"This time we would not intervene when you returned," Junius said. "We would let you go. An Assembler would get you right back to the soup without a blink. We'd do that over and over again. This world but a blur to you, as it is for most, as you specifically designed it to be."

Her stomach hollowed with a lurch. Her heart gasped for air as it sunk into her back. "Granddaddy, why are being so mean to me?"

"You asked me to," he said. "Among other things."

He paused, looking helpless to her. "Such as helping you create bathrooms and maps and isles of snow and glass. Everything planned. Everything."

"Wait. What?" She sat up in her chair. "What are you saying?"

"When you created this world," Junius said. "It was in response to the desires of that world. Everything you do is to serve the souls who serve humanity. You can trust that. You need not pretend not to believe it. I suspect when you were there, you were highly—as in oddly focused on—all of humanity knowing their potential. It is who you are. No matter how many bodies you fill, that truth cannot leave you. You must be who you are. The question now is will you allow yourself to become it or will you continue to cling to the thought that you are less than who you know you are."

"Truitt Skye, you mean?" Truvie said.

"I don't care about the name." He leaned back, his ribs hitting the rough edge of the dining room table. "Inside. Your true self. Brave. Smart. Worry-free. All-knowing. Confident. Devourer of unrest. Mover. Shaker. Doer. Inspirer—"

"I'm trying," she said.

"Try harder," he said.

"Why aren't you all busy in your own worlds?"

"Energy can be in many places all at the same time," he said. "No body, no limitations."

"Can we go to your world instead of mine?" Truvie asked.

Junius smiled but did not laugh. He had that stern, irritated look he had when she exploded the glass library. "You knew you would be Truvie Tucker," he said. "And exactly what she would need to succeed when you returned."

Truvie frowned deeply. "You and Truitt planned it all out?"

He inhaled, chest rising. "Miss Frank was pivotal, as always."

Truvie's heart knocked against her sternum. "You know my next move? What do I need to do? How to help Pel?" Her back ribs ached. "That means you know how to stop Eva from merging the worlds and destroying us all? Or if that will happen and it isn't some wild, crazy dream I'm creating for who knows what reason other than to drive myself completely insane!"

He lowered his gaze. "It's no dream. But that is all I know."

"Why? Why wouldn't I tell you everything?" Truvie shook her head. "That doesn't make any sense to me. If I knew the stakes—"

"You said Truvie would think we were manipulating her. Pushing you to do something you didn't want to do. Said you would fail if you weren't given the proper chance to believe it on your own."

"Still,' Truvie said. "You understand I'm drowning here, Granddaddy? I don't have a clue what to do with Eva or anything else in this place."

"Believe it or don't," Junius said. "But you told me this was exactly how this particular conversation would go."

22
Becoming Truitt Skye

Junius rose from the kitchen table and stared at her for a few moments. "Because of the precision of our discussion, my dear, I am absolute in my resolve to do exactly as Truitt told me to."

"Can't you think for yourself?" Truvie clinched on her back molars.

"She said you would say that, too," he said.

"Fine. You win. Truitt wins." Truvie relaxed back into her shoulder blades. "I don't care."

"That's what humans do. Deflect to manipulate. Don't care? You care. You care so much you don't know where to begin. You want to help Pel. You want to save both worlds. You want it so much you gave up everything that you know, everything and everyone you loved

to be here. You took on unbearable pain. You chose to
be devastated with loss in order to take care of souls.
Let me in. Let me help you, Truitt Skye, to become who
you long to be."

Truvie shifted and watched the fire. The molten
red embers were so familiar and so real. She got up
and took a small log from the stack and placed it on
the coals. Little red sparks flew and scattered, turning
black the moment they landed.

"Everything," she said. "All mapped out and
planned." She returned to the velveteen chair. "That
does sound like me." Her voice dropped as she choked
up. She cleared her throat. "My biggest dream. It's here.
This place is exactly as I imagined the world could be."

Junius' eyes bloodshot from his tears. "How about I
make us a tea?"

She nodded.

"Your grandmother still calls it that then?" He filled
a kettle with water from the sink, put it on the stove,
and lit the flame.

"Gram has tea every afternoon. Three thirty-three,
precisely."

"She likes threes," he said. "Always three of everything."

"I told you," he said. "Before you went how much
she thought three was a magic number. Her, me, your
mother."

"The trio of love-o," Truvie said. "She told me."

He placed loose herbs and tea in a glass teapot
then poured the steaming water on top. "You made me
tell you every last detail so you'd be sure to connect."

Lavender and pale pink roses floated among little black sprigs of tea, suspended briefly before sinking to the bottom. Junius lowered a scoop of honey into the brew and stirred the tea into a flurry.

"I chose your family as my family?" Truvie asked. "Truitt did, I mean?"

"For the last time, Truitt," he said. "You are one and the same."

"Go on, I'm sorry," she said. "Please."

"You asked me if I would be your grandfather before I understood what you were up to." He left the tea to settle. "I don't think you quite get the gravity of such a request. You wanted to be a member of my family. Granddaughter to my wife. Child to my daughter. I could hardly contain my energy. Of course, I told you I would be honored. I am honored."

"You didn't ask why?" she pressed.

He sat on the edge of the bench again. "I knew why, Truitt. I knew what it meant. But do you? Do you know what it means?"

"That we're family."

His cheeks rose to his eyes and he exhaled. "Connected through all time. No matter what, we would forever be intertwined. Souls come, they go, but there are some, families, lovers, great friends, that are inextricably together. They live every life together again and again and again. Never in the same way, but always together somehow, in some way. It meant everything to me that you wanted that kind of bond with me."

"I wasn't even going to know you," Truvie said.

"A grandchild does not need to know a grandparent

to feel the love they have for them," he said. "No one needs to know anyone to feel profound love that is sent to them."

Truvie took a deep breath. "I always felt like I knew you, and loved you. I thought it was because of my mom and Gram."

"My dear," he said. "We're talking about a love that is timeless. Constant unending pure love. That's what our bond means whether it is experienced or not."

Truvie wiped her eyes. "I'm sorry I'm so—so—clueless."

"It's time to let that go. Time to let your soul lead you." Junius went over to the tea. He poured two cups and lifted the lid from a ladybug cookie jar. "Oatmeal raisin or shortbread?"

"Either," Truvie said.

"I don't miss Helena and Sylvia like you do," he said. "Because I'm with them. But a body, with the sensation of touch. Nothing like it. Even the pain is worth it."

Truvie nodded.

He handed her a tea in a ladybug mug and a shortbread cookie.

"Wait," Truvie sat up. "I feel you when we touch. I feel your hugs."

"You don't, dear," he said, taking a sip of tea. "It's a memory. One of many—like this tea and that cookie—you asked me to perpetuate."

"I don't taste the tea? I don't hold the mug? Because I do, and I am," Truvie said.

"You are and can for as long you decide to remember to," he said. "We are energy. No bodies. No chairs.

No houses. No islands. No tea. When I say, you created this world, I do mean, you created this world."

"When?" she asked.

He took a bite of cookie.

"Can you taste it?" she asked.

"You're confused, but you warned me you would be." He set his tea aside and rubbed the crumbs from his pants. "Tell me about quantum mechanics."

"Now?" Truvie asked. "I don't—why? Can you taste the cookie or not?"

"The basics. What does quantum mechanics attempt to explain?"

"The relationship between energy and matter," she said.

"Matter. Yes. What is that again?" he asked.

"Granddaddy. You know what matter is."

"Humor me," he said. "I ate a cookie without hands or teeth or tongue for taste."

"Matter is a way to measure," she said. "Not weight, not mass, because neither are required to be matter. People think matter is mass, but it isn't. Matter is kind of the great mystery. It's gas, liquid, solid but it's also nothing. It only matters when it interacts with energy. Then it becomes something."

"Could not have said it better myself."

"Overly simplistic," she replied. "It's embarrassing. Dad would—" She stopped herself. "He likes to express things mathematically."

"Simple is always best," he said.

"Not with physics," she said.

"Truitt added mass to matter," he said. "Before you

263

left. In the crudest, overly simplistic sense of it: you made matter matter."

Truvie frowned. "I added energy to something?"

"You created here for this very moment," he said. "Give it a moment to sink in. Consider what Truvie Tucker might need to see in order to believe she created a world whose only purpose was to serve souls and thus, the unending growth of humanity."

Truvie looked out to the sea. "I created this place to understand who I am? A city of islands where like souls gather? A castle posing as a cave? Green crows? Wolves? Wish Listeners? Bathrooms? A suspended bedroom in a rainforest? Catters? Miss Frank?"

Truvie began walking around the room. "I made this glasshouse, not you? The contents in each house and building? The map in Dr. Blick's lab? The food in this kitchen? The plants in the atrium?"

"Come." He left the kitchen at a quick step.

She took a last sip of tea. The sweet tang of the wilted roses. The dense, stringent flavor of the black tea. She paused. "How can this not be real? I can taste the pungency and feel the heat on my tongue and teeth." She started to pour another—

Leaning on the door frame from the hallway. "Truitt! Don't mess with our momentum."

. . .

Junius stood in front of the mirror.

The red lights at her feet lit as she followed him. "I made this hallway?" Above her hung a delicate peony-like chandelier with teeny pink, white, and red lights glowing. She pointed to it. "And this?"

She stopped. "But why? Why did I go to all this trouble?"

Junius stopped in his tracks. "To become who you are. So that in your comfort and curiosity you would believe what you're capable of."

"What about your world?" she asked. "What goes on there?"

He touched his fingertip to her nose. "One day you'll find a way to visit. How about that? A puzzle for another day. We've got Pel to think about."

"But—"

"Let's keep our momentum in this direction. For Pel. Can you?"

"Yes," she said. "I'm sorry."

"Quite all right," he said, putting his arm around her shoulder and gave her a squeeze. "Ready?"

Snug to him, she nodded.

. . .

Slowly her reflection began to shift, not quite as fast as it had come before. A Middle Eastern soldier. A newborn in a tuxedo onesie. A chubby teenage Asian girl dressed as a boy looking around. A short African man in a suit. A baby elephant. An elderly woman with a cane.

Truvie was as a young dark-skinned man in athletic gear when she reached for Junius' hand. She missed, moving forward instead of back, to engage his clasp.

Junius took hold.

"Best if you close your eyes," Junius said. "It'll help you focus."

Truvie, a woman in her 50s now, closed her eyes. "I don't mind watching them all."

"You're not watching, my dear," he said. "You are them, and they are you. Energy. But it's time for you to be you, Truitt. Focused on what needs to happen next.

"You made this mirror to help you understand what it is you do here. The purpose of your soul. Specifically, how you help souls become whole. You help them release the past and reclaim who they are. You meet them, my dear, in their soul. And to do that, you morph into the fragment they need to set free. Do you understand?"

She asked her Truitt self to answer. Immediately she said, "I become what they need so they can move forward freely."

"Precisely," he said. "In a moment, when you open your eyes, you and I will stand here until one of my fragments appears. I want you to see if you can let go enough to serve my soul. Nothing to worry about, okay? My fragments are healed. You can't hurt me. This is not the Cave. In the Cave of Souls, the fragments you meet are real and you're helping them not only has consequences for them, but for the entirety of both worlds."

Truvie fought to keep her eyes closed. "Why would I do that? Why risk—"

"It can't be helped," he said. "We are beings in perpetual motion. There is no practicing. Or, one could say, there is only practicing."

Truvie tried to pull away, but Junius strengthened his grip.

"There's nothing a soul, and therefore any being, cannot handle."

"If I can't break a soul then what's the big deal?"

"When you work with a soul," he said. "You cross over. You merge into their world."

"If I stayed," she said, piecing it together. "The worlds would merge."

"Open your eyes," he said.

When she gazed into the mirror, her image was not her own, but it was familiar. And unchanging. She shifted her gaze to her grandfather. He gave her a nod and then he stepped out of the reflection.

As she studied herself, she remembered. It was the beautiful woman, in the white tunic and white pants with long golden locks that had been painted on the vanity in her suspended bedroom.

"Am I Truitt Skye?" Truvie asked.

"You're someone she thought Truvie would want to be," he said. "In preparation for what is about to come."

23
Fragments

Truvie remained in front of the image in the mirror. "It's like seeing a photo in a magazine and loving it so much you tear it out and hide it in a book."

"You're stunning," Junius said.

"How did Truitt know that this is the someone, the soul, I would want to become?"

"She knew the image had to have enough resemblance to Truvie that Truvie would believe it to be possible. That it would match her aspirations and dreams for herself. I take it it succeeds?"

"Very much. Most people would have seen in me in a lab coat with my hair pulled back. Glasses. Pen protector." She turned her gaze to her grandfather. "You made this possible? You let me be part of your family so I would become who I am."

"As is the case with all families, my dear," he said.

"But this was bigger, Junius," she said, calling him by his name for the first time. "I must have loved you very much to ask you such a thing."

"You loved me no more than anyone else," he said.

"Still," she said.

"Indeed," he said.

Staring back at her soul, she asked, "How did it work? How did I, how did we—"

"Set things in motion?"

Truvie nodded.

"That is between you and Pel," Junius said. "However, he remains silent on the matter. When I asked him if people select their parents, he said arrangements are made for what the soul wants to experience, what they prefer to feel with flesh and bones, who they want to become according to the desires of the whole of humanity. They don't know names. They know they will re-connect with the souls they've known because that's how energy works. However, they don't want to know which ones or how or when."

"Pel was part of the plan?" Truvie asked.

"Only moments prior to your jump," he said. "What else you may have told him, I do not know."

Unexpectedly, but naturally, Truvie's left hand extended to her grandfather's. "I'm not sure why, but I want you to join me here. In the mirror."

He smiled. "Just as Truitt said you would." He stepped into the mirror's reflection. His pink tie and navy suit. Baldhead. Strong hands, lean but fit build.

His black wingtips polished and pristine.

Truvie blinked and her grandfather started to become a young man. It didn't take long for his full head of blonde wavy hair and wrinkle-free skin to fill in. Not quite as lean, he wore khaki pants and a blazer with a yellow insignia, crisp white shirt beneath it. His feet bare.

"How old are you?" she asked.

"Eighteen," the young Junius in the mirror replied.

Truvie's body started to widen and bulge. "What's going on?" She looked down at her legs. They were fattening!

"Why can't I feel what's happening." Her hair darkened and greyed at the bangs. Her white outfit turned to a frumpy black dress. Her feet from bare to patent black low leather heels.

"It's working," Junius said.

. . .

The edges of the mirror slowly turned to shiny liquid. Traveling inward, the mirror completely melted away. Truvie turned to face Junius. He had vanished. No bald Granddaddy Junius. No eighteen year-old one either.

The room had gone as well.

She stood, not as herself, but as a plump woman in a black dress, in a gravel parking lot, alone. She knew she was Judy Stelae. Mother to Junius. Wife to Fletcher. Thirty-nine years old but felt a hundred and nine in this moment. Waves of information about Judy flew through her mind. All there. All accessible, but still fully herself, Truvie—Truitt—was completely present.

There were only a few cars in the sunken lot. Old cars. A long Cadillac in lemon yellow. A cartoon-ish green pickup truck like the ones Truvie had seen in parades where the backend was filled with stacks of hay and waving beauty queens, like her mother.

Judy's feet stamped over the rocks toward a crumbling cement staircase with a rusted banister. Truvie felt the weight of this woman's girth as her thighs rubbed together. She appreciated how skilled Judy was in heels. Her heart raced. She held her tongue to the roof of her mouth, nibbling it with her back molars. Judy climbed the stairs, using the rail to assist, and at the top spotted young Junius sitting on a picnic table holding hands with a young woman under a small cluster of oak trees. Within a step, the woman with her grandfather became clear: Truvie's grandmother, Helena.

The heat of the sun beat down on Junius' mother's forehead as she moved to the young couple. Blades of grass pricked the tops of her feet with each dip into the dry grass. She clutched a square purse to her stomach. Her hands shaking in her silk gloves. The air warm, but Judy Stelae shivered.

"It's okay," Judy whispered. Truvie was still there, but less there. Like a traveler on the woman's shoe. Distant. But wanting to rise and be part.

And so it was.

Judy's every muscle tightened. A surge of energy rushed through her.

Junius released from Helena and stood before his, "Mother. What is it?"

Judy embraced young Junius. "Don't worry," she said. "He didn't suffer."

"Who he?" Junius said, but his expression told the truth. "Dad?"

"Oh, Junius," Helena touched his back. He groped for her.

"It was an accident," Judy said. "I blamed him, but I was wrong to. I'm sorry."

"Mother," Junius said. "It was his fault. He knew better."

"No," Judy said. "He loved that car. Loved to drive it. Nothing to regret."

"He should have stopped and slept," Junius said.

"He wanted to get home," she said. "Nothing will change that."

"I hate him," Junius said.

"No, you don't," Helena said. "Don't say that."

"Hate him for a moment," his mother said. "Then remember you love him. Don't let his choice become a permanent resentment."

Truvie could feel herself doing the talking, not Judy. Yet Judy's body—her energy—sparkled and shined in full agreement. To Truvie, it felt like she and Judy were holding hands and madly in love.

"I resent him for everything. He was never here," young Junius said. "He didn't care."

"You'll need to indulge another line of thinking." Judy spoke the words but now, deep into this, Truvie knew they belonged to Truitt Skye.

Junius ran his fingers over his hair. "Like what? That I loved him? That I can overlook his callousness?

His disregard for putting his family first?"

"That you love him," Judy said. "Let his way of being serve your own."

"Be better than him?" Junius said. "I have loftier goals, Mother."

"To appreciate that he lived his life exactly as he chose, and that you have the same on offer," Truitt said through Judy.

Junius fell to his mother's chest. Helena lowered her head to his shoulder.

The sun brightened to blinding, devouring the sky, the oaks, the picnic table, everything.

．．．

Junius pulled away from his mother's arms and stepped away from the mirror. He returned immediately to his familiar baldheaded self in a tight, navy suit with a pale gray shirt and pink tie.

Truvie watched herself transform away from Junius' mother's body and back to the woman in white.

Junius smiled wide. "Powerful, hmm?"

"Extraordinary," she breathed. "Are you okay?"

"Oh yes," he said. "I don't mind repeating that moment again and again and again. That is not how it happened originally, of course. My mother merely told me my father was dead and I was left standing there. Helena was in class. I didn't tell her for days later. And thus, I was lost, exactly as I needed to be to become the man I did. My soul fragmented awaiting your repair years later."

Junius did not stop there. "It makes me feel like I could soar to the moon then drop back and float through the clouds doing backflips the entire way. I love the feel of my mother, the sweetness of her perfume, the softness of her frame. My mother hugged me twice that I can remember. And Helena there, with me so present, giving me every ounce of her love."

"What we just did, that was a fragment of your soul returning?" Truvie asked. "That's what Truitt does?"

"This was practice," he said, smoothing his tie. "It is not the Cave of Souls as I told you before. That bit wasn't recovered until after I arrived here—after my death."

"I don't understand," she said. "I thought I helped humans recover their souls?"

"You do," he said. "When they ask you to. If they do not ask, you meet them when they arrive here."

"How do I have time for all that?" Truvie asked, looking at her soul self in the mirror.

He laughed. "When you're free of a body and only energy—"

"You can be anywhere all at once."

Truvie's mind ran wild with wondering and with rushing energy from what had just transpired. She had been there, not here, giving the soul of his mother words and emotions he needed to feel and hear.

She stepped away from the mirror to focus on Junius. "How do people know I helped them? How do they know they're more whole?"

"They don't," he said. "They simply lose interest in their pain. It's a sensation of relief, of peace. It takes

274

over the hole they'd let form, often one they denied, or forgot, they created in the first place. They have lots of terms for it. Surrender, letting go, giving up. Quitting."

"They know something's off in them," Truvie said. "And then it's gone?"

"By the time they meet you, they're ready to heal," he said.

"But we healed it so quickly," she said. "Why wait?"

"That is how humanity evolves, for now. They hold onto their pain for years before they believe they can heal old hurts, sometimes entire lifetimes, like me. They cling to their anger or fear or fragility or not good enoughness or sadness. Never digging in and finding how strong they are, avoiding calling to their soul and connecting to this world and all it knows."

"Is it always forgiveness that heals their soul?" Truvie asked.

"It is a simple shift in their attention. 'If I can get them to realize mistakes and losses are good for them,' you loved to say, 'they will be unstoppable forces of nature. Impenetrable love-beings.'"

They took a few moments in silence.

Then Truvie abruptly asked, "Does the fragment ever break again?"

"Not in the same place."

Truvie stepped back into the mirror. She expected the images to shift and change, but she remained the woman in white with golden hair. She watched the image for several moments. Memorizing. Soaking. Savoring. Exploring. She let her thoughts drift to her house in Milwaukee, dinners that went on for hours with her family, watching her grandmother paint, and Fig asleep on her belly. She saw herself focused as her father explained the String Theory, black holes and asymmetry. She thought of prancing in the hall for Eddie. His coy smile and electric eyes, always on her, always by her side. His face so close to hers before they kissed. His breath, his love. Her hands began to tingle. She wiggled them. The prickling rattled up her arms, across her chest and into her throat.

"I wanted to experience love," she said. "That must be why I went, because it was all I wanted there, all I was ever after."

"And you found it?" he asked.

"Everyday."

"But?" her grandfather asked.

"There has to be something more," Truvie said. "Something else I was after."

"The only one who knows that is—"

"Eva," Truvie said. "I know."

24
There is No End

The slightly burnt crust of the wood-fired pizza cracked and split as Truvie's took a bite. They'd returned to the kitchen in silence.

"How could it be that none of you ever ate? What a waste," Truvie said.

"We weren't constructed to live as if human until you left, my dear," Junius said. "And, I have to say, we didn't practice nearly enough while you were away."

"When you see me, is it as light, or a seventeen year-old girl?" Truvie took another bite. The molten cheese threatened to burn the roof of her mouth. She stretched her lips and vented in some air through her teeth to cool it.

"I have to work to see Truvie, but I can do it," he

said. "It takes a lot of concentration, so usually I skip it. Your Truitt essence is distinct, and far more clear."

"Tots? Latham? You sense them distinctly, too? But you don't see them?"

He nodded, making her wonder what nodding looked like without a head or body.

"The energy transforms," he answered her thought, making her wonder about that too. "Sound vibration," he said. "Thoughts are energy."

Truvie frowned as she deciphered. "When you nodded, my light changed, and you heard my reply through sound vibration."

"It's all energy," he said. "I don't pick it apart. I receive it. Likely it comes as sound, light, heat, all of it, all at once."

"You're not eating because the food doesn't taste or smell to you?" she asked, the pizza was easier to understand. "How do you know when it's done?"

"Scent," he said. "I focus on the memory of it."

"You don't get hungry?"

"Never," he said. "I only want to work with you. To answer the questions you have. To create momentum for what's next."

"You're about energy only?" She shoved a big bite of pepperoni, mushroom and two Kalamata olive halves in her mouth. "I'm fueling. Even if it's not real."

"It's real, dear," he said. "You know how it works. Matter only needs an observer to make something real. Your memories will come to life constantly for you, until you decide to let them go."

"And if I don't want to?" Truvie rubbed her hands

together to rid the crust debris.

"Keep them for as long as they serve."

That was not the voice of Junius.

Miss Frank, clad in leather pants, boots and long jacket, stood in the doorway. Her cherry-red nails strumming a burnt red patent leather satchel.

"Don't you knock?" Truvie said then immediately added, "I'm sorry. That was rude. I didn't hear you come in."

"Souls don't knock," Miss Frank said. "You look better."

Truvie looked down. She looked the same. Not even a grease stain. "Oh!" she laughed. "You mean my energy is better? Do I look not as red?"

Miss Frank addressed Junius. "You haven't shown her?"

"It is time already?" Junius moved toward the smoldering fire.

"Time?" Truvie asked. "For what?"

"You called me, Truitt," Miss Frank said.

"I don't think so, Miss Frank," Truvie said.

Miss Frank set the satchel on the floor, leaning it on the doorframe. She stalked—click, click, click—into the kitchen. "Were you thinking about your return to the Cave of Souls?"

Truvie flashed a glance at Junius.

"I'll take that as a yes," Miss Frank said. "Which for me does not look like you looking shocked at Junius, rather, your heart, which is a pale green light illuminated and spread on all sides, indicating that yes, you had very much been thinking of a return. Of Pel and

Eva."

"I'm not only thinking about the Cave of Souls," Truvie said.

Junius laughed. "She has you there, Viveca."

"Because you are still clinging to the human girl," Miss Frank said. "I ignore that energy."

"Are you here to help?" Truvie knew Truitt was greatly influencing the rapid replies to Miss Frank. She had to admit she liked it.

"Believe it or not," Miss Frank said. "That is all I want to do. However, help doesn't always come in ways you want it to."

"What does that mean?" Truvie looked to Junius.

"Hear her out, dear," he said.

"You will return to the Cave, but first you must gain control of your energy. You mustn't help Pel. I told you that before—"

"I didn't listen," Truvie said. "I messed up."

Miss Frank took another step to Truvie. "You didn't break the glass and now you know what you're in for when you return. I'd say you did rather well. Much to my surprise."

"I felt like a freshly captured lion who'd broken from her chains."

"Only one lion?" Miss Frank said.

Truvie looked to Junius. "More than one."

"In other words," Miss Frank stepped closer. "Completely out of control."

"No," Truvie said. "Completely in control."

A flicker of a smile edged over Miss Frank's cheeks. "How do you think you'll do next time?"

"The same," Truvie said. "Is that a problem?"

Miss Frank and Junius looked to one another, nodded, and disappeared.

Truvie spun in a circle. "Granddaddy!"

She was alone.

"Granddaddy?"

She stepped into the hall.

"Where'd they go?" She walked a few paces more, leaning to see if they went to the mirror.

Searching as she returned to the kitchen, she stumbled on the satchel that had rested at Miss Frank's heels. Truvie reached down to pick it up but when she did, it evaporated into a thick, liquescent smoke. A burning smell filled her nostrils. She backed away from it.

The smoke grew and bubbled in heavy balls that popped. Boop. Pop. Boop. Pop. Until all the smoke dissipated and what remained, was a piece of luminescent paper resting on the table.

Written in script across the top, she read, "The Soul of Truvie Tucker."

But the page was blank.

With one final pop over her left ear, a pen appeared on the table.

"What the—" She looked around. "Miss Frank? Is that you?"

The paper lifted and drifted into her hand. The words, "Age seventeen. In need of repair," were now written on the page.

Truvie felt compelled to go to the windows to see if the wolves were huddled beneath the grove of aspens. They were not. She looked up to the sky. No green crows. Tots and Latham hadn't arrived.

All she could think to do was hide.

. . .

She left the paper and the kitchen behind as she traveled to the hallway. She paused to consider the mirror but turned the opposite way and hurried up the long staircase and into the atrium. She pressed through the fern jungle, annoyed by the gentle trickle of the spring, the high-pitched whistle of the robins, and the strong song of the wrens. She looked up to her bedroom, but had no intention of—

"Up," she said, testing Truitt.

And so it was.

Sprites remained balled up on the white bed. His white fur smoothed back and sleek. He blinked open his right eye, then his left. His light purple eyes squinted then grew wide as he stretched his front legs straight out toward her, claws engaged. A wild yawn revealed his long tongue that curled at the end. Truvie sat on the edge of the bed and let him come to her. He pressed his back to hers then wrapped around her side and purred in her ear. His chin to her shoulder.

"Hey, baby," she said, petting his closest ear. He flopped his shoulders into her lap and offered up his pale pink belly. "I'm in trouble."

Sprites' lips relaxed, leaving a little gap that revealed his tiger-like fangs. She bent forward to nuzzle him. He licked her cheek and ear.

"I don't suppose Truitt ever worried about going

into the Cave of Souls," Truvie said.

She caught sight of their reflection in the screen on the opposite wall. She remembered Junius telling her that she studied here, or thought, or something to do with those screens. She floated backward to rest her head and neck on the pillows.

"I should go for it, shouldn't I? Repair my soul, find Pel, reason with Eva ... Then what? Be part of life here? Work on souls? Is that all I do? And what about Eddie and my parents? I just forget them? Forget I was ever there?"

Sprites used his claws to stretch himself along Truvie's side. Lengthened nearly completely, Sprites was a foot longer than her. She liked his weight against her.

"I can't believe Truitt never felt matter before, never felt the warmth of a body next to her. I wonder what you look like, Sprites, a ray of violet light?" She scratched beneath his chin. His eyes half-closed, his mouth and whiskers looked to be smiling. "This is way better, isn't it?"

Truvie shifted her attention to the image of the woman in white. "Truitt was right to pick you."

She let her eyes fall closed and imagined hundreds of Wish Listeners flying around her head and heart gathering her asking. "How can I possibly be Truitt Skye?"

A breath later, without one bit of rest, she sat up, knocking Sprites off-kilter. She took hold of his jowls and kissed the top of his nose. "I'll be right back."

. . .

Stepping up the plantation stairs two at a time, Truvie called, "Dr. Blick! Are you here?"

She opened the screen door and bolted up the stairs like she lived there. "Dr. Blick! It's me Truv—it."

"Truvit, is it?" Dr. Blick was at the top of the staircase.

Truvie bent over to catch her breath. "I'm glad you're here."

"Where else would I be?" he asked.

Truvie straightened. "I need to talk to you. Pel—no—remember when we were talking? About my role here. And there. I thought. I mean I need—"

"Let's go in here," he said. "Have a seat for a second."

"No," she said. "I don't have time. I mean I do since there's no time here—but that's it—that's the thing. Why do you think I began again? Why would I do that?"

"I don't know," he said.

"I didn't tell you," she said. "Or you don't know?"

"You didn't tell me," he said.

"But you had guesses?" she said. "As to why?"

"I shouldn't have," he said.

"But?"

"I had guesses," he said.

"At first," she said. "I thought it was because she was—I was—afraid of Eva. Like she had pushed me—us—the world of souls—to no other choice. Like she had something on Truitt. On me."

He pulled his chin to his chest. "Something on you? That's—"

"Ridiculous, I know that now."

Truvie walked toward the copper wall near the tunnel entrance. "Then I thought, maybe Truvie—I mean—Truitt—was curious, you know, since she'd never had a body, she felt like she needed to know what she was talking about, especially if Eva wanted to merge the worlds. Eva and everyone else had a leg up on her because they'd had time in humanity. I can see that. Needed to do a field test, so to speak, so I had all the information necessary."

"Field test?" Dr. Blick paced near Truvie. "Seems a bit risky."

"Too irresponsible for our Truitt, right?" Truvie said. "I agree. Still, something about it makes sense."

"What something?"

"Sometimes when we don't know what might happen, we jump to find out. We surrender."

Dr. Blick lit up with a bright lime green light, so much light, Dr. Blick disappeared with it. Truvie gasped. "What—what's wrong? Where are you?"

"The green? You see it?"

"How could I miss it? It ate you." Truvie reached out to touch the light, but of course, her hand passed through it. She smelled her hand. It had no scent.

"Truitt," Dr. Blick said, his voice serious. "The light's been here. You're finally ready to see it."

"Turn it off, I want to see you."

"You are seeing me. The light indicates my agreement. Green, from the heart. What you're saying lights me up. It pleases me. I'm showing you that, and you're seeing it. It is not a bad thing."

"I want to see you," she said. "Please."

"Choose, Truitt," he said. "Choose what you want to see. Matter is the result of energy, the growth and evolution of it. Light or mass. Welcome it into being. That's how things work. Imagine no limits. Nothing is too small to become matter."

Truvie focused on her image of Dr. Blick. Corduroy jacket. Dark, mussed hair and glasses. Rumpled, wrinkled shirt and jeans. Loafers. Bit by bit, Dr. Blick came to be exactly as she wanted to see him once again.

An unexpected shiver rippled from her, "Do you think it's possible that I went over that edge because I knew no other way to see things differently?"

Green light leaked from beneath Dr. Blick's shirt collar. "Wanted us all to see things differently, perhaps?" he asked.

"Not because I knew what would happen," she said. "But because I didn't? Because it was the only way not to merge the worlds? Was I considering it? Was I thinking I might. . .That I might merge the worlds?"

"You know the answer, Truitt," he said.

Truvie took a few steps forward then double back. "Do I?"

"You know more than you're letting yourself," Dr. Blick said. "What would Truvie think about merging the worlds?"

Truvie didn't need to ponder this. "People don't find value in the discovery. They don't want to examine where they came from, or how important understanding the nature of things is to knowing themselves. They want to have things handed to them. They want life to be lived for them, not because of them."

She bit the side of her lip.

"Go ahead," he said. "Say it."

"Merging the worlds wouldn't be better. It would set us back. Way back."

Green light illuminated from every edge of him.

Truvie threw her arms around him and pecked him on the cheek. She took off down the stairs, gripping the railing as her footsteps thunked all the way to the bottom. Without looking back, she rushed out the screen door, jumped over the porch and steps. She took three giant footfalls, launched off the edge of the island, and dove into the sea.

25
The Glass

When Truvie's head hit the cool water, she felt more alive than she ever had as Truvie Tucker. She kicked her feet to gain momentum then flipped to her side and began to roll, just as Latham had done when she first arrived and was racing to escape Pel. Spinning like a drill offered faster, more direct speed and she had to get to the Cave of Souls as quickly as possible.

Truvie didn't know the route, of course not. She had to trust Truitt Skye knew the way. She had to surrender to the depth of knowing she could not touch. It wasn't far away. Many times in her life she had that sensation that she hit a nerve within, a glimpse into pure power. A sense of truth that she didn't need to hold onto because it wasn't going anywhere.

Her body burst from the water and catapulted high into the air. Her feet landed confidently at the dark, craggy entrance to the Cave of Souls. No Latham. No Tots LaRue. No haunting cries from Pel. Or crushing threats from Eva.

. . .

Truvie approached the opening to the black hole. The tips of her fingers caressed the sodden wall. Each step slow, deliberate, focused, and awake. At first, the darkness devoured her. She closed her eyes to let it pass. "When I open, I can see everything. Top to bottom, side to side."

Truvie opened her eyes. But it wasn't an illuminated path to Eva and Pel she saw. No long line of souls waiting to visit with her. No walls of dirt and moss.

Truvie stood underneath a streetlight on the wooded trail in the park across the street from her house.

In Milwaukee.

"What is this?" Truvie asked.

Suddenly she had a memory of the luminescent paper on the kitchen table. "The Soul of Truvie Tucker."

Truvie walked then picked up the pace to a jog. Overhanging lamps offered spots of light. Drops of leftover rain hit her arms as she rounded the corner, clipping a tree.

She pounced onto the bridge overlooking the crevasse where Fig's ball descended and dipped over the railing. "Fig! Eddie!"

She saw something moving at the bottom. Too far

away to hear her call.

Truvie climbed to the top of the railing on the bridge. Balanced precariously, she gathered her nerve. As she let go and jumped intending to make in all the way to the bottom, she remembered the kiss she and Eddie shared right near this very spot. His lips so soft against hers. Plump and slightly dampened. Had he practiced against the back of her hand like she had? Were his eyes closed or opened? Would they ever kiss again?

Her feet hit the grass with a reverberating swoosh. Before she could straighten, Fig tackled her and smothered her in kisses. Above her, the golden leaves of autumn trees. Eddie's hand reached out to her. She took it and let him pull her into him. Her heart thudded against her chest. From the belly of the ravine, a still Lake Michigan rested across the street, lit by the light of the moon.

"We found it," Eddie said as he pulled slightly away from her.

"My soul?" Truvie asked, shocked.

Eddie jerked back then laughed, "The ball. It was at the bottom, just like we knew it would be."

Truvie felt his laugh ripple through her, as if—

"Woof!" Fig wriggled at her side with the red ball locked in his teeth. He dropped it to the grass, scampered back with wiggles and barked.

"All is well in the world," Eddie said. "Right, Figgy?"

Fig barked eagerly, a high lilt at the end letting them know he was impatiently ready and two barks away from adding a deafening squeal to his cry.

Eddie grabbed the ball. "You knew it would be down here, didn't you, Figgers? Your magic red ball."

He gave it to Truvie. "Nothing to worry about now."

"But—" Truvie couldn't understand. His words . . . they—

Fig released an ear-piercing, eye-squinting wrench of a bark.

Eddie frowned and turned away. "Yikes, Fig."

"Woof!" Fig's bark deep and guttural to Truvie.

Truvie tossed the ball up a few feet then caught it with the same hand. "You want this? This old thing?"

Fig spun in a circle then raised on his hind legs, swatting at her with his front paws. "Woof!"

Truvie drew her arm up and back, shuffled forward and let the ball launch. Fig took off sending wet grass and soil flying. His every muscle flexed, racing as if his life depended on getting that ball. Nothing else mattered. He lived for it. Absolutely and completely.

"I shouldn't have gone after the ball that day," Truvie said. "I was careless."

"It was you being you," Eddie said. "Exactly as it should be."

As his words swirled, she knew he would not utter unless his soul was doing the talking. He wasn't there. No flesh. No bone. All soul. Only soul.

Fig had nearly reached his ball. Triumphant pounce so close. She couldn't bear to miss it.

"Good boy!" she cried as Fig closed in on his prey. "Good boy!"

Truvie wanted Eddie, the real one, not his soul, not her Truitt. Them. But his words sealed it and Truvie knew, "I'm not going to wake up in a hospital bed."

Fig's front paws reared up a couple of inches then dropped, capturing the ball.

"Get it," she said playfully. "Let me see!"

Fig collected the ball in his mouth, whipped around, and hauled ass back to them.

"Everything you do is to push yourself," Eddie said. "All the questions you ask. All the stuff you know. All building up to something big. Super big."

Truvie turned to face Eddie. "Is that how you see me? Something big?"

Eddie put his hands on her shoulders. "You know I love you, right? More than anything in the world."

Truvie's chin dipped down with a heavy sigh, her mouth stayed open. "I love you," she said. "I love so much, I hurt. I don't want us to be over. I can't leave—"

"You could never leave me. We're sealed. You and me. In this together. Always."

Truvie started to refute.

He touched his fingers to her lips then to the tip of her chin. "Don't worry." He lifted her gaze and kissed her tenderly. Shivers drifted through her heart and belly. She held his waist with her hands then wrapped them to the base of his shoulder blades. He kissed her deeply as he pulled her closer to him.

A shot of light blasted them apart. A cylindrical beam of golden light hit her straight in the heart. A flush of full, embodying warmth scattered through her. Her vision crystal clear. Strength rippled through her. An electric current surged inside her.

"Don't look back," Eddie said.

A bright flash of white consumed everything.

. . .

Truvie stood in a pile of autumn leaves. Light beaming in from all sides. The strength pounding through her made her invisible. Fragment recovered, Truvie was eager to let Truitt lead the way.

Without warning, the ground beneath her funneled inward and started to sink. Before she could grab hold of something, anything, her legs and waist descended. Her arms flailed above her head as she merged into the draining earth. Down and down she fell until her feet touched. Crimson, orange and golden leaves showered on all sides for a few more moments before settling into a pile once again.

Truvie now stood alone on a red rock platform in a constricted vertical cavern.

Peering over the side, she saw a chasm of slick rock walls. She leaned over the edge. The bottom was way down there—a couple skyscrapers' deep.

"Wait," she said. "Is that? Something's moving down there."

Teeny movements appeared as a dark dot along the bottom of the canyon.

"Pel!" she shouted.

The movement below ceased.

"Do not jump!" The words were male, and came from above, not below where Pel was. She turned. Tots and Latham waved from a ledge above hers.

"If you jump, you'll break the glass," Tots said. She

had on a magenta jumpsuit with lavender striped MaryJane heals and a lavender beret.

"You can see glass down there?" Truvie, not Truitt asked. "I barely see the black dot I'm hoping is Pel."

"It's called momentum," Latham said.

"It's the Crease, Truitt," Tots said. "The glass between."

"What do I do?" Truvie asked.

"Climb down and deal with it," Latham said. "We're staying here."

"Too much energy," Tots said. "Not on your side. If we get that close to them, we'll want to break through."

Latham cut in, "You have to resist the magnetism, like the pull of the silver pool. You have to want this world more."

Truvie peered over the edge.

"You do, right?" Latham asked. "Want this world more?"

"Of course she does!" Tots sang.

Truvie bit the side of her lip. "Guess we'll find out."

"Don't break the glass, Truitt," Latham said.

"Please, Tru," Tots said. "We can't merge."

"Truitt!" Pel's cry echoed off the chambers of the crevasse.

"Don't let Eva get to you," Latham said.

"I know," Truvie said, asking Truitt to take the lead. After a breath or two, she said, "I have to go before I launch over this cliff. The pull to help is driving me insane!"

"Don't break the glass!" Tots and Latham called out once again.

Truvie's insides trembled with a desire to bounce off the sides of the walls and down to the glass as fast as possible. Latham was right, momentum would win, and she'd crash straight through messing up everything, literally, Everything.

"I don't know what I'm doing, so—" Before she could finish, her own words corrected. "I know what I'm doing," Truvie said with apprehension. "Slow. Steady. Focused."

"Let Truitt in," Latham said. "Build momentum."

She peered over the edge. "I know what I'm doing," she repeated quietly. Tall walls of smooth, sandy rock. "I'm scaling a wall. No problem. I can do this. I'm doing this. All day. Me. And the wall. We're friends. I will not hit my head. I will help Pel."

Truvie got to her hands and knees and scooted backward until her feet went over the edge. She flattened onto her belly and used her hands and hips to slowly skid her legs over the sandy ledge. Dangling, she ceased all movement and arched to her far left to catch sight of a toe-hold. It was too steep to see her foot, much less a place to put it.

She envisioned a rock jutting out of the wall. She looked up to her friends. "Be right back."

Lowering down, the toe-edge of her shoes gripped tight to the wall in search of a landing. Down she stretched until her arms were almost completely extended and hanging. Her right foot tapped a small bump. Swatting at it twice, "Come on!" she screamed. Her toes caught. Another bump emerged to her left. She was solid. She pressed into the wall and took a few breaths.

"I should have imagined a rope. Maybe a ladder." She closed her eyes and let her forehead rest on the wall. Who was she kidding? A bump in a rock wall was all she could muster until she got the hang of this energy-to-matter thing.

Her fingers cramping, arms aching, she lowered her left arm into her chest.

"Beware of Induction!" Tots shouted. "Whatever that means!"

Truvie heard Latham begin to explain it to Tots as Truvie envisioned a dead grey branch coming out of the wall. And so it was. Her right hand gripped the limb.

With an exhalation, she imagined rocks and tree limbs all the way down the rock wall. Hundreds of holds. She lowered her left foot and easily found the next place to put it. Same for the right. Her arms, no longer spent, moved into place on either side with big rock handles to grab. She moved down into the depths quickly. When she gazed up, Tots and Latham looked far away. Over her shoulder, she made out the top of Pel's dark hair. She contorted to get a peek of Eva but didn't see her.

"Hang on, Pel!" Truvie continued her descent. "Almost there."

She moved with expertise down the final inches of the wall. "I know exactly what I'm doing."

And then the walls suddenly started to rumble.

The sides started to move toward each other.

"No," Truvie said with high-pitched panic. "I said I know what I'm doing!"

Closer and closer red sandstone walls closed in on her.

"Stop! Please!" She worked her mind to envision them expanding not contracting. They did not relent.

She pressed her back into the opposite wall, feet and arms completely outstretched.

Sandwiched between the walls with only a few inches on either side of her and nothing to hold onto, she dropped. Down she flew in a rapid free fall. She opened her mouth to scream for help, but she was too panicked to find sound.

After several hundred feet, her body skidded to a stop.

The walls collapsed into her, encasing in a solid rock box.

"I know what I'm doing," she cried. "I do! I know I do!"

The walls of the box transformed from stone to glass.

Before her, in a fitted red dress on the other side of the glass, stood Eva Kinde. "So do I."

26
Breaking Through

Trapped in glass too small to contain her, Truvie stared at Pel, who was trapped in an identical predicament across from her.

Truvie's bare palms and chin smooshed to the brink, she shouted, "Eva!"

"Get us out of these," Pel said. His cheek, ear, mushed brown hair, and sides of his swollen lips, were all she could see, but she clearly heard, "You are useless."

"Me?" Truvie cried. "You supposed to be the tough one. How'd she trap you?"

"Doesn't matter," Pel said.

"I used what Truitt gave me," Eva said. "Energy—"

"And matter," Truvie hissed.

"A game you played on me," Eva said.

"Truitt!" Pel groaned. "Get us out now!"

"Quiet!" Eva said. The glass wall tightened to Pel, smashing his knees and forearms into the glass.

"Don't hurt him!" Truvie called.

"If you were Truitt Skye," Eva said. "You would know he is in no pain. Stupid girl, this is an illusion you've created for yourself. But I can help. I can get us out of this. You did all of this for Truvie. Because she loves life. You want a body now, don't you, Truitt Skye? Think how strong you'd be as Truvie now? Don't you want to go back at her family? Be with humanity? We can do that."

"Pel? You're not in pain?" Truvie asked.

He shook his head, barely, since it was jammed to the glass—the glass illusion she had created but couldn't let go of, obviously.

"No, you idiot." His voice severely muffled and angry.

"Sorry." Truvie glanced to the sand under Eva's red heels.

Eva stalked before Truvie, sinking and growing. "You could be home in an instant. Right back in it."

"Sand," Truvie said.

Pel moaned.

"No, no," Truvie said. "Listen. The rock turned to sand then to glass. That's energy."

"Truvie," Eva said. "Don't you want to see your family? Your precious life? It can all be yours again. But better. You won't forget you're Truitt Skye."

"To get rock to change to sand, well, that would take years and years." Truvie paused, then said, "That must be where the concentration part comes in. That's why I couldn't stop the walls."

Eva clapped her hands in front of the glass encasing Truvie. "Listen to me!"

"I thought I was in control," Truvie said. "I gave myself all those holds on the wall, right? I was. I was in control. But so were you. You're better at it. I was imagining. You were creating. How—how so fast?"

"I don't overthink and get in the way," Eva said.

"Why are you so angry at me, Eva?" Truvie asked. "Why can't we work together?"

"Truitt!" Pel screamed, and though it was muffled, his red face captured his frustration precisely.

Eva said nothing.

"I'm the Truitt you want," Truvie said. "I promise. Or Truitt wouldn't have started all this in the first place. I must have jumped for us! For what we knew could be!"

"Let me lead then," Eva said.

"And what? We'll merge the worlds?" Truvie said. "Not a chance."

Eva squinted then dropped to her hands and knees and began digging into the sand.

Truvie pushed her forehead to the glass. "What in the? What are you doing?"

Eva didn't stop. She dug.

"Pel?" Truvie asked. "Do you understand this?"

The glass tightened around Pel as he started to answer. "She . . ." His breath condensed against the glass, fogging her view of him, but he managed to shout, "Break through."

Truvie thought for a moment. "Break through," she

whispered. Then without really knowing how the two connected, repeated Miss Frank's order, "Don't break the glass.

Mind racing, she took in a breath. Tell me what to do. She relaxed, and the answer came immediately.

The answer came into her mind loud and clear. Melt it.

The glass melted like wax into a pool beneath Pel's feet.

Eva stopped digging and looked back to Truvie. But her glass box had melted more than partway. Pel leapt for Eva. Truvie did the same. They piled in the sand until Truvie closed her eyes and shifted the air into a brisk, powerful wind, whipping the sand into a massive storm.

Pel, Truvie, and Eva fell backward as the sand swirled into a tornado, carrying them high into the cave, and settled back into the rocks from which it came.

. . .

Truvie was dropped on top of a window overlooking city lights hundreds of feet below her.

Eva and Pel were nowhere in sight.

"Pel!" She searched in all directions. The rock and sand walls gone. Nothing but glass below and blue above. No one. Nothing. "Pel! Where are you? Pel! Pellll!"

"Truitt!" Pel's voice echoed up ahead of her.

A surge of energy spread through her. She was up and running before she could consider any other alternative. "Not again."

She raced across the glass. Flashes of light scattered beneath her feet, below the glass.

"Slow down!" Her feet slowed enough for her to recognize the lights of a city, then plush green forest, then the vast blue ocean, then sunrise over a neglected neighborhood. She walked and soon moved above a small row of brightly painted houses on a canal.

"Truitt!" Pel's call sent her body rocketing. The glass dipped down as she traveled above tapered soaking fields of rice, palms swaying in the valley around them. She thought of the silky ribbon wave on the map in Dr. Blick's laboratory.

A vast waterway appeared beneath her toes. She wanted to get closer. She wanted to see people, cars, bikes, gardens. She wanted to be with life in motion. She suddenly knew Truitt had instructed Dr. Blick to show her that map—no—to create and then show her that map because she would be in the moment right here, right now with Eva. This was created long before Truvie Tucker ever existed.

"Truitt!" Pel's cry echoed and reverberated. "It-it-it."

Truvie raced into an empty horizon, fighting not to peek below her. "Pel! Where are you?" Sudden blurts of insight came. Hamster. Cage.

Stop.

Running.

In.

Circles.

Help.

Yourself.

Black.

Truvie halted, blinded by the darkness she created.

She stepped forward. She had not seen obstacles before, so no reason to think there would—

Truvie ran smack into something hard and rough, sending her head first and hugging it. She side-rolled free of what she thought was a boulder. The ground damp, muddy. Trying to lift herself, her hands and wrists, sunk. She hinged and splashed her bum to the muck.

"Come on!" she screamed.

"Truitt!" Pel called again.

"You are so on your own, Pel."

Lavender eyes popped in the darkness. Three sets to her left, four to her right. Creepy as all get out. But— she wasn't alone. That was good.

She took a moment. "How can I create light in the darkness?" She shook the first thought free. "Not philosophically. Literally."

Then it came to her. Ask.

"Light, please."

A thin ray of light emerged between her right index and middle fingers. She smiled with yes yes yes hissing in her head. Another burst shot over her left shoulder. A wider beam opened at her toes, and another, brighter still, above her head, but this light moved. She tilted upward from her sternum to find thousands of Wish Listeners dashing about the air. The enormous catters stalked in a tight circle around Truvie. The area was lush with vegetation like the atrium, ferns, jasmine, palms, and leafy green tropical shrubs.

She rose to her feet. "Thank you."

She waited for a gap in the catters to slip through and be on her way.

Truvie coned her hands to the sides of her mouth and shouted, "Pel!"

"Up here!" he called.

Truvie faced a ledge of giant, white-barked sycamore trees. There were aspen, cypress pines, and eucalyptus, too. And brush bigger than she was used to maneuvering through.

"Where?" she called. "I can't find the path!"

"Up!"

She gritted her back molars as she bent back branches and shoved her feet into the soft dirt for strongholds. The scent of soil and trees filled her as she ascended the pitch. Pel and Eva could be anywhere.

"Am I doing this to myself? I think saving Pel is hard, and so it is?" Truvie paused then added, "I should have asked Miss Frank more questions."

Heat and sweat pulsing through her and out of her.

Something furry flicked her arm. She looked down. The wolves. Pel's wolves flanked her. Three of them bolted out ahead, stomping down the bush, clearing her way.

With the additional help, Truvie covered ground fast.

"Truitt! I'm here!"

Pel balanced on a rock several feet up from her and the wolves.

"Almost there!" she called. "Where's—"

Eva stepped out from a grove of aspens and with

her pinky finger, pushed Pel over the edge.

"No!"

Pel launched over Truvie's head.

"No! Stop!"

Truvie rushed down the mountain. A crack of thunder rippled. Heavy, mean pellets of hail reddened her hands and forearms. She ran faster, but the ground soaked to a flood of white pellets in seconds. Her toes gripped the mountain, but she couldn't—

Whap! Nose, mouth and eyes to dirt and rushing mud. She, the trees, and the earth holding them released into a river heading straight down the face of the mountain.

Truvie pushed and fought to get to her feet. She could not fail. She had to create what she needed to save Pel and stop Eva.

Right.

This.

Instant.

The river vanished. Trees. Mud. Guck. Gone.

She stood on the glass with a vast ocean flowing beneath and an empty pale blue sky above, making it strikingly difficult to tell where one began and the other ended.

Twisting and searching atop the nothingness, she cried, "Pel!" one more time. She panned the horizon of glass, "He had to have landed."

"Move!" he shouted from above.

Pel catapulted directly at her, which meant he was heading straight for the—

"No!" Truvie shrieked. "You'll break the glass!"

Hoping he would suspend or maybe she would catch him, Truvie spread her arms wide and braced for impact.

"Move!" he bellowed.

"No!"

Eva appeared next to her and started to laugh.

Pel waved his arms wildly. "Move Truitt! NOW DAM- MIT!"

Eva raised her brows and smirked.

That smirk. It made Truvie cringe. But the Truitt in her welcomed it. Listening to her soul, Truvie stepped aside. "Let him crash."

27
The Line Between

Pel slammed his shoulder and side body into the glass. He did not break it.

He bounced off, rolled and came to his feet, inches from Eva.

"Back off," Eva said.

"Back on," Pel said.

Water suddenly rose on both sides but did not touch them. Then abruptly receded and shot upward, story upon story.

"Don't you dare," Pel said.

The waves held like converging reapers.

"Truitt!" Pel called. "Change the energy or matter or whatever—"

"I'm trying!" Truvie thought of ice, glaciers, polar

bears.

The tips of the waves turned to icicles, she tried to work them into freezing more, but—

The waves collapsed on top of them and exploded sending immeasurable tons of water to the glass.

Still.

The glass did not break.

Truvie created a swell of dry, hot heat. The water evaporated in an instant.

"You're getting better," Eva said. "But that doesn't change the game."

"What game?" Truvie asked.

"Choice," Eva said, lifting her arms and chin to the sky then to the ground. "Blue, though I'm sure you haven't spent enough time with Miss Frank to know again, is the color of choice. Of deciding. Of voicing your truth."

"Oh, come on," Pel groaned. "Blast her out of here and into the pool."

"No, no," Truvie said. "I want to hear this. You mean the choice of merging or not merging, or something else?"

"Your soul is not going to merge the worlds," Eva said. "Or it would be done."

"But?"

"And," Eva said. "I chose differently."

"I'm the only one who can break the glass," Truvie said. "Or you would have done it yourself. You wouldn't have to lure me here to save Pel."

"You can't help but help," Eva said. "It took no effort. No luring. However, your style of help differs from mine. You rescue. I empower."

"Bull—" Pel said.

Truvie held her hand out, requesting his silence. "I'm listening."

"She's playing you, Truitt." Pel crossed his arms over his chest, his camo tee-shirt tightened around his carved biceps.

"I don't mind," Truvie said. "She can't go anywhere. Let's listen. I rescue, even though I'm decently useless as Truitt."

"I don't think mending their souls is the best way to help them," Eva said. "I think they should have stronger, more resilient—completely resilient—souls to start with."

"Don't they?" Truvie asked.

"For about five minutes," she said. "Their creativity is obliterated almost immediately."

"Babies?" Truvie questioned. "They seemed pretty happy to me and get what they need without knowing how to yet."

"The diseased ones?" Eva said. "Ones born to despicable parents? Or worse, smothered in parental paranoia? They aren't loved. They're used. Thinking that kind of giving, tending to a helpless baby is love, sickens me. Broken souls clinging to freshly born ones. Until they break them, too."

"What happened to you?" Truvie asked, throat tightening.

"I'm awake!" Eva spun, her red dress lifted from her shins. "I want to give them what they want. Abundance. Power. Clarity. Joy. All the time. I thought you wanted the same."

Unexpected tears came to Truvie's eyes. She backed away, wiping them. Confounded, she did not dare speak. "I will not be weak," she whispered to herself. But the tears fell anyway.

"I thought we would take this world to theirs," Eva said.

Truvie had moved several steps from her and continued side-stepping.

Eva followed and kept talking. "All the work we've done to be the answer to everyone. No question too difficult. No trauma too great. Nothing we could not mend. No soul you could not make whole again. Still they break, again and again. Loneliness the dominant emotion of all humankind. We could eliminate it. We could give them our souls for all of time. Unbreakable. All-giving, all-loving souls for each and every one of them."

Pel suddenly appeared in step with Truvie. "What's wrong?"

"I don't know," Truvie said. "I can't stop crying."

"Tears are not a sign of weakness," Pel said. "They are a release."

Truvie drew in her breath then choked out to Eva, "How would we keep this world going if we gave them our souls? They will still die."

Pel gave her a quick nod of approval then kissed her forehead. "Keep going."

"Of course they will," Eva said. "They would leave knowingly, peacefully, without fear. Fully aware and prepared to begin again."

Truvie wiped her eyes with her fingertips. "Who would be here to greet them? Who would collect the lessons and return them to the soup for new souls to come forward to learn more?"

"There would be no need!" Eva shouted. "The worlds would move as one. In and out, no need for soups and pools. You die, you live again, as if death never happened. Complete perpetuity."

Truvie's tears stopped. Her vision focused with impeccable precision, down to each separate hair on Eva's head, each stitch of her ruby red dress, the freckles flat on the skin of her cheeks.

Shoulders back, chest forward, her entire being surged with energy. "How would we evolve, Eva? How would we grow?"

Eva's eyes opened wide. "Each one of them has at least a dozen lifetimes of wishes they are waiting to come true! You don't call peace and satisfaction growth?"

"Growth comes from adaptation," Truvie said. "Everyone knows that. It's asymmetry—the faults and flaws propel life forward—not symmetry. Symmetry only means we're on the right course, waiting to be knocked off again. Polarity is crucial to growth. Inherent differences force adaptation or mutation in order to survive."

"Suddenly the scientist," Eva said.

"Not suddenly," Truvie said. "Why would you want to disrupt the natural way of life? I don't understand how a soul in this place of souls would want such a thing? We can't force all of life to be perfect all at once. It is the difference among us that matters. All that matters. Everyone and everything in their uniqueness is what creates us. Homogenizing it would end it."

The tingling and surging let Truvie know she was coming into her Truitt self. She inhaled, hoping to soak in and fill more with her own soul.

Coming straight for Truvie, Eva roared, "You set the agenda, Truitt! Don't you get it?"

"They set the agenda," Truvie said. "Humanity is in charge. We simply listen and answer. You told me that, remember? 'We only respond to what they are asking for.' You claimed the merge was their idea, what they want. We only serve."

"You set things in motion, you set the speed, you determine the pace!" Eva cried.

"Do I?" Truvie asked, needling Eva.

Thin, pencil-size beams of red light shined from beneath the hem of Eva's dress and out the bottom of her heels, penetrating the glass.

"They don't know any better because we don't push their growth enough. We wait for them to catch up, but they never do!" Eva shouted then calmed as she continued. "Merging would be a fresh start. A base from which true, profound, immeasurable growth can occur. In unison. As one. Together. No one wants to be separated from their soul, from us, from the best of what is! How can you not see that? You were there. You asked and asked and asked. How many answers did you get?"

"I never wanted to stop asking," Truvie's voice caught. Tears stung her eyes. "That's living. To ask is to live. To seek and to not always find so we can—" Her lips quivered her to silence. "It's okay," she said inaudibly,

"I'm releasing you, Truvie."

Truvie drew in a congested breath then pressed on, "We keep searching more, keep loving more, learning more. Here, the answers are known. There is no need to worry or risk or sacrifice, we only want to serve. We answer to—" She shook her head in quick succession to quiet her weeping. She pinched her nose and exhaled, "We answer to watch them shine."

"You're almost there, Truitt," Pel said.

"When they fill—" Truvie sniffled then took in a couple of heaving breaths. "When they fill with the energy of this world, with the soul they embody, they are merged. They don't need me to do anything. They merge constantly!"

"No!" Eva cried. "It's not enough!"

Truitt smiled at her beloved friend. "They are here, and we are there. You know there is no separation. Just pauses along the way. Each time, a little more, a little deeper, a little closer to knowing how easy it can be to listen to what they already know. It is up to them to decide they have nothing to fear in living life. They are becoming. Always more."

"No!" Eva burst with red beams of light. "You aren't hearing me! We want the same thing! We want them to have it all—"

"No," Truvie said without emotion. "You want to tell them how to live instead of letting them discover and adjust on their own. A forced merge would destroy them. I won't do it."

Eva fell to her knees. The dazzling red light retracted back into her. She dulled to dingy grey.

"You ruined everything when you jumped," she said.

Truvie knelt beside her and touched Eva's shoulder gently.

She glanced up to Pel then back to Eva. "Are you ready to begin again, Eva? Ready to let go?"

Pel lowered to the glass on the other side of Eva, opposite Truvie.

Eva did not move. She slumped forward, bending her elbows, dropping her head. Her long auburn hair covered her face and chest.

"Take your time," Truvie said. "We're not going anywhere."

Pel edged his view right to left, trying to get a look at Eva, but she remained silent, and still. He looked to Truvie as Truvie looked to him.

Truvie shrugged and when she did, Eva thrust her elbow into Truvie's neck and flipped Truvie's back to the glass. A shattering crack rippled over Truvie's shoulders. Eva grabbed Truvie's wrist and pounded it to the glass, cracking it all directions. And suddenly, Eva let go of Truvie and vaporized into a red smoky mist.

Nothing could be done.

Eva Kinde slithered through a crack to the other side.

The red smoke hovered below the glass for a moment, then drifted down and was gone.

28
After

Truvie and Pel did not move. The glass sat shattered. They sat side by side, their fingers touching slightly, and watched the ocean sway beneath the glass. No speaking. No action. No nothing.

After many, many more breaths, Pel said, "You should repair it. And we should go."

"Don't you think she'll come back? Maybe we should leave it cracked for her?"

Pel turned to her. "Truitt, her soul will have to merge with another, or it will wither and fade, never to return to either world. She knows that. That's why she went."

"Wah—wait!" Truvie jiggered back a bit. "We have to stop her! We can't let her take over someone's soul!"

"Too late," Pel said. "She's already in one, I'm sure."

"But—but how?" Truvie asked.

"Easy," Pel said. "She'll slide right in. Same way she slithered through the glass."

"Won't they notice? Maybe the victim is somewhere here in the Cave."

"Trust me, Truitt," he said. "They will be. Many of them."

"She's merging into more than one soul?"

"No!" Pel forced himself to take a deep breath. "You've heard of something called influence? She wants the worlds to merge. She'll initiate more than one plan to do so."

"But—" Truvie stopped herself.

"Shouldn't you dive in and go after her right now?" Pel guessed.

"We both know that's a bad idea," Truvie said. "I won't get anywhere."

"Not now," he said. "But you'll get there. You'll figure it out."

"As Truitt wanted?" Truvie guessed.

"You broke through, though," he said with a dimpled smile. "You released almost all of Truvie."

Truvie studied him for a minute. Focusing, she could see he emanated a golden glow from his abdomen. "Why didn't you go? You must have felt the pull."

"I believe in you more than her," he said.

"But you did—you felt a pull to go once the glass cracked," she said.

"I felt compelled," he said, "Beyond anything I've ever known."

The glow in his belly grew with swirls. "What does

the color yellow mean for a soul?" she asked.

His eyes sparkling. He smiled wide and gave a chuckle. "It means a soul is offering their sacred truth. It means a soul can readily form boundaries, without harming another. It means I accept who I am, and no one can change me. I may decide to add to my truth, but nothing is said or done without my permission."

"You are who you've become," she said.

"Yes, Truitt, constantly," he said. "As are you."

"I hope so," she said. Glancing down, land filled with endless meadows of flowers, came into view. "Is it always like this?"

"I wouldn't know," he said as he smiled. "You wouldn't either. It's all new."

Moss filled trees overhanging a wide river zoomed underneath them as the wave of glass sped up and started to roll. Truvie and Pel's feet lifted a few feet above the glass then they floated down nice and slow.

"Should we get out of here?" Pel asked. "I've got work to do."

They walked with the rhythm of the swell and collapse of the wave of life beneath them. "What am I going to tell them?" Truvie asked. "Tots and the others."

"They'll already know," Pel said. "You did well. Who knows how long Eva would have kept you guessing? Kept me here. Now we know."

"All I know is she merged with some innocent person who will never know what hit them."

"I doubt they're innocent," Pel said.

"Why?" she asked.

"The soul would have to be. . . damaged."

"The person, you mean?" At the bottom of a wave, when they were closer to Earth, Truvie spotted a sailboat on a lake. She started to point at it, then retracted her finger.

"Same difference in this case. Very separate from here, from who they are," he said. "Not much to live for, totally disconnected, no sense of belonging, not paying attention to what is happening to them."

"Someone dying? An old person?"

"She wouldn't choose a body near its end. She'll want someone young. Criminal or someone in deep trouble is my guess."

Truvie took hold of his sculpted arm. "Pel! We have to do something!"

"You will," Pel said. "But not down here. This is a topic for you and Junius, Miss Frank, the rest of them. I'm not—it's not what I do, Truitt. Once you get Eva back here, I'll make sure she has a long list of lessons to cover and push her into the pool. Keep her away for years."

"Deal," Truvie said.

. . .

A few feet ahead, a stone staircase emerged.

Pel turned to it and ran up the stairs.

"Wait!" Truvie followed trying desperately to catch up with him. "Don't ditch me!"

"Catch me!"

She willed her legs to move fast up the high stone stairs. She skipped three at a time until she was by his side.

He slowed with a laugh. "Highly Truitt of you."

They climbed a few steps in synch and silence. Then Truvie couldn't stop herself, "What happened between you and me? Before I jumped? Junius said you were the last one I spoke to."

"You sound like you think I don't like you," Pel said.

"It's crossed my mind a couple of times," Truvie said.

"I don't not like or like. I perform on behalf of souls, like you do. It's everything to me," he said.

"And?"

He took a moment to answer. "When you came to me and told me what you were going to do . . . I wasn't prepared. I was torn. I still am. But you, the prior you? You weren't exactly open for a discussion—"

"I wasn't?" Truvie asked.

Pel laughed a little. "Truitt Skye doesn't—didn't—discuss what was right for souls. I did as I was asked and gathered up your requests for lessons."

"Do I seem—does she seem—" Truvie finally spit out, "I'm different now?"

"Extremely," Pel said. "Your essence is the same. But like everyone, you come back as more. That's how it works, by humanity's design. They want to grow and live and die over and over, always to become more."

"What lessons did I ask for?"

He stopped with one foot on the stair above and said, "You wanted to understand evolution. On every level."

"What else did I want to know?" Truvie started the ascent again.

Pel followed and said, "Physics. You wanted to see where they were really at, beyond the answering we give. You wanted to know the love of a grandmother. You wanted to see how to deal with difficult people, specifically rejection from your peers. You wanted to know harsh weather. You wanted a Labrador Retriever, and a best friend, which may have been the same. You wanted to believe in yourself fully. You wanted to have two parents that were highly different—that was the evolution in action, you said. You wanted to know compromise. You wanted to know what life was like without dreams fulfilled, with failure. You wanted to learn how to let go. You wanted to—"

"How big's the list?" Truvie cut in.

"It was small because—"

"I knew I wouldn't be there long." She took in a deep breath and said with an exhale, "Did I set the date, of my death?"

"You know a lot of souls, Truitt," he said. "You drew from your experience here. Seventeen years would give you enough time to understand life, but not enough to not sabotage that knowing. Experience, you said, tends to confuse humans for a few decades, sometimes the rest of their lifetime. You couldn't risk losing the lessons. You wanted to bring them back."

"I didn't fear that I would blow it? That I wouldn't learn what I thought I would?"

"Everyone learns what they set out to," Pel said. "It's whether they celebrate and become it that matters."

"Growth," she said.

"Evolution."

That was not Pel's voice.

Junius stood at the top of the staircase in a sunlit doorway with his hand extended.

. . .

The moment they emerged from the staircase, Pel disappeared.

Truvie took hold of her grandfather's hand and stepped into the light. She recognized the front gardens of the Cave of Souls.

Junius headed to the rose gardens. Truvie followed, searching out across the glistening sea. Butterflies and bees and dragonflies fluttered and zoomed from bloom to bloom. The scent of roses and ripe sea ever-present.

"Do you smell that?" Truvie asked.

He shook his head.

"Do you see the roses?"

"When I focus on my memory of a rose, of course," Junius said. "None of us sees anything exactly as another anyway. I don't need to see the roses, Truitt. It's perfectly lovely that you do."

Truvie pulled a rose to her nose and inhaled. "I'm keeping the roses and the castle—all of this—the sea—everything I created. Especially the kitchen in the glasshouse and the food. I want to see you all in clothes and bodies. A little light is welcome, so I know where your energy's at, but I want you, fleshy and stylish with expressions and hugs. I'm not letting go of Dr. Blick's maps or the creepy classroom on the Mint Isle or catters and green crows! I know how to help my dad with his equation now. And I know that I will learn more to share."

She lifted her chin to the sun and let her memory of its warmth soak into her not-at-all-there skin. "Even though there is no sun beaming down on you, I'm holding onto the one shining on me." She lowered her gaze to his. "I can work in both worlds, and I'm going to find Eva."

"Yes, Truitt," he said. "I know."

"Where do you think she went?"

"Haven't the vaguest," he said.

"But she'll show her colors soon," Truvie said.

"Quite literally, I suspect," he said.

"Are you worried?" she asked.

"Are you?" he returned.

"No." She knew the truth of her words because she felt nothing. "I don't want to hurt anyone, but I know, for now, I can't help that. I don't know enough of who I am."

She stepped deeper into the maze of rose bushes. Without turning to him, she said, "There's something I'd like to do."

"I know," he said.

"I told you?" Truvie asked. "Truitt did, I mean. Before she left?"

He shook his head. White light illuminated behind his neck and head. He smiled. "You just told me, dear."

"No, I didn't."

"You wouldn't like to have a BLT then figure out how to repair your mother, father, grandmother, and Eddie's souls?"

A bursting flutter caught in her chest. She twisted her lips side to side. "Oh," she said. "I guess I did."

Without another word, Truvie bent her knees, her bum out in a squat, and with an exhale released forward over the roses, the cliff, and onto the top of the sea.

. . .

A dolphin arched out of the water then dove back beneath the blue. Another emerged and did the same. Without hesitation, Truvie dove under the water and keeping her hands stretched in front of her, mimicking their style in a rapid, rush of a swim. She caught up with an entire frolicking pod. They zipped under and around her, spurring her to move faster in a game of chase.

. . .

Within a thought, the glass rocks of her home island sparkled from her reflecting sun. She rose up from the sea and landed her feet to the dock, dry head to toe.

Truvie casually moved down the dock admiring the art of the glasshouse she knew she, Truitt, created. "I wonder why she wanted it to be glass? Maybe that was the breaking through thing?"

"Talking to yourself?"

Pel.

She smiled and looked to him, prepared to say, "Maybe." But far more than Pel stood on the glass grounds of her home island. Hundreds, all dressed in gowns and tuxedos, had gathered.

And broke into applause.

Pel, in a brown suit with a grey shirt and tangerine tie, matched her stride and placed his hand on her lower back. "You said you wanted to celebrate."

"I did?" Truvie paused then said, "I said I wanted a BLT. To Junius, not to every—"

She cut herself off and smiled up to Pel and together they said, "Same thing."

"One of the many new gifts Truvie brings to the City on the Sea." He winked and showed his dimples.

She pulled at her tee-shirt, feeling a little—before another thought formed, Truvie's outfit transformed from tee-shirt, jeans, and Converse sneakers, to a long tangerine empire dress with pale pink flowers embroidered into the neck trim and thin ribbing a few inches above the waist. Her feet lifted a couple of inches in pale pink patent leather Mary Jane's, then she lowered back down again, replacing the heels with the purple glitter slipper boots her mother had given her. Her hair rose from her shoulders and twisted itself into a high bun.

"Can you see me?" she asked Pel.

"Clearly," he said.

"Is it from memory?" she asked.

"How could it be?" he returned. "I've never known this Truitt."

"What do you see?" Truvie asked.

"A beautiful young woman in a long tangerine dress and purple glitter slipper boots, never worn before now. Saved for this exact moment. Her eyes are blue, her hair is blonde, and she smells of roses. When she smiles, she melts me, a little."

Truvie's heart took flight in thousands of miniscule bursts. "Oh." She hunched with a breathy half-giggle.

"It's easy to see through your eyes now that you're here fully," Pel said.

"With your eyes you see me as—" she started trying to figure—

"I see the striking light of a sunset," he said without waiting for her to guess.

They drank each other in as a pale white glow emanated from him.

Tots skipped up wearing a black silk halter dress that tied at her neck. Her silver and diamond strapped heels glinted. Latham joined her wearing a black tux with a crisp white shirt.

"Orange," Tots said, pointing to Truvie's gown. "You're happy."

"Very much," Truvie said.

"Shall we?" Latham gestured toward the gathered crowd.

. . .

The four walked along a Tiki torch-lit path in the front of the glasshouse to join the party on the front lawn. Tea lights attached to flower-twined maypoles created a huge square with a wood-paneled dance floor in the center. Small cocktail tables with chairs surrounded the grounds, each with a candle and bouquet of orange and pink tulips. The guests, soul workers, donned elegant gowns and suits in every shade imaginable. One day Truvie might know what each hue stood for and might actually do something with it to help souls. Could she ever have imagined that deep within her she longed to help everyone, everywhere be more? She nodded. "Of course I did."

Among the hundreds of fancily attired souls stood Junius and Miss Frank, both in fitted black tuxedos holding flutes of champagne. Olivia, in a cherry A-line dress and steel corset heels, laughed at something the suited Dr. Blick said.

The creepy children looked shockingly normal in pajamas and slippers under fleece blankets. They watched an animated movie on a giant screen suspended from aspen branches. They tossed popcorn to the wolves snuggling among them. Keone, in a tux shirt and surfer shorts, and Leilani, in a violet tennis dress, both with tennis shoes on, ready to run, sat in beach chairs laughing hysterically at the film eating hot fudge sundaes.

Sussy Vox, in a purple striped suit and pink shirt, with a rainbow polka dot bowtie, and top hat, manned the bar without a bar—no drinks or bottles or glasses, handed out drink requests in rapid succession. On the far side of Sussy's bar was a banquet table with a smooth yellow tablecloth filled with plate after plate of bacon, lettuce, and tomato sandwiches. A blue and white frozen custard machine appeared on the end.

"Kopp's!" Truvie sang to Pel. "Kopp's is the best custard—it's like soft-serve ice cream but way better.

Creamy and rich. You have to—"

Pel took her hand and twirled her into his arms for a dance. At first, there was no music, but with that thought, an orchestra appeared near the front door of the glasshouse. She swayed in Pel's strength and closed her eyes. She thought of Eddie. But she did not ache. She knew he would grieve, and be lost off and on, but she would be there for him every moment of every day. Never, ever gone.

Others joined them on the dance floor. She inhaled the sweet vanilla scent of the candles and smiling, beaming faces all around her. Truvie wanted it to go on all night, but a glance at Olivia changed her mind.

29
With Love

Miss Frank and Olivia led Truvie down the glass stairs at the end of the dock onto a luxurious steel gondola with white cushioned seats. No one stood at the end with a giant oar, instead, the boat eased through the water on its own. There were no words exchanged. All three knew the purpose, and the destination.

Three moons illuminated the tips of the waves. The journey ended a few minutes after it began as the gondola slid into the sandy shore under the rocky cliffs of the back entrance. Truvie took the hands of Miss Frank and Olivia then bounded into the air touching down easily at the open archway to the Cave of Souls.

As they stepped in, their outfits changed. Miss Frank to black leather pants, a cropped leather jacket,

[2] and Jones[3]

and steel stiletto heels. Olivia, the same. Truvie now had on olive skinny cargo pants and a grey tee-shirt with brown lettering that she read upside down, "Cave Dweller."

"Ever the smart mouth," Miss Frank said.

"I thought it was clever," Truvie said.

"I know you did." Miss Frank lifted her sculpted eyebrows.

Truvie brightened the rocky, moist room with a quick thought for light.

"Thank you," Miss Frank said.

"Pleasure," Truvie said. "I'm not interested in being in the dark anymore either."

"I told you not to break the glass," Miss Frank said.

"I know you did," Truvie said.

"The advice still stands," Miss Frank said.

Truvie nodded. "Agreed."

"Go forward," Miss Frank said. "Whichever direction you like but be precise and clear about who you want to see first. Build yourself up by facing the one you want to avoid first. I've known you a long, long-long time. You work best once you get your jitters out. While it would be prudent and logical to begin with the most comfortable to create momentum, you can't settle until you've done what's difficult first. It's disappointing, but we must honor your limits."

Truvie started to speak but Olivia cut in, "It will loosen you up."

"I don't feel tense," Truvie said. "I'm excited to see them."

"That will pass," Miss Frank said.

"I'm stronger now. I know what I'm doing."

"You let Eva slip through the glass, and while the soul world didn't explode," Miss Frank stated. "It wasn't your finest moment. Pinned to the glass. Helpless."

"You'll be fine—" Olivia started but was cut off.

"She doesn't need indulgence, Miss Born," Miss Frank said.

"I don't mind—" Truvie smiled at Olivia.

"You are overconfident and therefore, contemptibly dangerous," Miss Frank said. "You know this or would not be here now with me as counsel. These are fractured souls, Miss Skye, broken off from all that they know and trust. The utmost respect is required."

"I know that," Truvie said.

Miss Frank started to say more but—

"Be yourself, Truitt," Olivia said. "You can do this and not—"

"Break the glass," Truvie said. "I promise. I won't."

"Do not crack, sliver, smash, melt, cut, put your fist through, or transform it in any way, shape, or form. Are you clear?" Miss Frank pressed.

"How do I—" Truvie paused, thinking. "I have to get through it, don't I?"

"Are we clear?"

"I have to get through it to reach them," Truvie said.

"It is a precise decision," Miss Frank said. "You will know what to do once you are there and stable. But you must come back, or this world will collapse and be gone forever."

"It would merge?" Truvie asked.

"Let's not find out," Miss Frank said.

"I'll be right back when I'm done," Truvie said.

"Keep it to one soul at a time, Miss Skye," Miss Frank said. "For your own good, do not stay long. Get to each repair and move on. No need to revisit Eddie, you had your exchange."

"But—he came to me—"

"Exactly," Miss Frank said. "Proof he knows how to find you."

"Fine," Truvie said.

Olivia embraced Truvie. "Good luck."

"Do try not to cause more disruptions," Miss Frank said.

"If I wasn't trouble," Truvie said. "What would you do with yourself?"

Miss Frank and Olivia vanished without another word.

. . .

Truvie walked down the last few steps she and Pel had climbed after Eva slithered through then gingerly placed her toes onto the top of a peaking glass wave. Beneath, fields of fresh cut grass and tiny moving dots. A schoolyard.

She moved over the glass counter-clockwise eager to see what would emerge below her.

In the flat valley of the glass wave, she got a close look of a mountain range with the faces of four Presidents. She'd reached the granite-carved Mount Rushmore in the state of South Dakota. Unsure which direction she was going when she moved, she waited to see what passed. If she hit fields of grain, she'd gone west, if she hit lakes, she was headed in the right direction.

Water. Deep blue water. With edges of ice and snow. Truvie Tucker was home.

Without thinking, she laid down on the glass.

And suddenly she knew.

"I don't change the glass. I become it."

She put her hands near her throat and cheek then gently pressed each finger and her palm to the pane and slowly merged into the glass. She lowered her forehead onto the cold and pushed until it took her. Her neck, spine, arms, hips, legs, and feet followed in a cautiously controlled press until Truvie Tucker was no more.

She felt nothing, was nothing, but energy rolling over humanity. She could not see anything, nor could she be sure how far she'd traveled east since seeing the wintery lakes, but that did not bother her. Calm and centered, Truvie let go. She needn't be the glass any-more. Finger by finger, toe by toe, she free-floated away as she fell to the Earth below.

. . .

Truvie waited outside her mother's advertise-induced SUV parked in the lot behind the community theater. The elf version of her mother painted on the door had been replaced with a flurry of roses and the announce-ment of a new show, "Collage of Love." Below the title, it said, "A Tribute to My Daughter, Truvie."

"Oh, Mom," Truvie said. Tears burned in the bottoms of her eyes. She forced a couple deep exhales out her nose and opened the door.

Sylvia Tucker sat slumped staring straight ahead, mascara-stained tear trails on her cheeks, hair uncombed, ratted into a bun.

Truvie got a whiff of roses. "You smell like you," Truvie said. "I've been holding to that."

Her mother stopped breathing and held rigidly still.

"It's me, Mom," Truvie said. "Turn to your right."

Deliberately and mechanically, Sylvia rotated her shoulders and neck to her right.

Truvie smiled and sent out as much light as she could muster, thinking, I want to blow her hair untangled.

It didn't happen, but her mother was able to see something. "Are you an angel?"

"Yes," she said. "Can you see me?"

"I see pink and yellow and green. Is that you, Truvie? It's blurry."

"I'm still getting my wings, Mom," Truvie said, choking up. "I'll get better so you can see me fully."

"It's okay, baby," her mother openly wept. "You're perfect. I know it's you. I feel you in me. All over me. Oh. Don't go. Don't ever go."

"I won't, Momma. I promise." Truvie squeezed her eyes tight. "You're going to get through this. Because I'm here. I'm right here."

Her mom sucked in her tears. "You aren't in any pain?"

"Oh no," Truvie sniffled. "I'm better than ever. I'm strong and smart and I'm helping. I'm helping everyone."

"That's a good girl," her mom said. "You're not showing off, are you?"

"I'm still a little out of my league."

"Good," her mom said. "You always needed—did thrive— with a challenge."

"Do, Mom," Truvie said. "I do need challenges to thrive. It's happening, don't worry."

"You're so beautiful," her mother said.

"You made a show for me?" Truvie asked.

"Soul music. Eddie insisted. Since you're all soul now."

"Will you sing me one?" Truvie asked.

Her mother wriggled up to erect posture, ever the star. She rotated her knees, hips and torso toward her daughter. "Hmm," she sang in a low voice to establish her starting point. Her voice stumbled and cracked. She cleared her throat.

After a few breaths, Sylvie belted out the same tune that bellowed from the kitchen of the glass house before she'd ventured into the Cave of Souls to face Eva. Truvie smiled at the thought that she and Junius had heard her mother rehearsing this very song.

"Is that how it works?" Truvie asked as her mother continued. "Always connected. Just have to be quiet and listen?"

Though the orchestra was not present in the car with them, the drums pounding in her chest to the beat of her mother's song. Her mom shimmied her shoulders as she sang with all she had.

"I love you, Momma," Truvie whispered and dimmed

her light. Her mother so happy, so proud, so joyous, she did not notice.

. . .

Her father stretched on Truvie's bed, his head propped under a folded pillow, feet dangling over the end. A splayed open black composition book rested on his chest, with the pages facing down. He had his tan Carhartt's and a flannel shirt on, and the socks she'd given him for Christmas a couple of years back with blue E=mc2 emblems all over them.

"Hey, Pop." She plopped down next to him.

He tilted his head to meet the top of hers.

"I've been missing you, kiddo," he said.

"What are you working on?" She tapped the comp book.

"Symmetry," he said. "And asymmetry."

"More asymmetry will help the equation," Truvie said. "People need to make mistakes to grow stronger and smarter. They have to mess up to correct. We don't know what is right without knowing what is wrong. And vice versa—"

"New worlds, new thinking, new logic, new everything," he said. "Comes from only one source. Incongruity. Conflict. Defeat. And tragedy."

"I'm sorry I had to leave you, Daddy," she said, taking his hand into hers. "So sorry."

"We break apart so we can mend," he said, a tear sliding to his chin.

Truvie closed her eyes and focused on calming

him. He drew in a deep breath and let it go. His eyelash tickled the top of her cheek as it closed. She lengthened her breaths. Easy and slow. Her father heaved and buckled. Squeezing her hand and weeping into her chest. Truvie stuck to her deep breaths until he did the same. Eventually, his body gave way and the rest he sought came.

She watched him from the doorway as he lay sleeping, the composition book curled up into his chest and waiting.

. . .

After a few moments, she moved down the hallway and without using any stairs or doors, arrived inside her grandmother's carriage house above the garage.

Fig snored at her grandmother's feet. Helena painted a single white rose against a pale blue background. She'd used a violet tone for shadowing and lit the blossom from beneath with the sparse use of gold and lemon. Helena hummed the song Sylvia sang to Truvie as she filled in a rose petal.

Truvie leaned close to her grandmother's ear and whispered, "Stick to the plan."

Fig opened his eyes and lifted his head.

Her grandmother dropped the paintbrush, sending white splashes to the floor and chair.

"The plan," she whispered to her painting.

Fig sat up and placed his paw on her thigh. He gave a mild groan.

Helena stood and glanced around the room.

Truvie pondered moving a curtain or asking a bird to perch on the windowsill. Too bad the crows had to stay in the City. But she knew she didn't need any of that.

"Come on, Fig," her grandmother said, grabbing her sweater from the back of her chair. "We gotta hustle."

· · ·

Helena donned a heavy fur coat and calf-high boots then out the door she flew, loaded Fig in her Volkswagen bug and backed out the driveway.

· · ·

It took less than two minutes for her to park the car in a spot across from Lake Michigan, mere steps from the bottom of the ravine. She let Fig out the passenger door and he took off running.

Helena shuffle-walked as quick as she could and when she reached him sniffing around the cavernous opening, she said, "Find it, boy. Where is it? Where's that red ball? Find it, Figgy. Find it."

Truvie positioned herself on a small pile of snow. Fig immediately began digging with fervor.

"Good boy!" Helena said. "Find it!"

Truvie bent down close to his head and said, "Almost there, Figgy. Keep going."

He plowed with every ounce of strength and after a few more rips, there sat the red ball. He took it with his teeth and wiggled his middle, wagging his tail as fast as it would go.

"Good boy!" Helena and Truvie sang together.

Fig jumped up and put his paws on Helena's chest, wriggling and whimpering, so, so proud.

She cupped his sweet face with her hands. "Off we go," she said. "One more stop."

. . .

Kopp's Frozen Custard was crowded, as usual at dinnertime. Her grandmother pushed the door with her bum to exit the milieu. She coveted two cups of vanilla. One for her. One for Fig.

"Good job, Gram," Truvie said.

Helena moved with a zip in her step to the car, set the frozen delights on the roof then opened the driver's side door. Fig's head and shoulders shot out.

"Scoot, scoot, so I don't spill."

Fig wagged himself backward to a seated position on the passenger seat. Truvie emerged in the elevated middle of the backseat. She leaned forward, elbows on the tops of the seats.

Helena held the cup for Fig as he licked and bit, vanilla custard covering his snout. She licked from her cup, not enough hands to use a spoon.

"Heaven, hey Fig?" Helena asked.

He stood up, crammed in the seat, to give her a wiggle. "Sit down, sit down," she said.

"Gram," Truvie said.

Helena did not answer, she continued devouring

her custard.

"I want you to come visit me," Truvie said. "You know how to do it. Just relax and let yourself dream. Ask to see me. Can you do that? I'll bring Granddaddy."

"Mm hmm," Helena said without thinking.

"Bye, Figgy. Thank you for helping me take care of everyone." She caressed the top of his head, kissed it, and slipped away.

. . .

Before Truvie needed to concentrate, she merged back into the glass and stood on top of it. She took a minute to watch the wave pass over the rest of Milwaukee then as she asked, a countless murder of green crows took flight from the glass.

They did not take hold.

Truitt Skye flew on her own.

Acknowledgements

Where to begin! I have experienced such a bounty of help getting this book to you, my beloved reader. I want you to know it's all for you. I write, I research, I work my imagination onto a frenzy for the sole/soul purpose of sharing it with each and every one of you. Writing is how I think, how I process, and feel, and become more. Thank you for being here with me. It means everything to me.

To Teff, who has been with Truitt and me since the beginning. Writing partner, dear, divine, magical, talented, extraordinary friend, I love and appreciate you.

To May, your illustrations always capture what I want to share. Thank you for your talent, your patience, your endless willingness to get it how I want it. I adore you! I appreciate you! I can't wait for us to create more together.

For Karen McDermott and the teams at Making Magic Happen and Serenity Press, this would not be without all of you. Period. End of. My gratitude radiates across the oceans straight to you.

To my early readers, Mollie, Erica, Therese, Bruce, Marsha, Nikki, Phia, Michelle, Laura, Kelly, Seton Hill colleagues, and the intrepid travelers of Lake Atitlan— Lea, Ann, Francesco, Leigh, Jami, Cissy, Chris, Emily, Judy, Joyce, Katie and Suzanne—you are treasures to me. To have your criticism, your praise, your confusion, suggestions and findings of typos and weird sentences, I am forever yours.

To Lauren Bell, my Tots. You are my heart. You give my strength and unfettered support whenever I need it. I love you.

Anj, thank you for staying with me on this journey. I appreciate you more than words, or worlds. Thank you. Thank you. Thank you.

To all of you that believed in this happening "someday," I thank you. I know it made the difference.

For more about how the Becoming Truitt Skye series came to be and how it will continue on, please visit www.adreapeters.com

About the Author

"We are the stories we tell.
Understanding you is understanding everything.
You are the world you create."
Adrea L. Peters

Adrea is a bestselling author-shareholder with KMD Books. She trained as a journalist, novelist and screen-writer. She earned a Bachelor of Science in Journalism from the University of Colorado at Boulder and Master of Arts in Fiction Writing from Seton Hill University.

Her bestselling book, *Quantum Thinkinφ*, released in September 2020. She recently co-authored, *When I Go Outside, I Go Inside* with longtime writing partner and dear friend, Teffanie Thompson. She is currently working on *Quantum Wealth* with Amber Lilyestrom.

Quantum Love and *Becoming Truitt Skye: The Equation for Imagination* will be released in 2021.

She lives amongst the trees in Vermont with her beloved boys, Skye and Fig.

Please visit her website at www.adreapeters.com for more information.

Other Titles by ADREA L. PETERS

Milton Keynes UK
Ingram Content Group UK Ltd.
UKHW040958080824
1159UKWH00030B/26

9 780648 728023